AGAINST THE GRAIN

THIRDS BOOK 5

CHARLIE COCHET

Against the Grain

Second Edition Copyright © 2019 Charlie Cochet

http://charliecochet.com

Cover Art Copyright © 2019 Reese Dante

http://reesedante.com

Proofing by Susi Selva

First Edition Copyright © 2015 Charlie Cochet.

AGAINST THE GRAIN

As the fiercest Defense agent at the THIRDS, Destructive Delta's Ash Keeler is foul-mouthed and foul-tempered. But his hard-lined approach always yields results, evident by his recent infiltration of the Coalition. Thanks to Ash's skills and the help of his team, they finally put an end to the murdering extremist group for good, though not before Ash takes a bullet to save teammate Cael Maddock. As a result, Ash's secrets start to surface, and he can no longer ignore what's in his heart.

Cael Maddock is no stranger to heartache. As a Recon agent for Destructive Delta, he has successfully maneuvered through the urban jungle that is New York City, picking up his own scars along the way. Yet nothing he's ever faced has been more of a challenge than the heart of Ash Keeler, his supposedly straight teammate. Being in love isn't the only danger he and Ash face as wounds reopen and new secrets emerge, forcing them to question old loyalties.

ONE

THERE WAS NOWHERE TO RUN.

Ash Keeler had faced a hell of a lot in his life. He'd come up against terrorists, extremist groups, dangerous criminals, and lethal feral Therians. He'd been stabbed, taken hostage, had the shit beaten out of him, been shot—twice—but he'd never come face-to-face with the pissed-off dad of a potential romantic partner. And because Lady Luck had a habit of being a real bitch to him, the pissed-off dad before him also happened to be his sergeant.

After their last—unsanctioned—investigation, Bradley offered to open Bar Dekatria exclusively to Destructive Delta for a night of much-needed rest and relaxation. They'd been having a great time, even if some of them couldn't drink thanks to Therian-strength antibiotics and painkillers. Ash was almost fully healed from his gunshot wound. Sloane still had a few weeks to recuperate, as did Cael, who was on crutches after that bastard Hogan fractured his leg. Luckily Cael was a quick healer, thanks to his cheetah Therian metabolism, so he'd be back to running full speed in no time. Ash couldn't think about how much worse it could have been after Hogan had taken Cael. It made him want to tear the son of a bitch apart with his bare hands. Good thing he was already dead.

Everything had been going well at Dekatria until Maddock had shown up with a baseball bat in his hand. Originally Ash thought the same as Sloane. That somehow their sergeant had found out about the mission. Instead, Maddock had come to kick their asses for dating his sons under his nose. The only problem was Ash and Cael weren't dating. Not that Ash hadn't secretly thought about it. A lot. It was the logical step for two Therians who happened to be in love.

Ash stood silently beside Sloane in the back end of Dekatria while Maddock glared at them, his nostrils flaring and the old beat-up baseball bat in his hand. How many others had come up against—what had Cael called it? That's right, Old Betsy. How many potential boyfriends had seen the rough side of Old Betsy? And now here he was, his every instinct telling him to flee. It was hardly the first time they'd seen their sergeant pissed off, but this was a whole other level of pissed.

This was stupid. Ash was a top agent for the THIRDS with twenty years of experience, skilled in entry tactics and close-quarter combat. He could handle one Human officer holding a baseball bat.

"Which one of you heartthrobs wants to go first?" Maddock growled.

Ash didn't hesitate. "Sloane."

"Wow." Sloane shook his head at him in disbelief. "Way to throw me under the bus, buddy."

Ash gave his best friend an apologetic smile. It was better to let Sloane do the talking. Knowing Ash and his propensity to piss people off, he'd open his mouth and make things a whole lot worse. Sloane was their team leader. He had experience in hostage negotiation. Most people liked him, the ones he didn't scare the hell out of at least. Meanwhile, the majority of people disliked Ash from the moment they laid eyes on him.

"Sarge, you have every right to be pissed," Sloane stated gently, his hands held up in front of him in surrender. He motioned to the bat in Maddock's hand. Their sarge appeared to give it some thought before he lowered the bat, though not completely. "I know I should've said something, but I promise you, Dex and I talked long and hard about this, about our relationship and the job. Whatever happens, we'll work through it. We're very serious about a future together. I love him, sir, and maybe I don't deserve him, but I'm going to try my damn hardest to be worthy of him. His happiness is important to me."

Maddock pursed his lips, and his eyes narrowed. "How long you been practicing that speech, son?"

Sloane shifted awkwardly despite his crutches. "A while now."

"Your honesty is appreciated, despite your dumbass attempt to keep something like this from me. I know those boys better than they know themselves. As far as your relationship goes, I have no intention of meddling or telling you what to do. I also don't have to tell you what's at stake. If Sparks gets wind of this—"

"I'll figure it out," Sloane said, his voice grave. "I won't let her break up the team. Not if she wants to keep me around. I know what I'm worth to her, to the Chief of Therian Defense. If I have to use that, I will."

"Shit." Maddock ran a hand over his shaved head. "You really want to go up against them?"

Ash had never seen Sloane look more determined. He wished he could be as confident about this as his friend.

"I'll do whatever it takes to keep my team together. My relationship with Dex is my business. What I do outside the job is my business. He's my partner, and I'm not going anywhere without him."

Maddock didn't look pleased, but he gave Sloane a nod. "Okay. Now get lost." He motioned to the door behind him. "Tell your boyfriend I expect assurances from him. I also expect him to help with Thanksgiving dinner. He wants to eat like a Therian, he can cook. I'll see you both there."

"Yes, sir." Sloane smiled and headed for the door.

Hoping his sergeant might not notice, Ash made to slip past. He should've known better. Maddock put a hand to his chest to stop him. Damn. So close.

"I don't think so, Keeler. You and I are going to have a little chat upstairs where it's more comfortable and Dex is less likely to listen in. That boy's like a damn ninja when he wants to eavesdrop, especially when it concerns Cael." He turned and marched out the door. Reluctantly, Ash followed. Outside, everyone pretended not to notice, but he knew his nosey-ass team was following his every move. He stole a glance in Cael's direction. His sweet face was filled with worry. Ash gave him a wink, hoping to ease his mind even if it didn't ease his own.

Ash was sorely tempted to make a break for it, but he'd have to face Maddock at some point. They headed upstairs to the second floor of Dekatria, which Ash had forgotten was there. He and his team spent so much time downstairs around the bar and that godforsaken karaoke machine that he tended to forget Dekatria had two other floors, one of them a rooftop garden. Maybe he should check it out one evening and invite Cael up for a drink. Lou had rambled on about how gorgeous it was, with its fairy lights and candles. All romantic and shit. *Romantic?* What the hell was wrong with him? Here he was about to argue the fact he wasn't dating Cael, and he was getting thoughts about having drinks with the guy up in a romantic roof garden. *Get your shit together, Keeler.*

He followed Maddock's lead and slid into one of the booths, taking a seat across from Maddock and Old Betsy, which was tucked on the bench beside him. Both of them sat in silence as Bradley placed coasters and soft drinks on the table without making eye contact. As soon as he was done, he darted from the place like it might spontaneously combust. All right, time to man up and grow a pair.

"Sir, whatever you might think, Cael and I aren't sleeping together. We're not even together."

Maddock's frown deepened. "That's what worries me."

Not what he'd expected. "I'm confused."

"Cael's in love with you, and I know you care about him, maybe even love him. Hell, you took a bullet for him. And that's not the first time you sustained injuries to keep him safe."

Ash couldn't bring himself to confirm Maddock's statement about him loving Cael. He shifted uncomfortably and took a sip of his Coke. What he really needed was some vodka. "How long have you known?"

"I had my suspicions for a while but felt it wasn't the right time to address it. With Dex, my suspicions were confirmed at the hospital." Maddock let out a heavy sigh and sat back, his gaze off in the distance at nothing in particular. "When I saw him at Sloane's bedside, his anguish clear as day as he tried not to fall apart, I knew he'd fallen in love. Broke my damn heart seeing him like that."

"For what it's worth," Ash offered, "those two are crazy

about each other. I've known Sloane since we were kids. Believe me. He's in deep. And I'm not just saying that because he's my best friend. You know Sloane. He might not be perfect, but he's a good guy."

"And you?"

God, he wished he were anywhere but here right now. He'd even take sitting in on one of Intel's long-ass boring-as-fuck presentations with all their mind-numbing algorithms and PowerPoints. They worked under the military branch of the government, and still they couldn't escape those fucking things. "What about me?" Did his sergeant really want him to answer that? Besides, judging by his expression, Maddock already knew the answer.

"Sloane has his issues, and although he might need some sense knocked into him every once and a while, he finds his way. More importantly, I can see how he's opened up with Dex. When things get rough, he turns to the man he loves. He's grown more confident in himself and their relationship. He smiles more. Laughs. I haven't seen him happy like this in a long time. It's good. You on the other hand..." Maddock leaned forward, and his hard gaze pinned Ash to the spot. "I know behind that fierce roar of yours is a guy who isn't as sure of himself as he pretends to be. You're aggressive and, let's face it, an asshole."

And there it was in a nutshell. "Thanks, Sarge," Ash muttered.

"I'm not done. You might be an asshole, but you're a good man where it counts and a damn fine agent. I'd be a fool to say your methods haven't provided results out in the field. There are no easy answers in this line of work, but you always find a way to cut straight through all the bullshit, and I respect that. But we're not talking about fieldwork here. We're talking about my son. I know you care about

Cael, but you've got some angry demons inside of you looking to claw their way to the surface, *and* if that wasn't enough, there's the fact you don't know who you are. Where does that leave Cael, besides on the road to a broken heart? You think I haven't noticed how miserable he's been since your undercover job? Or how he fucked up that training simulation?"

Ash straightened. This was the first he'd heard about it. "When?"

"While you were working undercover to infiltrate the Coalition. Sloane executed a breaching simulation. The usual training session. Cael had been so wrapped up in his own little world, he looked at the wrong screen and gave Calvin the all clear."

Shit. "Let me guess. It wasn't clear."

"Nope. Your partner shot him in the leg. Twice."

"Wait, Calvin got shot? How? And where the hell was Hobbs?" No Human got the drop on Calvin from that distance, especially with any kind of firearm. The guy was the fastest shooter on their team and a fucking sniper. What the hell was going on? As if reading his thoughts, Maddock spoke up.

"Yeah, Cael wasn't the only one who fucked up that day. Those two aren't your problem. I'll deal with them. The point is Cael's focus wasn't on the job, it was on you. Remember this, Keeler. Just because you don't hear me or see me doesn't mean I don't know every little thing going on with my team." Maddock sat back with a sigh. "Dex and Cael wear their hearts on their sleeves. It makes it easy to know what's going on in their heads. It also makes it easy for someone to hurt them. I like you, for the most part. What I don't like is where this is heading."

"And where's that?" Ash was curious. He wasn't exactly

a catch. Maddock had every right to be concerned. Ash's track record for successful relationships left a lot to be desired. With Cael, it was different. Man, was that an understatement. It had been so much simpler when they'd been friends. Being affectionate toward Cael had come easily. Cael had brought out emotions in him he hadn't known existed. Now Ash was having trouble figuring out which way was up.

"Let me tell you a little story."

"Sarge, as much as I'm enjoying this little one-on-one, this is between me and Cael." Ash turned to get up, surprised when Maddock put a hand out to stop him.

"Sit your ass down. You need to hear this."

Ash didn't question Maddock. He resumed his seat and listened, not liking the way his sergeant rubbed at the salt-and-pepper stubble on his jaw, as if he were reluctant to say whatever was on his mind. He seemed to come to a decision about it and nodded.

"Aside from the various boyfriends who dumped Cael for reasons ranging from his being smarter than them to things just not working out, there are two who are on my shit list. Those relegated to the Tony Maddock shit list are Therians I wouldn't piss on if they were on fire. One, Shane Cruz. Despite Dex's warning to his brother about falling for a straight guy, Cael fell for him anyway. The reason he's on the shit list is because he used Cael's feelings to take advantage of him, getting Cael to do his assignments. That dumbass not only graduated high school with high marks because of Cael, he earned himself a scholarship off Cael's hard work. Then he packed up, changed his number, and fucked off to California. Broke Cael's heart."

Ash didn't reply. If he did, only unpleasant words would come out. Wherever Shane Cruz was, Ash hoped karma came back to bite him on the ass or punch him in the balls. Ash preferred the latter.

"The second, he's at the very top of the shit list."

Maddock's expression darkened, and Ash braced himself. He really didn't want to hear this, but like an idiot, he sat there and listened.

"The only reason I didn't throw his ass in jail or the fucking Hudson River is because Cael wouldn't let me."

"*Jail?*" Jesus, it was worse than he thought. Why hadn't Cael told him? Cael shared everything with him, despite Ash's inability to do the same more often than not. "Shouldn't Cael be the one telling me all this?"

Maddock continued as if he hadn't spoken. "Have you noticed how Cael apologizes for everything? Even when he's done nothing wrong? When there's nothing for him to apologize for? Why do you think that is?"

Ash shrugged and sat back. "I figured it's just part of his nature. He's a sweet guy."

"It's *not* part of his nature," Maddock growled, surprising Ash. "It's what happens when a piece of shit like Don Fuller gets his claws into a guy like Cael. For nearly two years that son of a bitch put my boy through hell. You don't know what it's like to have your son come home with a black eye and know his boyfriend was the one responsible."

"What the *fuck?*" Ash slammed his fist on the table, and the drink glasses jumped causing the soda to spill. He caught himself, remembering who he was talking to. "Sorry." Ash swiped a handful of napkins from the dispenser at the end of the booth and promptly cleaned up the spilled liquid. He had to calm down. If he didn't... Fuck, he didn't even want to think about it. Before his thoughts could turn ugly, Maddock continued.

"I never told Cael this, but that night, Dex kept me from doing something stupid."

Ash pushed the soggy napkins to one side. There was something in Maddock's eyes, in his tone, that said maybe he wished he'd done whatever it was he'd meant to do that night.

Maddock shook his head, his eyes filled with a pain and silent rage Ash imagined only a parent could feel, knowing their child was in danger.

"You should have heard Cael. Apologizing for that bastard, blaming himself for whatever it was that set Fuller off, promising he could handle it, that it wouldn't happen again. After Cael cried himself to sleep, I went downstairs, grabbed the crowbar from my toolbox, and I headed out the door with every intention of beating the ever-living shit out of that son of a bitch. I didn't care that he was a Therian, and I was a THIRDS officer. The entire time, I kept thinking, 'How fucking dare he lay a hand on my boy?' I got my keys out of my pocket, ready to get in the car, when Dex stepped in front of me. He put his hand on my shoulder and said, 'Don't let that asshole break up our family. I'll take care of it.' Cael couldn't see what we saw. The only way to get him away from Fuller for good was for Dex to get through to Cael. Cael had to be the one to walk away, to really *see* Fuller for what he was." Maddock rubbed his eyes. "Most heartbreaking year of my life. But Dex never gave up."

Ash couldn't believe what he'd heard. Maddock was even more protective of Cael than he was of Dex. Cael was the baby of the family, always coddled by his big brother and dad. Dex wouldn't hesitate in taking someone down if they tried to hurt Cael. Hell, Dex had punched Ash in the face when he'd been undercover and said some harsh words to Cael in an attempt to keep him safe, and Ash was his teammate. Yet somehow that asshole Fuller had managed almost two years with Cael? God only knew what damage he'd caused in that time. Ash didn't know what to do with this information other than feel rage.

"How could you let it happen?"

Maddock narrowed his eyes at him. "I didn't *let* it happen, Keeler. You think if I'd known what was going on, I wouldn't have addressed it sooner? Cael spent more time with that bastard than he did with his family. At first Dex and I thought it was just young love. It wasn't. Fuller convinced Cael that he needed to devote all his time to him because he couldn't stand to be away from Cael. It was bullshit. Cael was falling hard, and Fuller knew it. He played it just right when we met him, said all the right things to come off as a genuinely decent guy. Something didn't sit right with me, but I put it down to my never liking any guy looking to be Cael's boyfriend. I pulled a background check on Fuller, and he was clean. The guy'd just been recruited to the THIRDS, for fuck's sake."

Ash could feel his anger threatening to burst free, but he maintained a firm grip. He needed to hear the rest of this, even if it killed him.

"Cael would make excuses every time we called about why he couldn't come to dinner or hang out with his brother. It hurt Dex, but he respected Cael's privacy. Of course, you know Dex can't be ignored for long. He grew more and more suspicious. And when that boy gets something in his head, ain't nothing gonna stop him. He'd show up at Cael's school, his job at the campus coffee shop, wherever he could. That's when we noticed little things. New insecurities Cael never had before. He was apologizing more. Seemed more skittish than usual, more down on himself. He'd always had confidence issues over his Therian form, but after some time with Fuller it was something else altogether."

"What kind of Therian was Fuller?"

Maddock hesitated before replying. "He was a lion Therian."

Fucking fantastic. Ash ran a hand over his hair. Because lion Therians didn't have a bad enough reputation as it was. Of all the Felid Therians, they were the ones who got the most shit, that they were lazy, possessive, chest-beating assholes and bullies who only got off their asses when it was to their benefit. Ash had heard it all. Had been hearing it all his life. Luckily he didn't really give a shit what people thought, but lion Therians like Fuller didn't help matters.

"Anyway, after Cael refused to press charges against Fuller, Dex and I kept an eye on the guy. Call it an invasion of privacy or whatever the hell you want, but that's my son, and I wasn't about to let Fuller hurt him again. That's when we realized what was really going on. The way Fuller talked to Cael? He made him feel like he was the only guy in the world, made him feel loved and happy. Then he would pull the rug out from under him and crush him. It went on and on. He'd convinced Cael he was the weakest of the Felids. How he was small and useless. How he wasn't as smart as he thought he was. Then one day, Dex and Cael got into an argument. Dex threw his arms up in frustration, and Cael backed up against the wall. We'd been under the impression the black eye had been the first time Fuller had assaulted him. Cael swore left and right that Fuller had regretted it since, and it had been the end of it. It was just the beginning."

Ash jumped to his feet. *"What?"* His hands balled into

fists, and he felt his vision sharpen, his fangs threatening to elongate. He had to get a grip.

"Sit down," Maddock ordered quietly.

"How could you not know? You're a fucking THIRDS agent. Dex was fucking HPF."

A host of emotions flashed through Maddock's eyes, and Ash backed off. It wasn't his intention to give his sergeant such a hard time over something that had pained his family so deeply, but Ash was finding it difficult to swallow all this. He couldn't get past someone hurting Cael and getting away with it. Reluctantly, he forced himself to sit.

"Cael was already training to be a THIRDS agent. He'd graduated top of his class. He's smart. He grew up in a cop house. Which meant he knew what we'd look for, knew how to conceal the evidence. What to do, what to say. Cael really believed Fuller was helping him be stronger, tougher. We tried to get him away from Fuller, but he was blinded by what he believed Fuller felt for him. The way the guy got into his head, twisted everything Cael thought about himself, about us? It still makes me sick thinking about it."

Ash was forced to close his eyes. He hung his head in an attempt to gather his thoughts and keep calm. He couldn't think about Fuller, couldn't think about Cael bruised and in pain at the hands of someone who was a worthless piece of shit. Compartmentalize. That's what he had to do, what he'd been doing all his life. There was a reason Maddock was telling him all this. His eyes flew open, and his head shot up.

"You think I'd harm Cael?" He couldn't help the hurt in his voice. "Because if you're telling me that after twenty years of knowing me you think I'm capable of laying a hand on Cael to hurt him, then you can have my badge right now."

"Relax. I know you wouldn't, and I'm not comparing you to Fuller. Like I said, you're a good guy, whereas Fuller thought he was. I needed you to know because you're not the only one battling demons. Cael just has a different way of dealing with them. The last thing he needs is someone adding to that pain. It took years for Cael to undo some of the damage Fuller had caused, and even now he's still healing. Some wounds may never heal. I'm telling you because even if you sort out all your shit, you need to know it won't be easy with him. He puts on a brave front a good deal of the time. Like Dex, he's an expert at evasive tactics. If he doesn't want you to see or know something, he will do what it takes to keep you out of the loop, and that's dangerous for everyone. There's still a lot you don't know about Cael. Believe me."

Ash frowned. "I know everything about Cael." Didn't he?

"Oh? So you know about the panic attacks?"

"What panic attacks?" Damn. Ash sighed. "No." In the five years he'd known Cael, not once had he seen Cael experience a panic attack. He'd had moments of panic but had never suffered a panic attack. Was it possible he had at some point and had kept it hidden from Ash? How much had Cael kept secret from him? How much of himself had Cael held back?

"It's been years since he's had them, but he used to get them all the time when he was with Fuller. Really bad ones. I thought you should know so you can be prepared."

"Thanks." A part of him wished he hadn't been told any of this. He hated not having been around to protect Cael. But then he could hardly look out for someone he hadn't met yet. He could protect Cael now, and he had every intention of doing so. Maddock sat pensively.

"What happened to Fuller? Please tell me he's not still with the THIRDS." The guy definitely wasn't Unit Alpha, or Ash would have recognized the name. He'd never heard it before now. The THIRDS wouldn't keep a guy like Fuller around.

Maddock shook his head. "He didn't last very long. Failed one of his psych evals due to violent tendencies and unresponsiveness where empathy was required. Ironically, it was during a Therian domestic violence scenario. Must have hit too close to home, and I'm guessing he couldn't fake his way through it. Especially since by this point, Cael had pressed charges.

"It was after Fuller put Cael in the hospital with a broken arm and a concussion. That wasn't what got him to press charges, though. It was seeing Dex tackled to the floor by me and four of my agents when Fuller had the fucking nerve to show up at the hospital. If we hadn't restrained Dex, who the hell knows what he would've done to Fuller. My guys got Fuller the hell out, and Cael managed to calm Dex down. Cael realized if he didn't do something, his big brother would, and the end result would most likely be Dex throwing his career and maybe even his life away, all to protect him from Fuller. Cael wouldn't let that happen. Fuller was charged with assault and battery. He failed his eval, was let go from the THIRDS, convicted of third-degree assault, and sentenced to a year in a Therian prison. That was years ago. Last I heard he was working construction in Carson City somewhere."

"Good fucking riddance." Ash took a sip of his drink. Though he would have preferred it if the guy had driven off a fucking cliff, he took comfort the guy had been sent to a Therian prison, or the Zoo, as some Therians referred to it. Locked away with the rest of the fucking animals. Maybe it was time to check up on Fuller and make sure his ass was still in Carson City.

They sat in silence, each lost in his own thoughts when Maddock broke through the quiet. "Son, do you want to be with him?"

Ash nodded and tried to swallow past the lump in his throat from having Maddock call him son. Not even his own father had called him that. He'd called him a host of names but never that. Maddock had always been good to him, but did he really want his sergeant to know the truth? Sloane was the only one who knew about his past. What would Maddock think of him? Ash had never been very good with authority, which was ironic considering where he'd ended up. Respect was something to be earned. Anthony Maddock had gained it from day one. Even when they butted heads, Ash respected Maddock and strived to make him proud.

"So what's the problem? Or is it none of my business?"

"It's personal," Ash replied quietly.

"Does it have to do with why you're so hung up on the whole gay thing? No one cares about that anymore. And you're both Therian, so you won't get the same level of shit Sloane and Dex will get once their relationship is out there." His frown deepened. "There's a lot of stupid in this world. I hope those two are ready for it."

"They can handle themselves. And I know no one will care that Cael's a guy. You're not the first to tell me that, believe me. The problem is *I* care, because the last time I gave into what I felt for a guy, my brother got killed."

Maddock cursed under his breath. "Jesus, Ash. Why the hell didn't I know you had a brother?"

"When Shultzon registered me, he made sure to keep certain personal information out of our files. I had a twin brother. Arlo. He was killed during the riots. We were just kids."

"I'm sorry to hear that. Can I ask what happened?"

"I fucked up, and Arlo paid the price. I was supposed to have been there the day he was killed, but I wasn't. I was with this boy I had a crush on. I sent Arlo home on his own, and he was killed."

"I'm sorry for your loss, but how do you know you wouldn't have been killed along with him if you'd gone home together?"

Ash grimaced. "Now you sound like Sloane."

"I would listen to him. He's a smart guy. Whatever happened that day, no matter how tragic, isn't your fault."

His parents hadn't thought so. They'd blamed him for Arlo's death. He remembered that day clearly. He'd wanted to die. To be with Arlo and away from his parents, who hated him, from all the horrible things his father said to him, from the pain his father inflicted on him. Then Ash had shifted, and his world officially went to hell.

"Either way, that fucked me up, Sarge. I've tried to move on from it, but the thought of what I did, of how I wasn't there to protect Arlo, it's been eating away at me year after year after year. When I think of being with Cael, I think about how giving in to what I felt all those years ago brought nothing but pain and heartache. It destroyed my family. When I'm out with the team, with Cael, I tell myself no one knows what I'm really feeling or thinking. They don't. Yet it feels like they do, like they're judging me, condemning me. How can I be the man Cael deserves when the thought of holding his hand in public scares the ever-living shit out of me?" How was it he could compartmentalize everything else in his life, but when it came to Cael, everything was a jumbled mess?

"Have you talked to Cael about this?"

"No." Ash frowned down at his fingers on the table. "I told him we'd sit down and talk, and we will. I need to figure things out."

"You do that." Maddock reached out and patted his arm before sliding out of the booth, taking Old Betsy with him. "Talk to each other. Let him help you. If you really care about him the way you say you do, then let him help you. Sometimes, no matter our strength, we need someone we care about to lean on, and that's okay." With that, Maddock headed for the stairs, but not before calling out over his shoulder. "Tell Sloane I expect you both over for Christmas dinner as well."

Ash turned in his seat. "You want us to spend Thanksgiving and Christmas with you?" After everything he'd just told him?

"Is that a problem?"

"No. Not at all."

"Well, all right then."

Maddock disappeared through the doorway, and Ash sat there for a moment. He couldn't believe he'd opened up like that to his sergeant. Now that he had, he was glad he'd done it. Besides, Maddock deserved the truth, especially since it concerned Cael. Ash still had no clue what he was going to do, but Maddock was right. He needed to talk to Cael. Soon.

Ash headed back downstairs. Thankfully the music playing from the sound system wasn't Dex's annoying '80s playlist, but a mix of classic rock and modern music. It was loud enough to enjoy but low enough everyone could talk to each other without having to shout, which Ash hated. It's why he rarely went to clubs. The music was so damned loud in those places he could barely hear himself think.

And despite what most people believed, he did think. Too much at times. He dropped himself into a chair at the table next to Sloane. Dex sat across Sloane's lap, and the two were so lost in each other, they hadn't even noticed him. Ash didn't interrupt. Instead he watched them, envious of the easy way his best friend smiled and laughed with his boyfriend. His love shone through his eyes, and there was no hesitation when he kissed Dex. No second thought. It was natural. An extension of himself. He was in love with the man in his arms and unafraid of who knew or who saw. Granted, there was only their team in the bar, but had the place been filled to the brim with people, Sloane still wouldn't have hesitated. His best friend's only worry regarding his relationship with his partner was the job. Ash couldn't see himself being so at ease out in the open with Cael.

Kiss. Ash turned away from Sloane and Dex as the memory of Cael kissing him entered his mind. He'd tried his hardest not to think about it, but it had been one of the most amazing experiences of his life. Cael had tasted sweet and warm. Despite the state they'd both been in, Ash had caught a whiff of Cael's intoxicating scent. Holding Cael in his arms... He hadn't wanted to let go. He hadn't been able to stop thinking about it since either.

"Hey, big guy. You okay?"

Ash blinked, his attention moving to Cael, who was watching him worriedly. Damn. He'd been so lost in thought he hadn't noticed Cael arrive.

"Yeah, I'm fine."

"I'm so sorry about my dad."

"Don't worry about it," Ash said with a warm smile. "Really, we just talked."

"I can't believe he totally freaked out like that." Cael

lowered himself onto the seat beside him, his crutch to one side.

"I can. He's a good man. You're very lucky."

"I know. But sometimes he can be a little overprotective."

Ash smiled and gave Cael's jaw a playful nudge. "It's hard not to be when it comes to you."

Cael's cheeks flushed that wonderful pink Ash loved so much. How could anyone hurt someone so warm and kind? The thought of that filth Don Fuller laying a hand on Cael had his blood boiling. He needed to calm down before he gave himself away. At some point he would tell Cael he knew about Fuller, but now was not the time.

"We're heading home," Sloane announced, sucking in a sharp breath as Dex helped him to his feet. "I hate to say it, but I could use a nap."

"Showing your old age, huh?" Ash teased.

"Fuck off," Sloane said, laughing. "We're the same age."

"Yeah, but I'm younger at heart."

Sloane scooped up a cheese cube from the table and threw it at him. "Ass."

His best friend still had some recovery to do after nearly losing his life to the explosion outside Dex's house. The car bomb had been planted in Ash's car by the same bastard who'd tried to kill him once before. Sloane had insisted Ash not feel guilty about it, but how could he not? The bomb had been in *his* car. It had been meant for *him*. What if he'd lost Sloane? A hand came to rest on his arm, and he smiled down at Cael. It's like the guy could sense when he needed to be pulled out of his thoughts. He gave Cael a wink and turned back to Sloane.

"Call if you need anything," Ash said.

"Thanks." The two started for the door when Dex

narrowed his eyes at him. "Just remember what I said. Alaska."

"I'm quaking in my boots," Ash drawled, turning back to Cael after Sloane and Dex had said their good-byes to everyone and left. Maddock was gone, and everyone else sat at the bar chatting and laughing as Bradley attempted to show Lou how to twirl a bottle in his hand without dropping it.

Cael prodded Ash's bicep. "Alaska? What's in Alaska?"

"Nothing. Your brother's being an asshat. As usual." Dex had threatened to annoy the ever-living fuck out of Ash if he hurt his baby brother, stating he'd drive Ash so crazy he'd end up asking for a transfer to Alaska. Like Ash wasn't already used to Dex annoying the fuck out of him.

"Oh." Cael let out a yawn and laid his head against Ash's shoulder. It was an innocent gesture. One Cael had done countless times. Usually Ash would rest his head against Cael's in return. Now he felt self-conscious. Like maybe everyone around him would know how he felt. He cleared his throat and gently moved away to stand.

"I'm gonna head home."

Cael stood and took hold of his crutch. "Want to share a cab?"

"Sure."

"Aw, you guys are leaving already?" Letty came skipping over and poked Ash in his side. She was clearly tipsy, though God only knew how many drinks she'd had. The woman could drink a Therian under the table. So could Calvin, for that matter. Pretty impressive considering they were the smaller of their Human teammates. Letty poked him again, and he gave her a playful shove away from him.

"Yeah, those of us on meds drinking nothing but juice have better places to be." On the third poke, he threw an arm around her neck and pulled her against him. "Is there a breeze in here? I swear I feel something tickling my side."

Letty laughed and punched him in the ribs before pushing him away. "*Cabrón.* Get lost, then."

Rosa came over and kissed Cael's cheek. "Rest up, *gatito.* Call me if you need me."

"He'll be fine," Letty said, watching Ash intently. "Ash will take good care of him."

"Speaking of. Are you two dating?" Rosa asked, looking from one to the other.

Cael opened his mouth, and Ash cut him off. "No."

Letty cocked her head to one side but didn't respond. His partner knew him well. She planned on accosting him later. Rosa was more persistent. "Then what the hell was Maddock going on about when he stormed in here?"

"It was a misunderstanding. Mind your own business," he growled, snatching his coat off the back of his chair.

"Fine. Jesus." Rosa waved them off and headed back to the bar. Ash said his good-byes to the rest of them, helped Cael into his coat, and then out of the bar. It was a chilly November evening, and Ash called for a cab. Cael was quiet at his side.

"Sorry about that back there. I don't want to stick a label on anything before we talk."

"I get it." Cael tried to straighten out the scarf around his neck while still holding on to his crutch. "Don't worry about it."

"Thank you for being so patient with me. I know I don't deserve it." Ash turned to face him and gently took hold of the scarf he'd given Cael earlier in the evening. It looked better on him anyway. The silver and dark grays brought out his eyes. Ash had fallen deep into those amazing silvery eyes from day one. "I'm sorry for pushing you away." He paused, his hand coming to rest against Cael's neck. His skin was warm and soft.

"It's okay, Ash." Cael leaned into Ash's touch, a shy smile on his handsome face. "We'll work it out."

"Yeah." Ash smiled when the cab appeared. He pulled away and opened the back door, then motioned for Cael to get in first, taking hold of his crutch for him. It was awkward with his leg, but Cael managed it, though Ash could have done without seeing Cael's ass in the air when he opted for crawling across the seat. *Lord, give me strength.* He passed Cael his crutch and climbed in next to him, doing his best to ignore how Cael put the crutch beside the window so he could sit closer to Ash. As a large Therian, there typically wasn't a whole lot of room for him in the back of these old New York cabs. His head touched the ceiling, so he had to slump a bit.

"So, what did you and my dad talk about?" Cael asked after giving the cab driver his address.

"You. He's worried about you. About us." He murmured the last part. Which was stupid. Like the cab driver gave a fuck. "He's afraid I'll hurt you, and he's right to be."

"Don't worry about him. He won't bug you," Cael said. "He knows you."

Ash wanted to point out that's exactly why Maddock was worried, but he didn't. Usually when they shared a cab, Ash would put his arm around Cael, and he hated that things felt different. He'd lived for those moments. The innocent touches that weren't so innocent. They had become a sweet form of torture for him. Now that the possibility of more loomed on the horizon, he couldn't shake his discomfort and self-consciousness. Their relationship had changed whether he liked it or not. They couldn't go back to the way things were, but if they couldn't move forward, where did it leave them?

Thankfully, the cab pulled up to Cael's brownstone, where he occupied the top floor apartment. It was spacious yet cozy, with a playful style befitting its owner. Ash told the cab driver to wait as he helped Cael climb out. He walked Cael to the front steps, careful neither of them slipped on any ice. Cael opened the front door and turned with a shy smile.

"Do you want to come in? You could stay for dinner. We could hang out."

"I would, but I need to sort out some insurance paperwork on my car. I want to get the new one before we're called back in." That had to be the most pathetic excuse in the history of excuses.

"Right. Sorry. Forgot about that."

Cael bit his bottom lip and leaned into Ash, who took a step back.

"I need to go. I'll call you later."

The disappointment on Cael's face hit Ash hard. *Please don't let this be the start of a disturbing trend.* He hated disappointing Cael. He hated hurting him even more. This wasn't how he wanted things to go at all, but no matter how much he told himself to man up, he backed off like a goddamn coward. Cael simply nodded his understanding.

"Have a good night, Ash."

There was no sweet smile, no hug, only Cael closing the door while Ash remained on the other side staring at the scuffed wood like an idiot. He lifted his fist to knock, then stopped himself. With a shake of his head at his own absurdity, he turned and descended the steps to the sidewalk and the idling cab parked at the curb. The whole way home, he stared numbly at the passing scenery from the backseat.

Maddock expected him and Sloane to spend the holidays with him and his family. It sounded less and less like a good idea. Last year they'd all had a great time, but things had been simpler for everyone then. Dex and Sloane hadn't been dating. He'd had fun with Cael like he always did, with no confusing emotions to muddy up the waters of their friendship.

Dex and Sloane had finally reached a stable point in their relationship, even if his best friend had thrown him for a loop by stating he was moving in with Dex. Of course, that hadn't surprised him as much as Sloane's admission to having marked Dex. Sloane was a Therian, but Ash wondered if his best friend was aware of how serious a commitment he'd just made. Neither of them had much experience with a committed functional relationship until now. Ash was still trying to wrap his head around Sloane in love, much less being all domestic and shit. From what Ash gathered, Sloane actually liked it. He liked getting up before Dex and making them breakfast. They took turns cooking or ordered takeout, took turns washing the dishes and clearing up, even doing laundry. Did his friend enjoy it because it was what normal couples did? Because all their life they'd struggled with finding a little piece of normalcy in the chaos that spawned them? Ash cooked and did chores around the house, but he didn't think of himself as domestic. He just liked taking care of his shit. Everything clean and in its place. But being told to take out the trash, wash the dishes, or pick up a gallon of milk on his way home? Ash didn't like the sound of that. At least not until he thought of Cael, and then everything he thought he knew flew out the window.

I am so fucked.

TWO

THE CAB PULLED up outside Ash's apartment building. He paid the driver and headed upstairs. His smartphone vibrated in his pocket and his heart skipped a beat when he saw it was from Cael. Jesus, what was happening to him? Cael texted him all the time, every day. Now he was going to feel like a damn virgin every time Cael texted him?

"Fuck this shit." Ash shoved his phone into his pocket and went inside. He closed his apartment door behind him, removed his shoes, and hung his coat up on the rack by the door. It was good to be home, even if a part of him wished he'd taken Cael up on his offer. By now they would have been huddled close together on the couch with Cael rambling on excitedly about the latest gadget. Cael was the only one who could talk tech to Ash without him wanting to shoot something. He padded across the hardwood floors to the kitchen to wash his hands. They were still a little sticky from when he'd spilled the soda at Dekatria. The thought had him clenching his jaw. Damn it, the last thing he needed was to get caught up in his anger at what he'd learned from Maddock.

Fucking double-edged sword. He was glad he knew about Fuller, but he also hated it at the same time. There was nothing he could do with that information. He couldn't kick Fuller's ass. He couldn't undo what had been done.

Ash walked to his couch and dropped down onto it, just staring at the ceiling. "Fuck." Then he remembered Cael's text and removed his phone from his pocket. He tapped the screen to open it and smiled like a dope. There was an image of two cute little green dinosaurs, one bigger than the other, and they were hugging, a little red heart above their heads.

Ash tossed his phone onto the couch cushion beside him and let his head fall back. Man, he was so screwed. He'd disappointed Cael. Again. They were supposed to be moving forward, not backward. Whose fault was that? His. As usual. His smartphone rang, and he considered not answering. The ringtone told him it was his partner. With a sigh, he scooped it up, tapped the screen, and held it to his ear.

"Yeah?"

"I'm coming over."

"Now's not a good time," he muttered. The doorbell rang, and he closed his eyes. "You're outside the door, aren't you?"

"I am."

He hung up and went to his front door. Just what he didn't need, a heart-to-heart with his partner. He should have known she'd have something up her sleeve when she'd stayed quiet after Rosa asked if he was dating Cael. Damn it, he really didn't want to do this. He opened the door and glowered down at her.

"Can we not do this now?"

"Nope." As expected, she ignored his displeasure and

slipped past him into the apartment, where she proceeded to chuck off her boots and leave them by the door. With a growl, he closed the door and followed her into the kitchen.

"Beer or wine?"

"Beer," Letty said, hopping up onto one of the chairs at the island counter.

He grabbed two beers from the fridge along with the bowl of black olives. His partner loved these things as much as he did. Placing the bowl on the counter, he snatched one and popped it into his mouth before he used his shirt to twist the caps off their beers. He slid one across to her and took a long swig as he waited for her to say whatever it was she came here to say.

"So, you and Cael."

"What about me and Cael?"

"*Is* there a you and Cael?" She popped a couple of black olives into her mouth and arched an eyebrow at him.

"I don't know."

"Kind of hard not to know if you're with someone. How long have you been into dudes?"

Ash took another swig of his beer before replying. Maybe he needed to break out the hard stuff for this conversation. He could have sworn he had a bottle of vodka left from Dex's birthday party. "I'm not. Never have been."

"Right. Last time I checked, Cael identified as a dude."

"It's complicated."

"Of course it is. Because it's you. You make everything complicated, Ash."

"Thanks. That really helps." Not that she was wrong. After working almost ten years with someone, having their back, always in each other's hair, you got to know them pretty well.

"You've always been different with him. It's sweet. So when did things change?"

"Letty—"

"No way. You've been twisted up inside for months. I'm your partner and your friend. None of this tough suffer-in-silence lion Therian bullshit. Talk to me, Keeler."

There was no way around it. She wouldn't let up until she was satisfied. Unlike Rosa, who fussed over everyone on the team, Letty was more reserved, but she was a great shoulder to lean on and had this pain-in-the-ass way of seeing through him. Next to Sloane, she was also the only one who could get away with pushing his buttons without running the risk of a punch in the face. Maybe he wouldn't punch Rosa, but he wasn't against swiping her legs out from under her.

"Fine. Nothing changed. It's more like I couldn't bury what I felt for him anymore. I'd pushed it down for so long. Since we met, basically. I convinced myself that I was lucky to have him as a friend. It got harder each year. Then all this shit happened with the Order and the Coalition. When Hogan took him..." The moment the words left his mouth, he regretted it. Shit. It was the first time the incident had been brought up. He took a gulp of his beer, feeling her intense gaze on him. She had this unsettling way of being able to get information out of him just by looking at him. There was no one who could outstare Letty.

"What did happen with Collins? How'd he take your gun?"

Ash had never minced words with his partner. He wasn't going to start now. "I let him take it."

"Jesus, Ash." Letty closed her eyes and pinched the bridge of her nose. "I don't—Fuck it. Tell me."

Ash shrugged. "He was going to shoot Dex. I had to take him out."

"No. You *wanted* to take him out. Fuck." Letty jumped off the chair and started pacing. "Do you realize what would happen if Sparks found out?" She spun toward him, her brown eyes blazing. "Damn it, Ash. What were you thinking?"

"That I was doing what I had to do."

"No." Letty jutted a finger at him. "You lost control."

Ash put his beer on the counter and confronted her. "Those sons of bitches tried to kill me and Sloane. They almost succeeded. You really think Hogan was going to let Cael walk out of there alive? What about Dex? That asshole Hogan was going to take down as many of us as he could. You think I don't know about your little outburst in Dex's office after Sparks pulled the team?"

"Yeah, I got pissed and wanted to punch something. *You* snapped Collins's neck!"

"Collins knew what he was doing. He pulled a gun on an agent with the intent of killing him while surrounded by armed agents. Neither he nor Hogan had any intention of being taken in alive."

Letty folded her arms over her chest. She knew he was right. He could see it in her eyes. Of all his Human teammates, Letty had the most explosive temper. She was sweet and kind, but when something pissed her off, she was a blazing inferno that felt no remorse for the fuckwit who'd earned her wrath. Ash had always admired her and her mettle. She was living proof that big things came in small, explosive packages. Right now her anger stemmed from Ash doing something that could potentially end his career.

"It doesn't change what you did."

Arguing with Letty would get him nowhere. He'd

learned that a long time ago. So he approached from a different angle. "Let me ask you something. Have you ever loved someone so much you would die for them? Without hesitation or a second thought?"

"I—" She sighed and deflated. It didn't last long. "And what about the next time Cael's life is threatened? You can't just go around snapping perps' necks, Ash."

Like he wasn't aware. Ash ran a hand over his hair and motioned to the couch. They took their beers and sat down. Letty sat facing him, pulled her feet up, and leaned against the backrest, waiting for his reply.

"I don't know. I haven't given much thought to what happened. I kind of have a lot on my plate right now. Maddock's worried I'll hurt Cael."

Letty scoffed. "I love the sarge, but he's not always right, despite believing otherwise."

Ash smiled. "Listen to you, defending my honor and shit."

"Fuck off. Seriously. The way you treat Cael? Shit. I wish a guy would put me on a pedestal the way you do with him. You've taken a bullet for him."

"Yeah, and I've broken his heart time and time again. I've been too much of a coward to step up and be what he needs me to be."

"Ash Keeler is not a coward. I should know. You've had my back for years. A lot of the other guys in Defense would have given me shit for being a woman. Not you. From the beginning, you supported me. You never tried to prove you were better than me or more skilled. You stood up to anyone who had shit to say about me."

Ash frowned. "That's because you're fucking scary."

"Shut up." Letty laughed, then sobered up. "Ash, you've had a string of one-night stands and casual hookups. This is the first time you've been in love. Why are you holding back? Why is Cael being a guy such a problem?"

"I don't *want* it to be a problem, Letty. You think I don't want to throw myself into this? Into being with him and say fuck everyone? When I'm with him, all I want to do is touch him. When I'm not with him, all I do is think about him. I fucking dream of him. I want him so bad it's killing me, but whenever I'm faced with him, my brain panics and pulls away. It's a vicious cycle." He sighed and put his beer down on the coaster on his coffee table.

"So what are you going to do?"

"Find a way to sort my shit out. See a therapist, I don't know. But I have to do something. We can't keep going like this. He deserves better."

"So do you," she said gently.

"You really think that, don't you?"

"You bet that grumpy ass I do."

"Thanks."

Not one to get too mushy, she swiftly moved on to something else. "I gotta go. I'm meeting Rosa and Lou for Christmas shopping at the mall. Want to come?"

Ash arched an eyebrow at her. "I hope you're kidding."

Letty jumped off the couch with a very indelicate snort. "Duh, but it was worth it to see the look on your face."

"Sadist."

She let out an evil cackle on the way to the kitchen, where she dropped her empty beer bottle into the recycling bin before heading for the front door. She tugged her boots on and threw him a kiss. "Be good. Love you."

"Get lost," he grumbled, holding back a smile. "And make sure Rosa doesn't get me any more fucking candles. There ain't enough candles in the world to make me get in touch with my gentler side, so she can fuck off."

"You know she does it to piss you off. What do you do with them?"

Ash shrugged. "I usually give them to Cael. He likes that sort of thing."

"And the ones you don't give to Cael?" she asked with a knowing smile.

"Why are you interrogating me?"

She laughed and waved good-bye, the door closing behind her. It was still pretty early. Maybe he'd take a nap and later order some takeout. He really didn't feel like cooking. His smartphone rang, and he straightened. Shit, it was Dex. There was only one reason Dex would be calling him. Something had happened with either Sloane or Cael. He quickly answered.

"Dex?"

"Ash, it happened again." Dex's voice was shaky, and he sounded out of breath.

The hairs on the back of Ash's neck stood on end. "What happened?"

"Sloane... he lost control again."

"Are you safe?"

"Yes."

"Okay, I'm on my way." Ash hung up and dashed to the front door, where he pulled on his boots and grabbed his coat off the rack. Shit. This couldn't be good. He locked up quickly and called for a cab to hurry the hell over. The company he used knew who he was. They'd send someone over in no time. As he took the stairs, he wondered what the hell was going on with his best friend. This had never happened before, and now it had happened twice. There was no reason it should be happening at all.

The only Therians susceptible to losing control of their shifting were adolescents, but the government had taken care of that a long time ago, developing a drug to help the hormone imbalance, which they provided free to parents of young Therians. The first time Sloane lost control had been after having an argument with Dex. No argument, no matter how big, should've caused Sloane's loss of control. Something was going on. When he got to the street, his cab was already waiting. He climbed into the back and gave the driver Dex's address, telling him it was an emergency.

Was it because Sloane was on Therian medication? Sloane was hardly the first Therian to be on meds. If there was a problem, it would have been all over the news, with mass breakouts of shifting. In less than ten minutes he was at Dex's front door, using his key to let himself in.

"Dex! Dex, where are you!"

"Upstairs. It's okay."

Ash took the stairs two at a time and ran into the bedroom, stopping when he saw Dex sitting in the middle of the large bed with Sloane passed out, his head on Dex's lap. Both were wrapped in white blankets from the waist down. Dex's eyes were red, and Ash could tell he was trying hard to keep it together. Dex gently stroked Sloane's hair, his lips pressed into a thin line. Beside Dex on the bed was a Therian jet injector.

"He's tranqed?"

Dex nodded. He picked up the jet injector and stared down at it. "I tranqed him. I put this thing against his neck, and I shot him."

Tears welled in his eyes, and Ash's heart went out to him. Tranquilizing feral Therian perpetrators was one thing. They'd trained for it, learned to detach themselves from the disturbing reality of taking citizens down like animals. But to have to tranquilize your Therian lover? Ash wished he was better at comforting or at least coming up with comforting words. Instead he gently took the injector from Dex's hands. He placed it inside the nightstand's open drawer.

"You had no choice." Ash took a seat on the edge of the bed close to Dex, mindful of Sloane curled around Dex, as if he'd been trying to protect his partner before passing out. Ash reached out to Dex and laid a hand on his shoulder. "Hey, look at me."

Dex blinked a few times, as if snapping himself out of it, and raised his head, his eyes searching Ash's. Most likely for reassurance Ash couldn't provide.

"You know he'd never forgive himself if he hurt you."

"I know. It's why he insisted I keep the injector in my nightstand. After what happened last time, he was afraid of what he might do."

"Tell me what happened."

"We were having sex, and everything was fine. Suddenly he screamed. Like, a feral scream. It scared the hell out of me. Right away, I knew he was about to shift. So I made a dive for the nightstand, pulled out the injector, and..." Dex blinked away his tears. "You should have seen his face, Ash. He knew what was happening and couldn't do anything about it. I'd never seen him look so scared. And there was nothing I could do to help him. I've never felt so helpless, sitting here, watching him suffer, hearing his screams as he tried to fight himself, the terror on his face."

Dex covered his face with his hands, and Ash pulled him into his embrace.

"It's okay. You did really good, Dex. You saved the both of you."

With a sniff, Dex pulled back. "Why is this happening? We thought the first time was a one-off. The stress, the meds, something. But now..."

"I know." The first time it happened, Ash had no idea what was going on. He'd arrived at Dex's house and shifted downstairs in the living room to the sound of Sloane's feral roar. He'd rushed upstairs, where his best friend attacked him. It had looked, smelled, and sounded like Sloane, but behind his amber eyes was only his best friend's feral half. Sloane was gone. It had scared the shit out of Ash. And then Sloane pushed him down the stairs.

"We need to figure something out," Dex insisted. "What if this happens while we're on duty or out in the field?"

"They'll suspend him and put him through enough evals to keep him off duty for months. We can't let Sparks or any of the higher-ups find out about this." Ash considered his next words very carefully. "I think maybe we should consider talking to Dr. Shultzon."

"Do you trust the guy?"

Ash frowned. "I don't trust anyone outside of my team."

It was the truth. He trusted those he worked with to an extent. Not because he believed they were shady or anything, but because he'd never been the trusting sort. Trust left you vulnerable. Ash had taught himself a long time ago to survive. His teammates, his friends, those lucky enough to be called family had earned his trust. He'd never admit it, but he counted Dex among his family. Sort of like the annoying brother-in-law. You're happy he's making your bro happy, but damn, sometimes you just wanted to punch him in his stupid smiley face. Who the hell smiled that much, anyway? A crazy person, that's who.

Dex worried his bottom lip, looking almost embarrassed. "Will you come with me?"

"Sure." Ash couldn't help the surprise in his tone. Dex never asked him for anything. It went to show how worried the guy was. There was also little Dex wouldn't do for

Sloane. Ash was coming to see that. "I'll put in a call. See if we can stop by sometime after Thanksgiving. I get the feeling Sparks is gonna call us back in any time now. Sloane's only got a couple of weeks of recovery left. I'm pretty good to go. Your bro will be back to his bouncy self in no time, and there's no longer an Order or Coalition to threaten us. Happy holidays to us."

Dex chuckled. "Guess we should enjoy it while it lasts, huh?"

"Yeah." Ash's gaze went to Dex's bandaged arm. "Didn't realize things were that serious between you two."

Dex followed Ash's gaze to his arm before moving on to Sloane. "Surprised the hell out of me too. I think that last mission was rough on everyone. Put things into perspective for all of us. One minute I was thinking he might never feel the same way I did, next thing I know he's telling me he loves me and that we should move in together." He brushed Sloane's hair away from his face and stroked his cheek. "It's scary, isn't it?"

"What's that?"

"How one person can become your whole world. One day you're going about your business, and next thing you know, you're handing someone all your trust, your love, your heart, everything you are. You're just handing it over and hoping for the best."

"Hope for the best, prepare for the worst," Ash said quietly. It's what he and Sloane had always done. They'd embraced it. Now things were different for the both of them. Ash never would have seen this coming, at least not for himself. Sloane had always wanted someone to love him for who he was. Despite what he was. Ash remembered his best friend confessing as much. One night back when they were kids in the facility, they lay on the floor staring up at their ceiling, painted like a starry night, and Sloane had opened up for the first time since they'd met. Ash had assured Sloane he'd find someone great one day, and Sloane had replied Ash would as well. Ash had nodded, but inside, he'd told himself no one would ever love him. He didn't deserve to be loved. After years of telling himself that, he started to believe it. Then he'd met Cael.

"Thanks, Ash. For everything."

"No problem." He got up and motioned to Sloane. "Will you be okay with him?"

"Yeah. He'll be out for a while. I'll get some dinner ready for him for when he wakes up. Even if he didn't complete the shift, he'll probably be hungry from the attempt and the tranquilizer."

"Okay. If you need me, just call. I'll check up on you guys tomorrow." He headed for the door, doing his best to occupy his mind with something other than the shitty day this had been, when Dex called out to him.

"Hey, Ash."

Ash turned, studying Dex and the wide smile on his face. He braced himself.

"You hugged me."

Ash held back a smile. "Don't let it go to your head. It was a momentary lapse in judgment."

Dex's grin got wider. "You hugged me, and I was naked."

"Thanks for the disturbing reminder. Next time I see you two, you'd better have some pants on."

"No promises." Dex beamed.

Ash shook his head, grumbling to himself as he left. He went downstairs, unable to help his smile. Looked like Sloane had found that someone he'd been hoping for since he was a kid. Maybe he hadn't exactly hoped for a Cheesy-

Doodle-crunching nut, but Sloane seemed content with the guy's peculiarities. Sloane was happy. It was all Ash needed to know. Now if he could only sort out his own love life, or whatever it was he had with Cael.

Outside, he decided to take a walk in the brisk late-night air before calling a cab. In a few days it would be Thanksgiving, and Maddock expected him and Sloane to spend the night, which was fine with Ash.

———————

CAEL WAS NERVOUS.

He was torn between trying to make everything absolutely perfect and pretending it was no big deal. And it wasn't, really. Ash had come over for Thanksgiving last year. Except last year they hadn't kissed or admitted to being in love with each other. Well, Cael had admitted it. Ash hadn't said the words yet, but Cael knew. He didn't need to hear the words. Or so he kept telling himself.

"So... Ash Keeler."

Cael stopped whipping the sugar frosting. He should have known this was coming. Frankly, he was surprised it hadn't come sooner, considering his brother's impatience. "Dex."

"I know." Dex held his hands up before wrinkling his nose. "But Ash Keeler?"

Cael put the bowl on the black marble counter and planted his hands on his hips. Were they really going to do this today of all days? They had a hundred things to do and prep before dinner. One of their dad's Therian-sized ovens was currently cooking a couple of forty-pound turkeys, casseroles, potatoes, and veggies, while in the second Therian-sized oven, Cael was baking cakes, cookies, fresh bread, and whatever Dex roped him into cooking next.

"What's wrong with Ash?" Cael demanded.

Dex smirked. "How long do you have?"

"Funny." Cael swatted Dex's hand away from the cookie tray he'd removed from the oven a minute ago. "No."

"Come on, bro. Just one. Pleeeease?"

Dex batted his lashes, and Cael shoved him out of the way so he could open the cabinet door for the box containing the food coloring. All the frosting and icing had to be handmade. Cael detested the premade supermarket stuff, and Dex hated marzipan. Everything always tasted yummier when it was made from scratch. He also enjoyed the process of making it. It was very therapeutic for him.

"I'm not Sloane. Batting those baby blues has no effect on me. You didn't answer my question. What's wrong with Ash?" He swatted at Dex's hand again. "I said no. Don't make me tell on you, because you know I will."

"Tattletale." Dex leaned against the counter and shrugged. "I don't know. I always pictured you settling down with someone less... Ash."

"First of all, no one said anything about settling down. Probably because no one says that anymore. What is this, Regency England? And why's this such a huge shock to everyone anyway?"

"Sloane's known Ash since they were kids. They grew up together, trained together, became the first members of Destructive Delta together. And according to Sloane, Ash has never expressed any attraction or romantic interest in another guy. He's had a long string of girlfriends. Granted, none of them lasted very long, but they were always women. I'm not judging him. If one day he wakes up and he sees this amazing boy and he falls in love, good for him. My issue isn't with his falling for another dude. My issue is why is it a problem for *him*?"

"He's got stuff to work out," Cael muttered, moving the chocolate chip cookies with M&M's onto a plate painted with a turkey and acorns. If his brother went for the cookies one more time, he was going to beat him with his spatula.

"No kidding."

Removing his oven glove, Cael turned to his brother, pleading. "I need you and Dad to support me on this. I love him, Dex. It can work between us. I know it can. He just needs some time to figure all this out. We're going to sit and talk about it. I don't want to push him. If we have to take things at his pace, then so be it. At least I know he wants to be with me."

"Hey, you know Dad and I will be here for you no matter what. I just worry, that's all."

"I can handle it."

Dex bit his bottom lip and averted his gaze.

What was this now? Cael folded his arms over his chest. "You don't think I can handle Ash?"

"I didn't say that."

Cael narrowed his eyes at his brother. "No, you were thinking it."

"He's got an attitude. I just don't want you to regret getting involved with him."

"Attitude. I know for you that translates to anger issues." There was something his brother wanted to say but was afraid to. "What is it?" Cael studied his brother and read between the lines. With Dex, you always had to read between the lines. Attitude. Anger issues. Regret getting involved. It dawned on Cael, and a lump formed in his throat. "This is about Fuller, isn't it?" An old wound he thought had long ago healed ached. He hadn't thought about Fuller in so long. Which was exactly how he preferred it.

"You can't deny the similarities," Dex said gently.

"Ash is nothing like Fuller! How can you even think that?" Cael was furious. How could Dex believe that of Ash, after everything they'd all been through together? Ash had proven himself time and time again. What was it going to take for his brother to understand? "Look me in the eye and tell me you think Ash is like Fuller."

Dex went pensive, and Cael waited.

"You're right. I'm being unreasonable and a jerk. I'm sorry. Ash might have issues, but he's a good guy. I genuinely believe that. I know he'd never hurt you like that. If anything, he's risked his life to protect you. I don't mean to give him a hard time. I just hate how he's keeping you hanging." Dex put his hand to Cael's cheek. "I'm sorry for being so insensitive."

Cael swallowed hard and nodded. The backs of his eyes stung. His brother was worried, and he had every right to be after what he'd been put through with Fuller. Years later, and Cael's guilt still ate away at him. All his life, his big brother had looked out for him, and Cael had pushed Dex away to defend a Therian who'd taken advantage of him in the worst way, who'd made him feel worthless. God, Cael had been such a despicable jerk to Dex. They'd had so many arguments. One in particular stood out among the rest. His hurtful words to his brother echoed in his head. He'd never forget them. *You'll never understand me. You're Human, and what's more, you're not even my real brother.*

"I'm so sorry, Dex." Cael wrapped his arms around his brother and squeezed him tight. "I'm sorry for the horrible things I said to you. I never meant them. You have to believe me."

"Hey, now." Dex held him close and placed a hand to the back of his head, comforting him like he'd always done. Cael had never regretted anything more in his life than he had in the two years he'd been with Fuller, not only for what he'd endured but for what he'd put his family through. "Of course I believe you. I never doubted you, Chirpy. I knew that wasn't you talking."

"I can still see your face, how badly I hurt you. Yet you never gave up on me."

"Never have, never will. It's all in the past. You don't have to apologize anymore." Dex pulled back and smiled at him. "Can I tell you a secret?"

Cael nodded. "You know you can."

"He may be far from perfect, with many, *many* faults, but I know deep down, Ash will treat you right."

Cael couldn't help his big grin. "You really believe that?"

"I do."

"Thanks, Dex."

Cael hugged his brother once more when their dad called out from somewhere upstairs.

"I don't hear cooking down there."

Dex huffed. "Because we were having a moment, Dad."

"Well, finish your moment, get back to cooking, and stay away from the cookies. That means you, Dex."

With a chuckle, Cael pulled back when it hit him. An odd yet familiar scent. He sniffed the air, catching a whiff of it among the smell of freshly baked cookies and the turkeys roasting in the ovens. He kept running into that scent but could never quite place it. Following his nose, he realized it was coming from his brother. That was weird. "Dex?"

"Yeah?" Dex removed a bowl from the cabinet and the

ingredients for their dad's super awesome green bean casserole.

"There's something... off about you."

Dex pointed to his head. "Too much hair gel? It's a new brand. Thought I'd try something that wasn't citrus. Therian agents can smell me coming from a mile away at work. I needed to shake things up."

"No. It's your scent. *Your* scent. Not your various manscaping products." He leaned into Dex and sniffed.

"First of all, I do not manscape. I'm not even hairy. I also happen to use an average amount of men's products. Second of all, don't sniff me. That's just weird."

"Sorry, it's just bugging me. You smell like you but not you. You smell like Sloane too."

"Maybe because we're always around each other?" Dex rubbed his chest sensually and thrust his hips. "And I do mean all up in each other. Ooh yeah."

"Ew, perv. No. That's not what I meant. Stop humping the air!"

Dex laughed. "What? You don't like my sweet moves?"

"Keep your sweet moves away from me and my baked goods." Cael shoved him again, ignoring his brother's laughter. "Dork." What was his brother hiding from him? And why? "This is different. Like you've been permanently—" Cael gasped. "Oh my God, Dex! Did Sloane mark you?"

"Um... I was going to say something, but I'm still trying to figure out how to tell Dad." Dex hesitated before pulling up his shirt sleeve, revealing a white bandage around his forearm.

"You bonded?" Cael couldn't believe it. His brother had been marked as a Therian mate.

"You *what?*"

Cael and Dex both gave a start. They spun to face their dad, and Dex hid his arm behind his back.

"Dad, hey. Sloane and I had a bonding moment. You know, heart-to-heart."

Their dad's laser-beam stare bore into them. "Boy, you must think I was born yesterday."

Dex shook his head. "No, not at all. I think you were born way back when. What were the dinosaurs like?"

"You're looking for a grounding."

Cael held back a laugh at Dex's scandalized expression.

"You can't ground me!"

"Try me."

Dex opened his mouth to reply but seemed to think better of it. They both knew their dad would totally find a way to ground him. With a deep frown, Tony reached behind Dex and took hold of his arm, causing Dex to suck in a sharp breath. Therian marks took forever to heal on a Human.

"Ouch. Damn it, Dad."

Tony's nostrils flared, and Cael took a slight step back. He knew that look. His dad was trying to keep his cool, and there wasn't a whole lot that made him lose it. Unsurprisingly, Dex was the exception. His brother could send most anyone off the deep end. It was a talent.

"Do you know how serious this is? Did you ask Sloane to do this?"

"No." Dex pulled his arm away. "It was both our decisions, and before you ask, it's not something either of us has taken lightly."

Cael was glad to hear his brother and Sloane hadn't rushed into it, but Cael shared their dad's concerns. This sort of thing wasn't taught in school. It wasn't even talked about out in the open. It was a parent's responsibility to have "the talk" with their kids about markings. Preferably a talk not accompanied by a five-hour sex education class with visuals and gay porn. No one needs a play-by-play on how the prostate works from their dad. At least he and Dex could laugh about it now. Back when they'd been fourteen, not so much. Mortifying didn't begin to cover it. There was more to being a Therian than having the ability to shift into a feral creature.

Tony leaned against the island counter and ran a hand over his jaw. "You two are going to be the death of me. You thought keeping your relationship secret at work was going to be tough before? Now every damned Therian agent is going to know you've been claimed as a Therian mate by an Alpha who will tear their throat out if they come sniffing around you with less than wholesome intentions. Do you know what this does to the dynamics of your partnership with Sloane at the THIRDS? And what the hell are you going to tell Sparks when she gets a whiff of that?"

"Sloane and I will deal with Sparks when the time comes. Granted, I don't know what we're going to do yet, but we'll work it out. As for our work partnership, why should this change anything?"

"Son, you took the Therian courses at work. You know how fiercely they feel things in their Therian forms. How protective they get of their partners. I went over Therian marking when you were fourteen."

"Yeah, well maybe you shouldn't have used porn as a teaching aid because a good deal of what you said got lost in the pizza guy's ass."

Cael cringed and took another subtle step away from his brother. He could practically see the steam coming out of his dad's ears while the gears in Dex's head spun furiously in an attempt to figure out why this was such a big deal.

And it was. Maybe not to most Humans, but it was a hell of a big deal to Therians.

"I don't get it, Dad. What Sloane did is meant to keep other Therian's paws off, not invite them to challenge his claim on me."

"In their Therian forms, their animal instincts are at their strongest. Correct?"

"Yeah."

"And when you have two Alphas and one mate, what happens?"

"Hold up. I only have one mate. Sloane."

"And when another Therian decides he likes how a Therian's mark smells on you. When he wants to challenge an Alpha like Sloane or when a Therian perp gets a whiff of that and decides to get to Sloane through you? What do you think happens then?"

"Um..."

"Therian cage match," Cael offered quietly. He understood his dad's concerns, but he also understood his brother's struggle to comprehend something that was a natural instinct for a Therian. Their Dad had seen it all after being with the THIRDS since the beginning. Cael was a Therian. Dex had never even dated a Therian before Sloane. It wasn't Dex's fault. There was still an overwhelming amount of information the world had yet to uncover about Therians. First Gen Therians were only in their late thirties now. Who knew what the hell else might develop.

"No one's going to challenge Sloane in his Therian form." Dex pursed his lips in thought. "Okay, at least not at work," he conceded.

"Oh?" Tony folded his arms over his chest. "What about Taylor?"

Dex mirrored their dad's pose. *Uh-oh.* Cael looked from

one to the other. He slowly reached behind him and plucked a cookie from the plate, then brought it to his mouth for a nibble. This was going to be good.

"Taylor knows I'm off-limits."

"His Human side does. If he's in his Therian form and he gets a whiff of that, he's gonna go all feral, and he might challenge Sloane. Why do you think we have a no fraternizing rule?"

Ooh, Dad's puffing up his chest. It's on now. Cael nibbled some more of his cookie. He really wished he had some milk, but if he got their attention, he'd get dragged into this mess, and he was *so* not taking sides. When he was little, they'd tried a few times to drag him into taking sides. He'd burst into tears and scream at the top of his lungs. They stopped trying to get him involved real quick after that.

"Because of what happened with Seb and Hudson?" Dex asked. "The kid that got killed when Seb broke protocol to save Hudson from getting shot."

"That, and Seb marked Hudson."

Dex's jaw dropped, and he put up a hand. "Whoa, hold the phone. You're telling me Sebastian Hobbs claimed Hudson and marked him?"

"Yep."

"Why didn't I know this?" Dex frowned and looked at Cael. "Did you know about this?"

Cael simply nodded and took another nibble. His brother frowned at him and nabbed his cookie.

"Hey! That's my cookie, you thief."

"For not telling me." He stuffed the whole thing into his mouth.

"Mature," Cael muttered, grabbing himself another cookie. "And I didn't tell you because it's not my place to say anything. Seb told me the night of your party. He was a little drunk. I don't think he meant to. You should have seen his face. That whole mess just crushed him."

"Why haven't I seen it?" Dex asked through a mouthful of cookie.

"Boy, don't talk with your mouth full. What's wrong with you?"

Cael grinned widely. "How long do you have?"

Dex's eyebrows nearly reached his hairline. He jutted a finger at him in mock warning, making Cael laugh. Their dad ignored them both, answering Dex's initial question.

"You haven't seen it because it's on his back. He never showers in the employee locker rooms. His office has a private bathroom and shower. He's self-conscious about it."

"That's horrible. Poor guy." Dex let out a sigh.

Maybe this wasn't going to be one of their epic three-hour grudge matches after all. Cael could only put it down to Sloane's calming influence. Dex would have irritated the hell out of their dad by now and ended up in a headlock.

"It gets worse," Tony said, deflating. "That kind of bond isn't broken easily, Dex. Instinct might have a Therian challenging an Alpha, but if the marked Therian has lost their mate, it changes things. Many Therians don't want a partner who's been marked by someone else and abandoned. By ending things with Seb, Hudson's pretty much condemned himself. Seb can find another mate to claim. Hudson... he's tainted." Tony shook his head sadly.

"That's ridiculous," Dex replied angrily. "Hudson is an awesome guy. Why would Therians reject being in a relationship with him because of a few scars?"

"Those scars run deep for Therians, Dex. It's a very delicate and complicated matter. Do you understand my concerns?"

Dex nodded, but he looked no less determined than he had when they'd started the conversation. "I do, Dad, but we're not going to let anyone dictate how we should live our lives or how we should conduct our relationship. If some asshole Therian can't keep a grip on his feral half around me, that's his problem, not mine. Being Therian is no excuse for that behavior. If things don't work for me and Sloane, well, that's something I'll have to deal with, and I'll do it the same way I've done with everything in my life. I'll face it head-on."

"You're absolutely right. I guess I'm just not as prepared for this as I thought I was."

This was the first time Cael had seen their dad look so worried. Other than the time Dex had landed in the hospital after he'd gotten jumped by Isaac's goons, over a year ago.

Tony put his hand to Dex's cheek. "If things don't work out, that mark will make it tough for another Therian to get close to you too."

Dex nodded, replying quietly, "I know." He smiled at Tony. "Thanks, Dad. For looking out for me. Whatever comes our way, Sloane and I will get through it together, but it means a lot knowing I have you guys to turn to as well."

Tony brought them both in for a hug, and Cael squeezed them in return.

"When did you boys get so grown up?"

"I think it was after the pubes grew in," Dex said.

Cael closed his eyes with a groan. "You just had to do it."

"Yep." Dex beamed brightly and ruffled Cael's hair.

"I may have spoken too soon about the grown-up thing." Their dad pulled away and headed for the stairs. "I'm going back to putting the laundry away."

"Does everyone have their headphones like we discussed?" Dex called out after him.

"Yes. Thank you for the horrifying reminder of why we'll need them," Tony grumbled as he stomped up the stairs.

"Come on. It's just sex."

Cael and his dad groaned in unison. Cael's room was right next to Dex's as well. Perfect. "You can't just not have sex for one day?"

"You two need to get laid. Seriously."

"You know what, eat some damn cookies," Tony called down from upstairs.

Dex cackled in amusement, snatched another cookie from the plate, and bolted before Cael could whack him in the arm. The doorbell rang, and Cael froze.

"Oh my God, they're here!" He grabbed another cookie and started munching away before Dex took it from him.

"Stop binge eating."

Cael swiped his cookie back. "Pot, meet kettle."

"Yeah, well, I have to actually work to keep the weight off, unlike you who burns through the calories just by breathing. You and your freaking cheetah Therian metabolism," Dex grumbled.

He'd always envied Cael's ability to eat whatever and however much he wanted without having to worry about his weight. Cheetah Therians had the highest metabolism of all Therians. It meant their bodies demanded a great deal of food, especially when in their Therian form. Post-shift was especially important. It also meant cheetah Therians were more prone to health issues if they didn't look after themselves.

"Why're you nervous?" Dex asked, heading for the front door with Cael trailing after him.

"Because everything's changed this year. Things are kind of tense with Ash right now. What if he has a terrible time tonight and things get even worse between us? Should I act like nothing's changed? Should I give him space? Should I try to ease him into the idea of being together? He said we'd talk, but we haven't. I don't want to push him."

Dex turned and took hold of Cael's shoulders. "Relax. I'm here, okay? I won't let things get weird."

Cael couldn't help himself. "But you said *you'll* be here."

"Funny. Okay, weirder."

"Really? No awkward silences?" He'd never had any with Ash. He really hoped they didn't start now.

"When is there ever silence when I'm around?" Dex asked, heading off once again for the front door.

"Good point."

"Don't worry, Chirpy, it'll be fine. Who knows? Ash might surprise you."

"Please don't call me that in front of anything with a pulse."

"No promises."

Dex opened the door, and Cael tried to relax like his big brother had wisely suggested. He felt like an idiot. Dex was right. It would be fine. He had his family and Sloane to take the pressure off. What would it say about them and their relationship if they couldn't make it through one meal without things getting uncomfortable? He'd never felt uncomfortable around Ash before, and he hated the thought that the amazing friendship they had might change.

All right, enough of that. Cael straightened and smiled when Dex stepped aside to let Sloane and Ash in. His brother all but threw himself at Sloane, being mindful of his leg. Cael was sure if Sloane were fully healed, Dex would have climbed him.

"For fuck's sake," Ash growled, raising the large insulated bag over the pair's heads as he pushed past them. "It's been like six hours since you've seen each other, not six months."

Cael was going to say hi when Ash kissed his cheek.

"Hey, sweetheart."

Don't freak out. It's just a kiss on the cheek. And a pet name. And oh my God, someone scoop me off the floor. Cael chastised himself for being such a dweeb.

"Hi," he managed cheerfully. If this was any indication of how the evening was going to go, Cael was in big trouble.

THREE

"Happy Thanksgiving. I made pie. Cherry, pecan, and your favorite, apple and cinnamon." Ash had spent the whole morning baking. He'd been so damned nervous he'd ended up with enough baked goods to last him well into the new year. He handed the warm insulated three-tiered bag to Cael so he could take off his coat.

Dex stared at them. "Ash Keeler *bakes?*"

Ash removed his hat and scarf and shoved them into his coat pockets. "Shut up, Daley." There was a reason he didn't go around announcing his hobby to the world. Just because he didn't look like Martha Stewart didn't mean he couldn't fucking use an oven or follow a recipe.

"Wow. You bake. Ash bakes. I did not know this." Dex turned to Sloane. "Did you know he bakes?"

Sloane hung his and Ash's coats on the hooks behind the door. "He's really good too. Like, really good."

Dex opened his mouth, then closed it before opening it again. "I got nothing."

Cael elbowed Ash playfully. "Dude, you left Dex speechless."

"Christmas miracle's arrived early this year," Ash muttered.

Dex let out a sniff and headed into the living room with Sloane in tow. "The only reason I'm not telling you to bite me is because you brought delicious, warm pies."

"Apple's mine," Cael declared, smacking Dex's hand away from the bag.

He took it into the kitchen with everyone following behind. On the way there, Ash noticed the table was all set. Cael mentioned how they were just waiting on their dad to come downstairs so they could start putting the food out. Cael left the bag of pies on the counter, and Ash stepped up beside him, his hand resting on the small of Cael's back as he spoke.

"How's your leg? I noticed you're not using your crutch."

"I'm feeling much better. I should be up for training once we're back on active duty."

"I'm glad. Don't push yourself too hard, though, okay? If you need a little extra time to rest, no one's going to hold it against you."

Cael turned to smile at Ash and appeared to have misjudged their proximity. Their bodies ended up pressed against each other, and Cael's face flushed pink. Not wanting to embarrass him, Ash pretended he hadn't noticed. Cael patted Ash's bicep.

"Don't worry, big guy. I'm doing great. Thank you."

Ash pulled him closer and kissed the top of his head. "You're welcome."

"Glad you boys could make it."

At the sound of Maddock's voice, Ash stepped away, noticing how Cael's smile faded. Cael wasn't an idiot. Ash couldn't even have his arm around Cael in front of his family. How pathetic was that? Having Cael so close and being unable to touch him was painful. Ash had loved the feel of Cael's body against his. He'd dreamed of having Cael in his arms, of holding him and making love to him, and now Cael stood beside him, waiting for him to give them both what they'd wanted for so long. For now, he'd work on spending a nice Thanksgiving with Cael, his family, and friends.

Maddock shook Sloane's hand first, then Ash's, lingering a little on Ash before letting go. Ash noticed the way Maddock's eyes narrowed slightly. Had Maddock discussed their conversation at Dekatria with Cael? Ash figured he hadn't, considering Cael hadn't brought it up. He imagined Fuller was most likely a sensitive topic for Cael, and rightly so.

"All right, let's eat," Maddock declared. "Everyone grab the potholders, and let's get this show on the road."

They hopped to it. The whole thing resembled more a military procedure than the setting of a table. Under Maddock's command, they all lined up, potholders in hand. Maddock pulled out a dish from the oven and handed it to the next person in line. The line moved, others returned from the dining room and joined the line once again to pick up their next dish. This continued until the table was set, leaving a large gap in the center for two turkeys. Once everything was in its place, Maddock motioned to the chairs.

Ash pulled Cael's chair out for him, and Cael once again blushed. God, he loved how sweet and beautiful Cael looked when he blushed. It sometimes annoyed Cael, but the guy had no control over it. Ash always noticed when Cael blushed. He tended not to bring it up so Cael wouldn't feel self-conscious about it. Ash winked at Cael and nudged his cheek playfully before taking a seat at the table beside him, their chairs closer than he was certain they'd ever been before. Dex and Sloane sat across the table from them, and Maddock sat at the head.

Maddock said grace, giving thanks for all they had, for their family, friends, and good health. While they served themselves and passed different dishes around, they all chatted and laughed. Most of it tended to involve Dex's shenanigans. After they'd all eaten their fill, or in Dex's case eaten his weight in turkey, Dex tapped his fork against his glass.

"So, um, I—*we* have an announcement of sorts." Dex took Sloane's hand in his. "Sloane and I are moving in together."

"That's awesome!" Cael got up and rounded the table to hug his brother and Sloane. "I'm so happy for you guys!"

"What's the arrangement?" Maddock asked curiously, and Ash noticed how Sloane subtly squeezed Dex's hand.

It always amazed him the kind of effect Maddock's presence commanded off duty. Ash didn't think Sloane was intimidated, but he respected Maddock. Everyone did.

"I'm moving in with Dex," Sloane replied. "It made more sense. Plus the labyrinth of '80s memorabilia in Dex's basement would never fit in my apartment."

Maddock nodded his agreement. "And your apartment?"

"I might have a friend who's interested in renting it."

"Congratulations, then. I'm happy for you," Maddock said sincerely. He took his wineglass and lifted it in a toast. "To Dex and Sloane. Here's to a future filled with love, happiness, and health. May there be many nights in each other's arms and very few on the couch." Maddock gave Dex a pointed look.

"What? Why are you assuming *I'll* be the one who ends up relegated to the couch?"

Cael arched an eyebrow at his brother. "Remember when you ran up the down escalator at the mall, fell on your knees, and had to get stitches?"

Sloane patted Dex's hand. "Aw, I'm sure he didn't know any better."

"He was twenty-three."

The table burst into laughter, except for Dex, who turned his nose up at them.

"I thought I could outrun it." Dex held up his glass. "All right you bunch of jokers, we were having a toast."

Everyone cheered and toasted and promised to help them move. They talked and ate. At one point, Ash felt Cael's leg pressed up against his, and it was ridiculous how happy the tiny gesture made him. If it was even a gesture. Ash swiftly pushed it off as an accident, but then a little later, Cael reached over and wiped a thumb over the corner of Ash's mouth, telling him he had a breadcrumb.

"You should have seen him," Dex said with a laugh. "He looked so adorable with his cheetah fuzz shaped into spikes, from his head down to his back. Like a little spotted punk rocker."

Maddock shook his head at Dex. "It took me two hours to wash all the hair spray out of your brother's fur."

"We were pretending to be Guns N' Roses," Cael explained. "Dex was singing 'Welcome to the Jungle,' and I was backup sing—er, chirping."

Ash laughed and playfully bumped Cael's shoulder. "I'm going to have to agree with Dex. That's adorable." Even in his Therian form, Ash thought Cael was the sweetest thing he'd ever laid eyes on. Cael could be in his Therian form among thousands of cheetahs, and Ash would be able to point him out. His little gestures, the heart shape of his nose, or the way he chirped away, as if anyone not in their Therian form might understand him if he tried hard enough.

Dex grabbed Sloane's arm. "Tell me you recorded that. Doesn't matter. I have witnesses." Dex stood and motioned to all of them. "Witnesses! You all heard it. Ash said he agrees with me."

"Oh, good Lord. We're never going to hear the end of this," Maddock sighed, getting up to clear the dishes.

"Do you realize how epic this moment is?" Dex said, helping clear up.

"It's not really that epic," Maddock replied.

Dex let out an exaggerated gasp. "Where have you been living? Ash Keeler has agreed with something I, Dexter J. Daley, said."

"About your brother being adorable. Not exactly earth-shattering. He's thought that since they met."

The table fell into silence as they all gaped at Maddock. Well, this was news to Ash. What the hell? Seeming to notice the quiet, or more likely the lack of Dex talking, Maddock looked up.

"What are you, fish? Close your mouths."

Four mouths promptly closed.

"It's not rocket science. I've known that boy since he joined, and he's threatened every agent he's ever met with kicking their ass. Except for Cael."

Hard to argue with that. It was the truth.

Dex frowned at Ash. "You threatened to kick Hobbs's ass?"

Ash nodded. "Yep." Was it his first week of being on the job? He was pretty sure it was the first week.

"Dude, that's not cool. Hobbs is awesome."

"He can also be a pain in the ass. Plus when we first met, I didn't know he had selective mutism. I asked him a question, and he wouldn't answer me. He'd whisper to Calvin, who'd answer for him. I got pissed off and told him if he didn't tell me himself, I'd kick his ass." Ash had never met a tiger Therian as big and insecure as Hobbs. The whole encounter had left him confused. Here was their new demolitions expert, and he couldn't talk. How the fuck was he going to communicate with his team? Ash wasn't proud to admit he'd had a shit fit. He understood the THIRDS was about equality and representation when it came to hiring, but he had been genuinely concerned about the safety of his team. Not long after, Ash had seen how wrong he'd been about Hobbs. Not that he'd admitted it.

Dex let out a sound of disgust. "Dude, not cool."

"I said I didn't know. I apologized afterward, and that's saying something."

Ash got up to help clear the dishes, with Dex going on about how he should really think about using some of those scented candles Rosa had gifted him. Ash proceeded to flip him off.

When Cael stood to help, Ash put a hand to his shoulder.

"Relax, I've got this."

He gave Cael a wink and walked the dirty dishes to the kitchen with Dex yammering on behind him. The guy was like a fucking mosquito buzzing in your ear and trying to suck the life out of you. Ash placed the dishes in the dishwasher, giving grunts and one-word replies. He grabbed the dishes from Dex and put those in as well. He wished he could stick Dex in there. Finally someone up there decided to give him a break, and Dex left the kitchen, singing some stupid song about a lion sleeping tonight or something.

Ash frowned at Maddock. "Does he never shut up? How the hell did you live with him for so long?"

"It's called patience," Maddock replied. "Not exactly your forte."

"Oh, I can be patient. That's not what's required when dealing with your oldest. I'd say 'sedative' is more the word you were looking for."

Maddock laughed. "Just get in there, Keeler."

Ash did as he was told, heading back into the dining room and resuming his seat beside Cael with a smile.

"Miss me?"

Cael chuckled and gave him a bashful push.

Dex patted his full belly. "I think we should chill in the living room for a while. Come back for dessert in a bit. What do you guys say?"

"Sounds good to me."

Sloane got up and followed Dex into the living room. Dex didn't miss a beat, going on about some movie he wanted to see before Christmas. Cael followed his brother with Ash close behind him. Was it him, or was Dex talking more than ever? Ash sneaked a glance at Cael, who appeared to be lost in thought. Maybe he was overreacting and everything was just fine.

A few hours later it was evident he'd spoken too soon. When Cael's family was around, everything was great. There was never any time for things to get weird between him and Cael, what with Dex driving them all crazy as usual, Sloane running interference, and Maddock attempting not to throttle all of them. Then there were the few instances when he and Cael were alone. Like when Maddock went upstairs for a post-Thanksgiving-dinner nap, and Dex got all cuddly with Sloane. The two got to talking about something, and things got quiet between him and

Cael. Ash used the opportunity to clear up the living room from the aftermath of Dex's turkey sandwich. The guy might not be a Therian, but he put food away like one.

Baking wasn't the only thing Ash turned to when he was feeling anxious. Cleaning helped. There had been several instances around the house, usually when Dex and Sloane were sucking face or being all cute together, that things had gotten quiet between him and Cael. It was almost like Cael was relying on his brother to fill every second of silence, which was beyond Dex's capabilities, despite his talent for never shutting the hell up. At some point, Sloane needed some quiet, and that's usually when he'd kiss Dex. Worked like a charm every time.

Cael had gone off to the kitchen to prep dessert, seeing as how everyone would be waking up from their turkey-induced coma soon, and Ash decided to join him. His hands were shoved into his jeans pockets, and he tried his best to appear casual.

"Hey. Need help?"

"Sure. I was about to remove the pies from the oven if you want to grab them for me. Just pop them on the counter." He went back to sorting out leftovers into Tupperware containers and stacking them in the fridge. Ash removed the pies from the oven where they'd been keeping warm and placed them on the counter beside Cael.

"Anything else I can do?"

"Cabinet up top and to your right, there's some serving dishes. Could you take half of each pie and place them on the dishes? The rest goes in the fridge."

"Why not just leave out the whole pie?" Ash asked curiously.

"Because then Dex will eat the whole pie."

Of course. "Where the hell does he store it all?"

Cael shrugged. "I have no idea."

"Then again, the way his mouth runs, he's probably burning mass amounts of calories."

Cael chuckled. "And this is news to you?"

They went back to their duties, and the room went quiet again. It was driving Ash nuts. Cael was being quiet, and Ash had no idea what to say to break the silence. What the hell should he talk about? What had they talked about before? It was like he was in uncharted territory, which was absurd. He'd known Cael for years, and they'd never had any trouble holding a conversation. Even when neither of them spoke, the silence had been comfortable.

Cael caught Ash's arm, took the pie from him, and placed it on the counter. "This is ridiculous. We've never been uncomfortable around each other. I know things have changed between us, but has it changed that much? I miss my friend."

He searched Ash's eyes, pleading. All at once, Ash felt himself relax. He smiled down at Cael and put his hand to his cheek.

"I miss my friend too."

"How about for the holidays, we put a hold on all the complicated stuff and just enjoy each other's company? Do whatever feels right, and we'll take it from there. No expectations, no waiting for the other shoe to drop, no over-thinking things, and no pressure. Let's relax and have some fun."

"I like the sound of that." Just when he thought he couldn't be more amazed by the wonderful young Therian before him, he was proven wrong. How could Cael be so insightful to his needs, so unselfish and understanding?

"Good. Now let's join the others before Dex eats all the

cookies. He always hogs all the macadamia chocolate-chunk ones."

Cael narrowed his eyes, and Ash chuckled.

"I'll make sure he leaves you some."

Cael turned away to pick up one of the pie dishes when Ash gently caught his arm and pulled him back.

"Question." He should probably give more thought to what he was about to say, but fuck it. He couldn't let Cael put in all the effort. Ash had to do his part, so he went with his gut.

"Yeah?" Cael cocked his head to one side, and Ash hoped his face wasn't as red as it felt.

"If I get the urge to sneak a kiss at any point, would that be okay with you?"

Cael brightened, and Ash's silly heart did a flip.

"I'd like that."

"Me too."

Ash pulled him into his embrace and kissed him. Not the peck on the cheek or the brief press of lips Ash had been expecting to give, but a kiss that had him all but dropping to his knees. It was sweet, warm, and tasted deliciously of Cael. Ash never wanted it to end. He felt Cael's tongue against his lips, and Ash opened his mouth, inviting Cael to taste and explore. To his delight, Cael accepted, deepening their kiss. He pulled Cael against him, his arms wrapped tight around Cael as if he might try to escape. A low rumble of a moan reverberated from Cael's chest, sending a shiver up Ash's spine. So much adoration and need, with more passion than Ash could have imagined. Tentatively, Cael wrapped his arms around Ash, his fingers digging into the firm muscles of his back. Damn, it felt so good.

As much as he told his heart not to give in so quickly, it was no use. Having Cael in his arms, feeling his strength, knowing the depth of Cael's affections, had Ash surrendering himself without a second thought. He left himself bare. Every nerve ending, every vulnerable, tender inch of him. Ash brushed his lips over Cael's as he pulled away, his thumb caressing Cael's cheek. "You're blushing," he murmured breathlessly.

"Sorry."

"I like it. I especially like that it's because of me."

That certainly didn't seem to help poor Cael's blushing situation. His cheeks burned crimson. "It's always because of you."

"I've never met anyone like you. You're so beautiful. And the best part is, you're not even aware of how wonderful you are."

Cael shrugged bashfully. "I guess you bring out the best in me."

"That's where you're wrong." Ash took Cael's hand in his and placed it to his heart. "*You* bring out the best in *me*. I had no idea what my life was missing before I met you." He felt it down to his core. What he was, what everyone thought of him, meant nothing compared to what Cael believed of him.

"Are the pies ready?"

Ash quickly pulled away as Dex entered the kitchen. He was torn between wanting to tell Dex what he could do with his pies and picking his heart up off the floor. This was how it had to be for now. For a slip of a moment, it had all been so perfect and right. Dex reminded him of the reality of their situation. Ash was grateful Cael had taken the first step in moving their relationship forward and reminded himself he couldn't mess this up. For years he'd been denying to himself what he felt for Cael. Even when he'd resigned himself to the fact nothing could ever happen between them, the tiny flicker of hope never went out. Having Cael in his arms, kissing him, was more than he'd ever thought possible. Patience. He needed patience.

Dex looked from Cael to Ash and back. "Shit. I interrupted something, didn't I?"

"No," Ash replied, though he knew Dex would be able to see past his smile to the "I'm going to kick your ass later" look.

Cael smiled sweetly, and Ash actually took a step to the side. *Uh-oh.* He knew that look. Cael was the sweetest guy he knew. He was also a little hellcat. Those claws were damn sharp. Ash had found himself at the receiving end of those razor-sharp claws and knew firsthand the sting they were capable of leaving behind.

"Now that you're here, you can go wake Dad from his nap."

"Aw, man. Seriously?" Dex whined. "Come on. You know he won't throw anything at you. Why do I have to do it?"

Cael folded his arms over his chest. "Tough. I called it. Go."

"Fine." Dex stomped off to wake Maddock, which from the sounds of it was no easy feat.

Cael turned to Ash with an apologetic smile. It had been so good while it lasted. With a smile, Ash motioned toward the pies.

"You want me to help with these?"

"Thanks. I'm going to grab the ice cream."

Ash took the pie dishes while Cael fished out spoons, bowls, paper towels, and the ice cream from the freezer. Together they walked into the living room, a loud thump causing Sloane to sit up in concern.

"What was that?"

"That was Dex falling over. Dad gets very cranky when woken up from his nap. It's all cute and bearable when your kids are little and jumping on your bed to wake you, not so much when they're thirty-five years old. My guess is Dad pulled the covers from under him." Cael placed everything on the large coffee table and turned to Sloane with a big grin.

"Expect lots of pouting."

Just as Cael had predicted, Dex entered the living room with his bottom lip jutted out as he rubbed his arm. "He could have at least pulled the blankets out when I was facing the carpet."

"That's what you get for not waking me up like a normal person," Maddock growled, dropping himself into one of the armchairs. "Grown man," Maddock mumbled, "jumping on the bed like he's five. You wanna jump, I'll give you jump. Just don't come bitchin' to me when you hit the hardwood floor."

"It's the only way you'll wake up," Dex groused, snuggling up to Sloane with a pout. "I hurt my arm."

"No, he didn't," Maddock countered, pointing to the pecan pie. "He's just saying that so you'll coddle him. He used to do that when he was little and he'd done something he wasn't supposed to so he wouldn't get in trouble."

Dex gasped. "So not true."

"Really?" Maddock scooped up some ice cream and plopped it down on his plate next to his pie. "When you took apart the VCR to see how it worked and I yelled at you, you started crying and saying your head hurt because the video shelf fell and hit you."

"It did fall."

"You were in the dining room, and the shelf fell two days earlier."

Ash couldn't help joining in the laughter with Cael and Sloane. Dex and Maddock continued to argue over Dex's convenient ouchies until Sloane did them all a favor and distracted Dex with pie. In the end, Dex got his way and then some, with Sloane coddling him and feeding him. Ash had a feeling that had been Dex's intention the whole time. He'd give the guy credit. He was damn sneaky.

After they all had their pie, Cael grabbed Dex by the ear and pulled him along to the kitchen to help him with the dishes, stating he wasn't getting away with it this time. Apparently, Dex was an expert at avoiding chores. He'd somehow managed to get away with it since they were kids.

The rest of the evening was filled with fun and laughter. They played games and teased each other. Soon Maddock had said good night and turned in. Sloane and Dex would be staying in Dex's old bedroom. Ash said he'd be fine on the couch. It was big enough for him. Maddock had brought plenty of blankets and pillows, and the heating would keep him warm. Dex was fighting sleep, so Sloane declared it was time for bed. Soon it was just Ash and Cael. The TV was on, and they were watching some holiday movies.

Ash opened his duffel bag and fished out his pajamas. "I'm just going to change and brush my teeth."

"Me too. Meet back here for some TV?" Cael asked hopefully.

"You got it."

Ash used the guest bathroom downstairs, in the basement outside Maddock's office. He changed into his pajama bottoms and T-shirt and sat on the couch with the Therian-sized fleece blanket pulled around him. He waited to see which pajamas Cael would be wearing. He had almost as many pajama bottoms as he had socks, and they were all quirky, ranging from bacon patterned to Angry Birds. He'd seen plenty of them while crashing at Cael's after a night of boozing at Dekatria.

The house was completely silent for the first time since Ash had arrived. It was nice. He watched TV until he heard Cael's socked footsteps drawing near. Cael leapt over the back of the couch and landed gracefully beside him. This time around, he was wearing his Captain America pajama bottoms and T-shirt. Ash took hold of the blanket and opened his arms.

"Come on. It's warm in here."

Cael smiled and cuddled close, his legs pulled up on the couch. Ash brought his arm around Cael with the blanket, holding him against him and covering them both up. It wasn't as though they hadn't sat together watching TV before, though this was the first time they sat so cozy together. It felt right.

"I like your pajamas," Ash said, giving him a squeeze.

"Thanks. I always pictured you more as a boxers and T-shirt kind of guy for pj's."

"Nope. Actually, I don't wear anything to bed."

Cael pulled back and stared at him. "You sleep naked?"

Ash nodded. "I thought you knew that."

"Why would I know that? Anytime I've crashed at yours or you've crashed at mine, you're always awake before I am and dressed."

"Oh." Ash shrugged. "I sleep naked." It wasn't really the sort of thing he went around advertising. Who the hell cared how he slept? Except for Cael. He seemed particularly interested, which was fine with Ash.

"So you go commando, and you sleep naked."

"I don't like underwear. It's too constricting. And sleeping naked is more comfortable."

Cael turned to face the TV. Ash waited for him to say

something, but he just sat there, staring at the TV, but not really watching it.

"You okay?" Ash asked. Had he said something wrong? Was it weird? He was hardly the first guy to go commando or sleep naked. He liked how the sheets felt against his bare skin, and he hated feeling hot. He especially hated collars or tight things around his neck.

"Sorry, I'm rebooting my brain because you just short-circuited it with that information."

Ash chuckled. "I did?"

"Well, yeah. I mean, I know how you look in your pj's, and then I find out you don't wear anything at all to bed, and that's just... You, sir, are a meanie."

"How am I a meanie?" Ash asked, amused by Cael's pout.

"Because now you've put these images in my head, and I can't get them out, and they're going to drive me crazy."

Ash chuckled and tried to pull him close, but Cael was having none of it.

"Aw, come on. Don't be mad. You're the one who brought it up. What's the big deal?"

Cael got up and turned to face him, his hands on his hips. "What's the big deal? I'll show you what the big deal is, Ash Keeler."

Ash cocked his head to one side, wondering what Cael was going on about. He opened his mouth to ask when Cael stepped up to him, shoved his knees apart, and stepped between them. Ash's eyes widened, and his pulse shot up. He wanted to ask Cael what he was doing, but nothing came out. His brain ceased to function. Cael removed his T-shirt and threw it onto the couch. A strangled noise was all that escaped Ash as he sat there, mesmerized by Cael's smooth, sinewy torso. He was so distracted, he hadn't realized what Cael was doing until Cael straddled him. *Oh sweet Jesus.*

Cael took hold of Ash's hands and placed them on his ass before thrusting down against him, his hard erection pressed up against Ash's now-stiff dick.

"This is the big deal," Cael said in a husky tone. "You have no idea how bad I want to touch you, taste you, feel you. Do you know how long I've dreamed of being with you? Years, Ash. For years I've tortured myself with thoughts of you kissing me, taking me to bed, making love to me, fucking me."

Cael thrust his hips down against him, and Ash groaned. Oh God, this wasn't good. It *felt* good. Fuck, it felt so damn good.

"I'd close my eyes and picture myself running my hands over you." Cael slid his hands up Ash's chest. "If you knew all the things I dreamed of doing with you..." He pressed himself against Ash, his arms wrapped around Ash's neck.

Ash's fingers dug into Cael's plump ass cheeks. Oh fuck. There was nothing but thin cotton between them, and Ash could feel Cael's hard cock against his own, the sweet pressure. A rolling wave of desire thundered through him, and he wanted nothing more than to throw Cael down onto the couch, to taste and feel every inch of his beautiful body, to bury himself in between those gorgeous cheeks. Cael's lips touched Ash's neck, drawing a gasp from him. The most delicious shiver went up his spine, and he slipped his hands up Cael's body, feeling the contours of his back, the curve of his spine, his firm muscles and soft skin.

Just do it. Give in. You want him. He's yours. He's offering himself to you, so take him.

"I can't." Ash took hold of Cael's shoulders and gently

pushed him away. "I'm so sorry, Cael, but this is... I can't do this right now."

Cael nodded, and Ash could see him trying his hardest to put on a brave front.

"Guess it's going to have to remain a dream a little longer. Excuse me." He pulled away from Ash and got up. He picked his T-shirt up off the couch, swiftly tugged it on, and made for the stairs.

"Cael, wait."

"Good night, Ash. Sleep tight." Cael hurried toward the stairs, and Ash couldn't stand to see him go, especially not upset like this, so he followed him.

"Stay. I'm begging you."

Cael stopped in his tracks, remaining there silently for several seconds. Straightening, he took a deep breath and released it slowly. He turned around, his heartache and disappointment hitting Ash hard. It was all there on his sweet boyish face for the world to see.

"I'm sorry I broke my promise. I said no pressure, and then I pushed you like that. I'm really sorry. I am. It was too much too soon. It's probably best if we sleep in separate rooms tonight. I hope you won't be angry with me in the morning."

"Never. And don't apologize. It's me. It's all me."

Cael shook his head. "That's very sweet, but it's not. I'd like it if we could pretend this never happened and just move on."

"Cael—"

"Please, Ash. I'm feeling a little humiliated right now, so please, don't make it worse."

Ash swallowed hard and nodded. "It's forgotten."

"Thank you. Good night." Cael turned and disappeared upstairs.

It took several seconds before Ash could get himself to move from where he stood. He walked back to the couch and sat down. Damn it. Everything had been going so well. All he'd wanted was to watch some TV with Cael and maybe fall asleep together, something they'd done countless times over the years. God, he was such an asshole. Cael had put himself out there, taken a chance, and he'd made the guy feel like shit for it. The worst part was that he'd wanted it. He'd wanted Cael so bad it hurt. And then his fucking brain had to mess things up by panicking. They were safe. This was Cael's childhood home. The only people here were family. It wasn't like they were going to have sex. At least he was pretty sure Cael had no intention of having sex on his dad's couch, but even with that in mind, Ash couldn't bring himself to give in.

With a sigh, he turned off the TV and lay down, then pulled the covers up to his chin. There was nothing that could be done about it now. He'd promised Cael he'd forget about it, and he would. Thank fuck this night was over. He closed his eyes when he thought he heard a faint cry. Instinctively, his thoughts went to Cael, and he sat up, listening. He heard another cry, this one a little louder. He got up and went to the stairs. Halfway up, he heard it clear as day.

"Oh fuck. *Fuck*. Please, Sloane."

You have got to be fucking kidding me! Ash hurried down the stairs. He reached the bottom and stepped on his pajama pant leg, nearly tripping and colliding with the floor. He managed to regain his balance and stomped over to the couch, where he got under the covers. With a grunt, he rolled over, taking his pillow with him in the hopes of drowning out the sex noises coming from upstairs. Just icing on the fucking cake. The last thing he needed was to hear his best friend and that menace fucking. He should have known this night could get worse. It was clearly a punishment for what had happened with Cael. He shut his eyes tight, but he could still fucking hear them. How fucking loud could one guy be? Very, apparently.

"Goddamn it!" Did those two have no shame? How did Maddock not get up and kick Dex's ass? Could he not hear them? He had to hear them. Why didn't Cael tell his brother to shut the fuck up? After gathering the blankets and pillow, Ash headed for the basement. Fuck it. He'd sleep downstairs in Maddock's office. Earlier, when he'd changed, he'd seen a couch down there.

He grabbed the cushions off the couch in Maddock's office, which was too small for him to sleep on, and he chucked them on the carpeted floor. He was so going to kick Dex's ass tomorrow. He readied his makeshift bed and lay down. He'd slept on worse. With a grumble, he closed his eyes and prayed Christmas wouldn't be such a fucking disaster.

FOUR

THANKSGIVING HAD COME AND GONE, leaving Ash with mixed feelings about spending Christmas with Cael. He'd had a great time until his spectacular fuckup at the end of the night. Maddock, Dex, and Sloane knew about them, so why hadn't he been able to relax? If he couldn't get himself to feel comfortable with Cael in front of family, how the hell would he be able to do so out in the open? This wasn't how he wanted things to go with them. He'd barely slept that night, thinking about how he'd hurt Cael, about how he was letting the most wonderful thing to ever happen to him slip through his fingers, all because he couldn't get his head out of his ass.

The next morning at breakfast, while Ash had been more miserable than ever, Cael had been his usual sweet, chipper self. Ash saw through the façade. Cael was hurting. Ash's rejection had stung. Even so, Cael had served Ash breakfast and brought him coffee just the way he liked it. He'd smiled warmly and even hugged Ash when he and Sloane said their good-byes.

Now Ash stood outside Shultzon's house with Dex, and

he was in a foul mood. If it wasn't for Sloane, he wouldn't even be here. He was glad his best friend had received some kind of closure from having chatted with Shultzon, but Ash had no desire to see the doctor. Not after he'd spent most of his life trying to forget what he'd suffered at the hands of this man, at least until Isaac Pearce had brought it all crashing back by kidnapping Dex and taking him to the research facility. Again, Ash had compartmentalized and closed the doors for good on memories and information that were of no use to him. His THIRDS-appointed therapist said it wasn't healthy. Fuck that. It kept him functioning.

Silence snapped him out of his trance. Dex had been quiet the entire ride over. It was freaky. Lord knew the guy never shut up, which was why when he did, it felt wrong. Was Ash actually getting used to having Dex around? Thankfully the door opened, stopping any more ludicrous thoughts from entering his mind. Ash had called the doctor while Sloane was at his therapy appointment for his leg, and they'd been in luck. The guy was home and invited them over for a chat.

"Ash, how wonderful to see you." He held his hand out, and Ash reluctantly shook it. With a bright smile, Shultzon turned to Dex. "Agent Daley, what an absolute pleasure to meet you. I've heard so many wonderful things about you."

Dex shook the man's hand, his jaw clenched so tight Ash was afraid he might break something. "Thank you."

"Please, come in."

Shultzon motioned for them to enter, and Dex did. Ash followed. The doctor led them into a neat and elegant living room and showed them over to a large couch.

"Can I get you both some coffee?"

Before Ash could answer, Dex answered for them. "No, thank you. This won't take long."

Daley sporting an attitude *and* refusing coffee? That was weird. Dex was usually all smiles and charm, even when dealing with someone he didn't trust, *especially* when dealing with someone he didn't trust. He knew how to get under their skin, gather intel without them knowing what he was doing. Ash was always able to spot the intensity behind his pale-blue eyes, despite the smile. It wasn't the same smile Dex had for Sloane, his family, or even his friends. Ash had seen it enough to know the difference. Dex was a complicated man with many faces. He was an expert at playing oblivious and a master of evasive tactics. Ash was starting to see through the class clown façade hiding a potentially dangerous man.

Shultzon took a seat in the armchair across from them. "Is Sloane all right?"

"Why wouldn't he be?" Ash asked, wondering how much Shultzon knew about what had happened the last few months. Sloane had told him how Shultzon was still connected to the THIRDS, working for them in the Therian youth centers. Was he still helping them recruit? He'd told Sloane he liked to know what was going on around him, but how much was he involved?

"Well, you're both here without him. His lover and best friend."

"He had an appointment," Dex replied somberly.

"Right. For his leg. How is he?"

Ash studied the doctor. "How'd you know it was for his leg?"

"Like I told Sloane, I like to keep myself informed." Shultzon turned his attention to Dex. "You look uncomfortable, Dex. May I call you Dex?"

Ash felt Dex shift beside him.

"I'm going to be honest with you, Dr. Shultzon."

Shit. What the hell was Dex going to say? Ash had been so wrapped up in his and Sloane's past with Shultzon that he hadn't given any thought to how Dex might react around the guy.

"Please do."

"You might reconsider when you hear what I have to say."

Ash clasped his hands together and remained silent. He could have told Dex now was not the time, but if Dex wanted to get something off his chest, who the hell was he to deny the guy that? A part of him was curious. The other half told him Shultzon deserved whatever Dex gave him.

"The only reason I'm not punching you in the face right now is out of respect for Sloane. You tortured him. You experimented on him. I don't care what your reasons were. They were children. Kids who'd already been put through emotional hell by parents who, instead of protecting them, had them taken away and locked up like animals. And then you come in, their hero. You rescue them, feed them, clothe them, give them toys, but at an unspeakable price. You put them through a physically and mentally excruciating experience they'll have to live with for the rest of their lives *if* they live through it."

Shultzon didn't look fazed in the least. "How much did Sloane tell you?"

"Enough to know eighteen years later that what you did to him still haunts him."

"I understand," Shultzon replied, his tone remorseful.

"Do you?" Dex asked angrily. "Do you understand what it feels like to be woken up by your lover's screams in the middle of the night? To see him distraught and lost in a world of pain and anguish, fighting a force out of your reach? Do you understand what it's like to watch the man you love begging for the pain to stop but knowing there's nothing you can do because it's in his mind? No, Doctor. You don't *understand*, and if it were up to me, you'd be rotting away in a jail cell somewhere. Lucky for you, it's not up to me. From this point on, Ash will do the talking, because nothing that comes out of my mouth while we're in the same room will be pleasant."

Holy. Fuck.

Ash forced himself to stop gaping at Dex and quickly snapped himself out of it. Okay, they came here for a reason. He turned to Shultzon. "Doctor, we're here because we're worried about Sloane. He's lost control of his feral side twice."

Shultzon's hand flew to his mouth, a look of genuine concern on his face. "Oh dear God. How did it happen?"

Ash explained about the first time Sloane had lost control after getting into a fight with Dex, and then the second time when Sloane had been in the middle of being intimate with his lover. He explained how Sloane's memory was fuzzy in some places while completely blank in others.

Shultzon looked thoughtful. "It seems to me the problem started after his injury."

Ash agreed. "We can't figure out what could have caused it. Could it be the combination of Therian medication and his emotions? He's been on meds since then." Although he'd pretty much ruled this out, he wanted to know if Shultzon agreed. There could be something he knew about the meds that maybe Ash wasn't aware of.

"It's possible. Therian medicine is still in its youth. There's no telling what effect it can have in the long run. However, if it was the medication, we would have had vast breakouts of Therians experiencing similar incidents.

Though it does make me wonder..." Shultzon pursed his lips and shook his head. "Never mind."

"What is it?"

Shultzon appeared reluctant to continue. He shook his head as if talking himself out of it, but in the end, he gave in. "When Sloane came to visit, he asked me about the First Gen Research Facility and whether that was truly the end of it. I'm afraid to say, I didn't believe so then, and even less so now."

Dex straightened beside Ash but remained silent. This wasn't what Ash had been hoping to hear.

"Are you saying what's happening to Sloane might have something to do with the First Gen Research Facility?"

"Not the facility, but perhaps whatever the THIRDS was working on inside of it. I know I shouldn't be discussing this, and I ask that it not leave this room, but now that I know about Sloane, I'm concerned for him and his safety. I believe the THIRDS, or at least someone with quite some influence, is still experimenting with the scopolamine drug Pearce used on Dex, attempting to perfect it to control Therians."

Ash frowned. "That's a very serious accusation, Doctor. Do you have evidence to back up this claim?" If the doctor truly believed this, he had to be getting his information from somewhere. An unsanctioned drug? And one powerful enough to control a Therian? Shit. They'd all had their suspicions regarding the facility and whatever had been going on, but Ash had hoped they'd heard the last of it after the facility had been decommissioned the second time. He'd almost believed it, and then during their mission to track down Hogan, Austen had shown up with a powdered concoction containing scopolamine, confirming it was all far from over.

"I've been trying to gather intel, but it's very slow going. Mostly it's where I've managed to glean snippets of conversations held in the shadows. I have to be cautious. Not everyone can be trusted." Shultzon spoke his next words quietly. "I believe someone is using specialist agents to get the work done without the THIRDS' knowledge."

"So you're saying whoever's working on this drug is doing so off the books?" Ash didn't like the sound of that. If what Shultzon was saying was true—and that was a big fucking *if*—then it would have to be someone with a high level of security clearance. Those officers were the only ones who could assign cases or tasks to specialist agents. Though it made sense. Specialist agents didn't function in the same capacity as THIRDS agents, since they technically didn't exist.

Shultzon nodded. "I had been hoping to speak with Sloane about it, but then there was that unfortunate incident, and he was injured." He opened his mouth to continue but seemed to think better of it. "I've said too much already. This is a very dangerous situation, and I have no intention of putting you or any of your agents in any danger. Until I have something solid to present you or the Branch of Therian Defense, I shouldn't say any more."

"The Branch of Therian Defense?" Ash and Dex exchanged troubled glances. If this shit went that far up, then it was big.

"I'm afraid—if my suspicions are true—this could have a dire impact on the THIRDS, especially if the involved parties are discovered by someone outside the THIRDS organization. I fear they may be putting their trust into the wrong hands, and I can't allow the lives of good agents to be placed in jeopardy. I will say this." Shultzon looked from Ash to Dex and back, his voice grave. "Someone may not be who they say they are. Be mindful of the orders you're given." Shultzon stood and motioned to the door. "I'm sorry, but I think it's best any future communication between us be arranged elsewhere."

Ash had more questions now than when he'd come in, but it was clear Shultzon had finished talking. He escorted them to the door, promised to call if he received any significant information, and once again told them to be cautious. Ash and Dex remained quiet until they were inside Dex's car. They sat quietly for a moment before Dex erupted.

"This is fucked-up. Do you really think someone inside the THIRDS is still working on that drug? Sorry, that's a stupid question. Of course they are. Shultzon said they were perfecting it. Perfecting what? That shit did its job on me just fine."

"He said they were perfecting it to control Therians. Maybe what you were given doesn't have the same effect on a Therian."

While in their Human form Therians might appear Human, but inside there were vast differences, which was why Therians had their own medicines. Hell, there were some Therian over-the-counter drugs that Humans needed prescriptions for because they would fuck them up if they weren't careful.

Dex let out a frustrated groan. "None of that explains what's happening to Sloane. He wasn't exposed to the drug. And that was months before the explosion. It doesn't explain what's happening to him now. Shultzon's right about the meds, though. If they were causing the problems with shifting, there would be mass breakouts of Therians losing control. They're Therian antibiotics. That shit's prescribed to God knows how many Therians. We'd have definitely heard something."

"So we're back to square one, not knowing anything about Sloane, except now there's the possibility something fucked is going on." Ash shook his head and motioned for Dex to drive. "Looks like we're going to start the New Year with a fucking bang."

"Shultzon said someone wasn't who they said they were, and we should be wary of the orders we're given."

Ash thought about that. "We're only given orders by Sloane, your dad, and Sparks. For something like this, it would have to be at least an officer. Someone with high-level security clearance."

"Well, Sloane's not involved in any of that shit, and neither is my dad."

"So what are you saying? That Sparks is somehow involved in this? That's insane."

"I don't know. To be honest, I don't know what to think. We went to see Shultzon in the hopes he'd shed some light on the subject of Sloane's shifting, and he drops this fucking bomb on us. What are we supposed to do now? Investigate? Ignore it? We're not even on active duty. Seriously, man. We're not even fucking working, and this shit falls in our laps. What the fuck?"

"Hey. Relax. Which reminds me. What the hell happened back there? I don't think I've ever seen you so pissed."

Ash discreetly watched Dex as they drove from Shultzon's upscale neighborhood toward Dex's brownstone. At this time of morning, traffic wasn't too bad. They still had about an hour before Sloane would be home from his therapy session. His best friend had bitched and moaned that he didn't need the sessions anymore, but Dex had convinced him to go to the remaining appointment while he and Ash went to visit Shultzon.

"How can you guys be so calm around that dude after everything he did to you?"

Ash shrugged. "What can we do? It happened. Yeah, it's fucked-up, but all we can do is move forward. Sloane and I got off lucky."

"Lucky?"

"Yeah. I would consider having a career at the THIRDS, a somewhat normal life, friends, a family—even if they are a pain in the ass—all things to be grateful for. Sloane and I had each other to get us through the rough times. We got out of there with our sanity because of it. Some of the others weren't so lucky."

"You know what happened to them, don't you?"

Ash nodded. "Sloane and I did a run through Themis back when Sloane was promoted to team leader. It kept haunting us, so we had to check, even if we knew it was a bad idea. Remember, the First Gen Research Facility spawned the THIRDS First Gen Recruitment Program, so a number of them got recruited young, sent to college, and hired by the THIRDS, same as me and Sloane. They were spread out throughout the country, a few sent abroad. Some of them..." Ash shook his head. "They weren't so lucky. There were several suicides. Some ended up hospitalized, some sent to prison, and a few others just fell off the grid."

"Yeah, but—"

"Look, I know if you could, you would make every one of those bastards pay, but all you'll end up doing is hurting Sloane. He's come a hell of a long way since you met him, and I'm man enough to admit you played a major role in that. Don't undo all the good you've done by trying to change something that can't be changed."

To Ash's surprise, Dex nodded. "You're right. The last

thing I want to do is cause Sloane pain. He's been through enough."

They'd driven to Shultzon's in Dex's Challenger. It was as loud and ostentatious as its owner. Trust Dex to buy an orange car. Some big-hair-band song came on the radio, and Ash rolled his eyes. How did Sloane listen to this shit? Thank God Cael had better taste in music. There was a lot of cheerful pop, but Ash didn't mind. The music reminded him of Cael, and he loved the way it put a smile on the cheetah Therian's sweet face. He wondered what Cael was doing right now. Most likely ruing the day he'd fallen in love with Ash Keeler. Or baking. That's what Ash would be doing.

Dex pulled into a parking spot not far from his front door. He turned off the engine, and Ash sat there, frowning.

"You okay?"

"I dunno. I can't shake this feeling. Like we're being watched."

Ash observed as Dex subtly scanned the street on his left, behind them, and then pretended to fix his rearview mirror. Ash checked the passenger side mirror, focusing on the cars parked down the street. The trees and garden shrubs were bare, improving visibility. He got out of the car and closed the door behind him, waiting for Dex. Discreetly, he assessed their surroundings, making note of any place someone could be hiding or watching them. It was quiet, not a soul in sight.

"Anything?" Dex asked.

"Nothing. Maybe I'm just being paranoid," Ash muttered.

"Which probably means you're not. Let's get inside. We need to tell Sloane about what we learned."

Dex headed for the front steps, and Ash followed.

"You sure you want to tell him?"

"Yeah." Dex unlocked the front door and turned to him with a smile. "No more secrets. That's our new motto."

"Sounds like you two are finally getting it. Took you long enough." He followed Dex inside and closed the door behind him. He hung up his coat and scarf. "I really hope Shultzon is wrong about this." He joined Dex in the living room and took a seat. "I remember the good old days when we issued high-risk warrants, knocked down barricades, and kept watch at Therian peace marches. Now everyone's trying to fucking blow us up."

"I've been thinking about something Shultzon said. How whoever's working on this off the books is using specialist agents. Remember the scopolamine Austen had?"

Ash nodded. "Actually, it crossed my mind earlier. When you asked him if the THIRDS gave it to him, he looked pissed and avoided answering."

"Do you think Austen's involved?" Dex asked worriedly.

"I hope not. I'd like to think he's smarter than that."

"Smarts have nothing to do with it. We don't even know what the hell Austen's job entails besides spying on us. I know Sloane trusts him, and the two go way back, but Austen's not a kid anymore. What if he's not the same guy he once was?"

Ash let his head fall back against the couch's backrest with a sigh. He sure fucking hoped Austen wasn't involved in this shit. Dex had a point. Austen wasn't a little kid anymore. He'd been with the THIRDS since Sloane found him. Who the hell knew what he'd learned and done in the time since joining? Austen was skilled. He had to be in order to cut it as a Squadron Specialist agent. Those agents were fucking shadows. Deadly shadows. Ash could hazard a guess what kind of black-ops shit they were involved in. One thing was certain, if it turned out Austen *was* involved, it would break Sloane's heart.

How THE FUCK did he get himself into these messes? This was all going to end so damn badly. He just knew it. Austen heard the faint click of the lock and cautiously lowered the handle. The hallway of the office building was shrouded in darkness. Not a problem for a Therian. He listened intently. Nothing. Slipping inside the east wing, he kept close to the wall. He pressed himself against the hard surface and silently stalked toward the closest empty room. Operating quickly, he worked the lock and hurried inside, then closed the door quietly behind him. With his lock-pick set secure in the pocket of his black tac pants, he hopped onto the metal table, snatched his collapsible steel baton from his belt, and snapped his wrist. It extended and locked into place. Standing on his toes, he reached up and used the end of the baton to release the vent cover. Thank goodness for old buildings.

There wasn't much time. He returned the now collapsed baton to his utility belt, jumped, and grabbed hold of the edges. He swung his legs and used the wall in front of him to push himself up into the vent. It was a bitch due to his height, and he struggled, but he made it in without any noise. Once inside he closed the latch and crawled three feet until he was above the room he needed. Holding his breath, he lightly tapped the side of the vent once. Seconds later there was one faint knock. Receiving the signal, he unlatched the cover and peeked through. His contact was alone in the room. Austen slipped through the opening and dropped down onto the floor, landing without a sound.

"I don't have long," his contact whispered, handing Austen the credit-card-sized case. "We're going to have to move sooner than anticipated."

"Shit."

"Word is some THIRDS agents have been asking questions about the drug. If they start snooping around, ten years of hard work goes down the pan, and we have nothing. Tell the boss we need to move on this."

"We've kept it from the THIRDS this long, so don't worry about them. We'll take care of it. I'll get this back to the boss. You just get ready to move." Austen headed back toward the vent he'd come from. As soon as their contact had slipped out, Austen did the same, returning the way he'd come in through the office building and its piss-poor security. Then again, too much security would end up drawing unwanted attention. In the cover of darkness, no one saw him or suspected he was even there, same as his previous visits. Damn it. It was too soon to move. Everything had been planned out to the smallest detail, and now they'd have to deviate from that plan. His boss *hated* deviating from the plan.

Making sure no one had seen him, Austen hailed a cab and gave the driver directions. He switched taxis three times before he ended up at his appointed destination. He sat on the bench and pulled out his smartphone. After he tapped in his security code, he turned the phone on its side and scanned the case. Small blue letters scrolled across the screen at unreadable speeds until it stopped. The words "Scan Complete" flashed green. No tracers. Good. He tucked the case into the hidden pocket inside his winter coat and sent out a text.

Plain bagel.

Austen waited for his boss to show up. Why did he always have to be the bearer of bad news? A black Suburban with pitch-black windows pulled up to the curb. This was it. He tugged his wool hat low over his eyes and climbed into the front passenger seat.

"We've got a problem," Austen said, removing the case from the hidden pocket inside his winter coat. The car took off, and Austen pressed the case to the console's digital screen. It scanned the device and beeped once. Clean. He already knew it was, but his boss was very particular. "Apparently, THIRDS agents have been asking questions."

As expected, his boss was pissed, judging by her white-knuckled grip on the steering wheel.

"Find out who it is and do what you need to do to put an end to it."

"Come on. I think we both know who it is."

"Damn it. Those boys just don't know when to quit."

Austen smiled. "That's why you like them so much."

Sparks pulled into an empty parking spot down a quiet street and put the car in park. She turned to look at him, her blue eyes cold as ice. "We've worked too damn long and too damn hard to let this fall apart now. I want you to keep an eye on them. Make sure they don't cause us any problems. They're back on duty Monday morning. I'll keep them busy. No more close calls. We get this done. Anything else?"

"Yeah." *Here we go.* "Our man thinks we're going to have to move on this."

"Goddamn it, Austen."

Sparks slammed her hand on the steering wheel, catching him by surprise. She was never anything but calm and collected. Then again, if he'd been working this job as long as she had, he'd be pretty pissed to find out things might be heading south at the eleventh hour.

"This is unacceptable."

Austen narrowed his eyes at her. "Hey, you're not the only one living a double life here. You get to sit in a cushy office playing lieutenant while I'm out here risking my neck, getting chased by homicidal maniacs, and running interference with your boy toys."

Sparks arched an eyebrow at him. "My interest in Destructive Delta is purely business, whereas your interest in a certain Agent Zachary is not."

What the hell?

"Oh, Austen." Sparks let out a husky laugh. "Did you really think I wouldn't find out you've been keeping tabs on him? Are you getting sentimental on me? Is it because he took care of you after your injury? He's very nurturing. Though I have to admit, I'm a little surprised. Zachary's a bear Therian. You don't normally go for such large Therians. But you know what?" She put her hands up. "It's none of my business. I'm glad to see you're finally moving on from Sloane."

Austen congratulated himself on not telling her to fuck off. She always had to have the last word. "Stay away from Zach," he warned. "He's a good guy." There was no point in trying to deny his recent activity where Zach was concerned. The truth was, he didn't know why he was keeping an eye on Zach, but now that Sparks knew Zach meant something to him—despite him not knowing what that something was—she would use him against Austen if she had to.

"Then do your job. If I'm overworking you, just say so. I can arrange some permanent vacation time."

"Please," Austen laughed. "You can't bullshit a bullshitter. You need me. And if this shit blows up in our faces, you're not the only one in deep shit. Zach risked his safety to keep me safe. I don't take that kind of thing lightly." His expression darkened as he leaned toward her. "If someone goes near him, I will take them out. You know me better than anyone. I don't fuck around." He just liked to pretend he did.

Sparks smiled, but it didn't reach her steel-blue eyes. "Looks like I've taught you well."

"Maybe too well," Austen said, lowering his cap once again. He opened the car door and got out. "I'll be awaiting your instructions." With that he closed the door, shoved his hands into his coat pockets, and walked away. His phone buzzed, and he removed it from his pocket. A text from Sparks.

Don't get too close.

Austen sighed and shoved his phone back into his pocket. *Story of my life.* Either way he had no intention of getting close to Zach. He was simply showing his gratitude, even if Zach had no idea he was even around. Friendships were a luxury he couldn't afford. Relationships were out of the question. Zach intrigued him, but that was all it was. A passing curiosity. Austen stopped in his tracks when he realized he didn't know where he was. He'd walked half a block from where Sparks had parked. He turned to the house in front of him, and his gut twisted.

Zach's house.

Son of a bitch. Sparks had brought him to Zach's neighborhood. Austen walked off at a brisk pace. He had to get out of here before someone saw him. Half the damn block was occupied by Zach's ginormous family. Austen couldn't fathom having six brothers and three sisters, much less all the nieces, nephews, cousins, aunts, uncles, in-laws, and grandparents that made up the colossal Zachary clan, a good portion of which occupied this block. Austen had always been on his own. The thought of having all those family members in his hair terrified the ever-living fuck out of him. Why was he even checking up on Zach? The guy was seven feet tall and weighed over three hundred pounds with six equally ginormous siblings.

Granted, none of them possessed the skills he did or the connections. Maybe it was best if he kept an eye on Zach. From a distance, of course.

FIVE

Now this was more like it.

Ash delivered a right hook to the black leather bag in front of him. His brow was beaded with sweat, his T-shirt clinging to him as he pummeled the swinging punching bag. Man, it felt good. It had been too long since he'd hit something. Back at the grain terminal when he'd been up against some of Hogan's goons in their Therian forms, he'd been forced to use his wits to outsmart them, since his body had still had healing to do. Some Humans truly believed if a Therian was shot, they'd bounce back up. Fuckwits. Therians might be stronger and heal quicker than Humans, but they weren't indestructible.

For weeks he'd been told to take it easy, rest, don't overexert himself, like he was made of fucking glass or something. On Friday, everyone on his team had been called in for a physical. They'd all been cleared for duty, with only Sloane being sentenced to desk duty for a couple of weeks just in case. His best friend had been pissed, but Ash was secretly glad for it. Sloane had been impaled by a piece of jagged metal and had almost died. Ash didn't want him out in the field before he was ready.

Their return had been met with cheers. Ash had never expected it. The whole of Unit Alpha was there to greet them when they stepped foot on the floor. HR had even arranged a party with "Welcome Back" banners, balloons, and cake. Everyone was happy to see them. They'd even been happy to see Ash, which was probably the biggest shocker of all. Sparks had given them all a speech, thanked them for their bravery and service, and then after the party, called them in individually for an assessment.

Despite being on active duty and having been cleared by the THIRDS physicians, Sparks had Destructive Delta's Defense agents benched. They were to resume their training regimen for another two weeks before they'd be assigned a case. That was fine with Ash. He'd had enough of resting. He bounced on his toes, pulled his elbows in at his sides, and delivered a roundhouse kick to the bag. His body was raring to go. After a good stretch, he'd started with basic punches and now kicks. He still had a good hour left to practice some routines before it was time to hit the pool, then the shooting range. Maybe tomorrow he'd get in the ring with someone who could give him a good workout. He'd just delivered a side kick when he caught a whiff of something fruity.

"No," he growled.

"You don't even know what I'm going to ask." Dex stepped up beside the bag, his hands on his hips.

"Doesn't matter. It's coming out of your mouth, so no." Left hook, right elbow, left knee.

"Even if it's about Cael?"

Ash stopped and turned to Dex. "You really think that's going to work every time?"

Dex blinked at him. "Yes. I really do."

"Fuck off." Ash turned back to the bag, then sighed. Who the fuck was he kidding? "What about Cael?"

"I need you to train him."

Ash jabbed the bag with his right fist. "He's already trained."

"Yeah, but he was put through Recon's training. Anything beyond that is because Sloane's insisted on it. Even then it's not the same training you, Sloane, and Hobbs go through."

"Yeah, because we're Therian Defense agents." They were the muscle behind Defense. It was their job to take the brunt of the physical danger for their partners. Their Human partners did what they could to neutralize a threat, but as past experiences had proved, that was easier said than done. It was a Therian Defense agent's job to go up against feral Therians and keep their partners from getting mauled.

"Hogan proved assholes like him don't give a shit what kind of agent you are."

Ash straightened and turned back to Dex. "So this is because of what happened with Hogan?"

Dex's pale-blue eyes flashed with anger. "You bet your ass. Hogan kidnapped Cael. What if we hadn't gotten there in time?" he spat out, and Ash understood Dex's frustration, not to mention fear. They'd had one hell of a close call.

"Hey, relax. He's okay now." It seemed like he'd been saying that to Dex a lot lately, which was disturbing. Dex was always annoyingly cheerful.

"And the next time? Please, just do this. Not for me, but for him."

Ash thought it over. He wouldn't admit it, but Dex was right. Cael wasn't trained the way Defense was. The Recon department had a training program for its agents. They weren't trained to take down lethal Therians because that wasn't their job. Although Rosa and Cael tended to accompany Destructive Delta's Defense agents more often than not, they did so in a medical and technical capacity. Their main objective was investigating and collecting intel. Maybe it was time for Recon's training program to evolve. The world had become a far more dangerous place than it had been when Ash first joined.

"Okay, but what am I supposed to tell him? You know he'll just walk away if he thinks it's because he's weak, which he isn't." He could see Cael's reaction now. It was not going to be pretty. Maybe still adorable, because even pissed off Cael looked perfect to him, but Cael would still get mad as hell.

"First of all, don't tell him it was my idea, because then he'll get defensive for sure. If it's coming from you, he'll listen. You care about him, right?"

Ash gave him an uninspired look. "That's a stupid question."

"Right. I can't believe I'm saying this, but tell him. That's all the reason he'll need."

"And you're okay with that?"

Ash studied Dex. Was it just him, or was Dex coming to him for help on a regular basis? A few months ago, Ash was pretty sure Dex wouldn't have been caught dead asking Ash for help. If he did, it was usually begrudgingly and because he had no choice. And he'd make sure to let Ash know it. Now he didn't seem to think twice about it.

"You're okay with me and Sloane?"

"Only because for some reason beyond my understanding you make him happy," Ash muttered, removing the wraps from his right hand.

Dex grinned broadly.

"Yeah, all right. I get it. Now fuck off back to your boyfriend. He's already called me twice today asking where you are. Tell him I'm not your goddamn chaperone."

"You can tell me that yourself." Sloane approached them with a wide smile. There had been a time when Ash thought he'd never see his best friend smile again. Now he was doing it all the time. Ash shook his head in shame at Sloane.

"Seriously, man? You can't go five minutes without being on your boy's ass?"

"What can I say? It's a mighty fine ass." Sloane winked at Dex, whose cheeks went pink.

Ash let out a sound of disgust before turning back to his punching bag and waving them away. "You two make me sick. Fuck off, both of you. I got shit to do."

The two of them laughed as they walked off, and Ash discreetly watched them go. He held back a smile at the playful way Sloane shoved Dex away from him, laughing at something his partner said. They were good together, those two. Without Dex, Sloane would be far too serious. Like Ash, Sloane was always in danger of losing himself to his dark thoughts. They needed to keep themselves busy, distracted, or their heads would go to places no sane person would want to live in.

Cael's sweet smile came into his thoughts, and Ash found himself smiling. Even when he wasn't around, Cael managed to save Ash from himself. He finished removing his wraps and shoved them into his duffel bag. He left it on the floor by the punching bag, knowing no one would dare move it. It had his name on it.

He pulled on his socks and sneakers and headed down the hall, not bothering to do more than wipe the sweat off his face with a towel he'd grabbed on the way out of the boxing bay. He walked into the gym and toward the back where he knew Cael, Rosa, and Letty would be using the exercise bikes.

On the way there, he spotted Calvin running on the treadmill, no Hobbs in sight. With a frown, Ash made a detour, stopping beside Calvin, who removed his headphones when he saw Ash approaching.

"Where's your shadow?" Ash asked, looking around the gym. It wasn't like Hobbs not to be where Calvin was, and he hadn't seen much of him since they'd reported back to work.

Calvin adjusted the speed on his treadmill. "He wasn't up for it."

"Haven't seen much of him today."

"He's not left the office today."

That was strange. It wasn't like they had a case to work on. They were supposed to be getting back into top form. Ash nodded. "He should really get in a workout. You think he might be up for a sparring session tomorrow?"

Calvin pressed his lips together. He looked worried, and that was never a good thing. Ash didn't know what the hell was going on with those two, though he had his suspicions, especially after what Maddock had said about Letty getting the drop on Calvin. Calvin slowed the treadmill until it came to a halt before hopping off. "I'll tell him. Don't be surprised if he doesn't show. He's been feeling a little... tense recently."

"Everything okay?"

"He'll be fine." Calvin gave Ash's shoulder a pat. "Thanks, Ash."

He walked off, and Ash didn't like the vibe he was getting. Whatever had been going on between Calvin and Hobbs had nothing to do with what he'd just witnessed.

Something else was worrying Calvin. Maybe Ash would drop by their office after what was sure to be an interesting session with Cael.

The trio was cycling and chatting to their fellow agents when Ash walked past Letty, giving her ponytail a tug along the way.

"¡Oyé, cabrón!"

She swatted at him, and he jumped out of the way with a chuckle and gave Rosa the finger in greeting. She rolled her eyes at him before carrying on her conversation with Letty.

"Hey," Cael said brightly.

Man, he looked sexy in his charcoal-gray THIRDS T-shirt and black workout pants. Cael used the end of his T-shirt to wipe his face, exposing his torso and the thin dark treasure trail that disappeared beneath the waistband of his pants.

"Come on." Ash motioned for Cael to follow him, and his heart swelled when Cael stopped pedaling and got off the bike to join him. He didn't ask any questions. Ash asked him to follow, and Cael did. Truth be told, Ash would have done the same. Wherever one led, the other would follow. Ash had never had that level of trust with anyone but Sloane. Cael told Rosa he'd come find her later and followed Ash out of the gym. "We're going to train," Ash said as they entered the boxing bay.

"We are?" Cael stopped beside Ash's bag, which was exactly where he'd left it. The boxing bay wasn't very busy, which was how he preferred it. Anytime he sparred with someone, agents would gather to watch him kick his opponent's ass. Ash only kicked someone's ass when they deserved it. Unfortunately, there was always someone who deserved it. Why? Because they were stupid enough to challenge him.

In Unit Alpha, there was always someone who wanted to prove how hard they were, and what better way to do that than trying to take down Destructive Delta's Ash Keeler? Ash had a reputation. He'd lost count of all the names he'd been called. He really didn't give a fuck. He had a job to do and a way of doing it. Whoever didn't like it could kiss his ass. He had no time for inflated egos. Most of their fellow agents respected him and his skills, but there were always those asshats who thought Ash was their personal Everest to climb.

"What kind of training?"

Cael watched intently as Ash reached into his bag and pulled out a pair of clean hand wraps. He tossed them at Cael, who caught them, his expression puzzled.

"My kind of training."

"Up close and personal? Why?"

Ash took one roll from Cael and took hold of his hand, smiling at the way Cael's cheeks flushed ever so slightly. Ash proceeded to wrap Cael's hand. "Because you need to be prepared."

"I am."

"You could be prepared better."

Cael's eyes narrowed. "Does this have to do with Hogan?"

"Yes." Ash readied himself. He firmly wove the wrap around Cael's knuckles, under his thumb, around his palm and wrist, making sure there was enough flexibility. Cael's frown deepened.

"You don't think I can take care of myself?"

"You know that's not it." Ash finished up and took hold of the other roll and Cael's hand again. He lingered slightly, his thumb stroking Cael's palm. He wasn't sure his distraction would work. Not when he could see the little wheels in Cael's head spinning furiously as he put two and two together.

"Then why do you want to train me all of a sudden? Did Dex put you up to this?"

With a sigh, Ash went to work wrapping Cael's hand. "He's worried about you." He could have lied, but if their relationship was ever going to get started, he wanted it to be on the right track. No lies, no secrets, no bullshit.

"I knew it. I can't believe this. He keeps telling me he's going to stop treating me like a kid, but it never ends."

Cael tugged his hand out of Ash's grip, the wrapping unraveling. Ash snatched a hold of it before it could hit the floor.

"Hey, your brother loves you. You can't be mad at him for wanting you to be safe."

"Yes, I can," Cael huffed, turning to march off, his one hand still wrapped.

"Come here. Please." Damn. How was it that Cael looked adorable even when he was pissed off? "Cael. Please."

With a frustrated groan, Cael turned and headed back to Ash. "What?"

Ash lowered his voice so no one else could hear him. There were no Therian agents anywhere near them, but he didn't want to risk it. "Had Dex not approached me, I would have suggested it myself anyway. When I found out Hogan had you, I wanted to tear all those bastards apart with my bare hands. I couldn't stand the thought of him hurting you. It's not because you can't handle yourself, but things are getting rougher out there. The Order, the Coalition? It's only the beginning." He put his hand to Cael's shoulder, his thumb finding a small patch of skin to stroke. "Please. I need you to do this for me. For my peace of mind. But I also need you to want this for yourself."

Cael wrinkled his nose. "Fine."

"It's not going to be easy." Ash took hold of Cael's hand again and gave it a small squeeze. Cael knew what he was agreeing to. What he was getting into.

"I can handle it," Cael stated firmly.

"I won't hold back." If they were going to do this, they were going to do it right. Ash only had one way of training. All or nothing. His opponent could either hack it or they couldn't. He never cut corners, and he sure as hell wasn't going to start with Cael. "Do you trust me?"

Cael's expression softened. "You know I do."

"Okay." Ash finished wrapping Cael's hand. "I promise you, this is going to hurt me as much as it does you."

"You're going to kick my ass to get me ready. I get it. We gonna get started, or we gonna stand around talking about our feelings all day?"

"Ooh." Ash held his hands up in front of him. "The claws have come out."

Okay. This was good. He could work with this. Cael, much like his big brother, had a bit of a temper. Ash could use that to his advantage. Unlike a lot of agents, whose anger made them sloppy, Cael and Dex's anger made them focused and determined. Ash remembered the first time Dex had sparred with Sloane. Little bastard refused to stay down no matter how many times Sloane floored him. The more Sloane had pissed Dex off, the more Dex was determined to kick his ass.

Ash stepped on the mat and motioned for Cael to follow. "Hit me. And don't hold back."

Cael gave him a deadpan expression. "Darn, and here I was planning on using my knockout punch."

"You planning on carrying a stepstool around with you to use it on a dude my size?"

Cael arched an eyebrow at him. "Oh, I see. It's going to be like that, is it?"

Ash grinned. "It's gonna be like that." He put a hand to his chest. "Unless that hurts your feelings? I've heard more and more criminals are taking sensitivity classes these days."

"Okay, then."

Cael rounded his shoulders. He did a few stretches, and Ash could have sworn Cael was doing his best to look as seductive as possible while he did it. Once he was done, Cael bounced on his toes to loosen up before he charged Ash and threw a right hook. Ash stepped out of the way with ease. Cael came at him with a series of hooks and jabs that Ash was able to easily deflect. He grabbed Cael's wrist, twisted his arm behind his back, and kicked at the back of his leg, forcing him down onto one knee. He released Cael and stepped back.

"I saw that coming from a mile away."

"That's because you're so freakin' tall," Cael complained.

"No, because you pulled back a fist two feet away from me. By the time you reached me, I knew how you were going to hit me and figured out what my countermove would be."

"It was not two feet."

Ash took hold of Cael's waist and pulled him closer. "We're talking close quarters, so it might as well have been. You're also swinging with no purpose in mind. When you're dealing with someone up close and personal, it's about putting your opponent down. You already know everything you need to know to subdue a perpetrator. You're not training with me for that. You're here to take down someone my size. Most perps won't be trained the way we are or even the way Hogan was, and sometimes you might not have anything available to use as a weapon. If that is the case, you'll be using your fists, elbows, and knees to cause the maximum amount of damage." Ash lifted his elbow and moved it slowly toward Cael's head.

"Elbows cause a shit ton of damage. You'll want to go for your attacker's most vulnerable areas." He pointed two fingers to each part of Cael's body as he listed them. "Eyes, neck, liver, kidney, groin, and knee. And when I say groin, I'm not talking about punching the guy in the balls. It might hurt like a motherfucker, but eventually he's going to get back up. So not only will he not be out, he will be fucking pissed."

Ash moved away from Cael and stood to face him. "You can't rely on your punches alone. Look at me. Think about what I just told you, and attack me."

"What, just come at you?" Cael looked uncertain.

"Yes. Use whatever you think would take me down."

"But what if I hurt you?"

"You won't."

Cael frowned at him. "Thanks for the vote of confidence."

"This is my proficiency. You're just learning. So come on."

Taking a deep breath, Cael charged. Every punch Cael threw, Ash was able to dodge or smack away. The force behind Cael's punches was good. His form was good. But he was relying on his strength in a scenario where strength alone wouldn't cut it. Maybe it would against a wolf

Therian but not against a larger Felid Therian. He might get some good hits in, but he wouldn't take them down. Ash thought about Hogan and that asshole Fuller. He needed Cael to be ready. *Fuller.* That son of a bitch had pretended to have Cael's best interests at heart, using his supposed love for him to hurt him. The moment the thought entered his mind, Ash pushed it behind a door inside his head and slammed it shut. He wasn't Fuller. He loved Cael, and he was doing this to protect him. To give him a better chance out there in the wild streets of the urban jungle. Ash grabbed Cael around the waist, hoisted him off his feet, and slammed him down on the mat.

Cael gasped and wheezed, rolling onto his side before coughing. With a groan, he pushed himself into a sitting position. "Shit."

"Get up," Ash growled.

Cael glared at him. "I'm coming."

"That's what she said."

Cael picked his jaw up off the floor and pushed himself to his feet. "You dick! What the hell?"

"What's the matter, baby?" Ash leered, slowly circling Cael. "Hurt your feelings?"

Cael narrowed his eyes. "What did you just call me?"

"You heard me." Ash smiled wickedly as he took a stance. "Let's go, baby. Come at me fast and hard."

He could see Cael's temper flaring, see the anger flash in his steel-gray eyes. Cael took a stance and slowly circled Ash. Finally, he was getting it. Ash could see him assessing, looking Ash over, trying to work out his vulnerabilities, where he might be able to get a good hit in. With a growl, Cael charged. Instead of going for a hook, he went low and turned at the waist to get a jab against Ash's ribs. Ash blocked with his elbows. He didn't attack. This was about Cael trying to land a hit.

Cael moved quickly. When he saw he was unsuccessful, he moved out of the way and approached from a different angle. He side kicked at the back of Ash's knee, but Ash was already jumping over his leg. If he did the same with an opponent, he might have just hurt the guy. Good.

With every punch and kick Ash blocked, the more pissed off Cael became. He wanted to land a hit, to show Ash he could do it. The harder Cael tried, the more Ash patronized him. Prodding him, poking his ribs, ruffling his hair as Ash avoided getting hit.

"Would you quit it!" Cael snapped, charging Ash only to have Ash step to the side and smack his ass. Cael let out a yelp and spun, his steel-gray eyes blazing. "Asshole."

"Just let me know when you're ready to start, sweet pea."

"Fuck you!" Cael advanced, jumping as he neared Ash and throwing a punch. Ash ducked out of the way and threw his arms around Cael's waist. He knocked him onto his back, straddled him, and pinned his wrists above his head. With a smug grin, he forced his weight down, purposefully sitting on Cael's thighs so he couldn't move.

"What's your move, Chirpy?"

"Kiss my ass, you bastard!"

"Ooh, ouch. That hurt." Ash smiled sweetly. "Emotionally, obviously, not physically. Which really doesn't help your current situation any. Get angry."

"I am angry!"

"Not angry enough," Ash growled fiercely. "Get angry, Cael! Some asshole has you on the floor. You've been disarmed. He's going to fucking kill you. What are you going to do? Whatever it is, it better be a fucking step up from what I've seen, because if not, you're as good as dead."

Cael pulled at his wrists and writhed, trying to get free.

"That's not going to help you survive, Cael."

"You want angry? I'll give you angry!" Cael smacked his head hard against Ash's, momentarily stunning him. The distraction lasted mere seconds, but long enough for Ash to release one of Cael's wrists and end up getting punched in the balls.

"Motherfuck!" Ash let out every swear word he knew as he was shoved off Cael. He held on to his balls and curled up on himself. Cael crouched down beside him.

"That angry enough for you, Ash?"

A pleasant voice resounded from the speaker system. "Destructive Delta's Agent Cael Maddock and Agent Rosa Santiago, report to dispatch."

Cael smacked Ash across the cheek hard just for good measure before storming off.

Fuck! Motherfucking son of a bitch asshole fuck-buckets. Ash pressed his head against the mat, his cheek stinging and his balls feeling like they might crawl up inside him. He closed his eyes tight when he sensed someone looming over him.

"Keeler, you okay?"

"Fuck. You," he ground out. He didn't know who it was, and he didn't care.

"Holy shit!" someone else piped up. "Did you see that? Cael just punched Keeler in the fucking nads, bro."

Ash opened his eyes and glared up at his fellow Defense agent. "Herrera?"

"Yeah?"

Ash used his recuperated powers of speech to threaten the agent hovering over him.

"Unless you want me to rip off yours, you'll get the fuck away from me. *Now*. Don't think I've forgotten about you trying to take a piss on my fern during Daley's party at my apartment."

Herrera jumped to it and made like the wind, taking the other half dozen or so agents who'd gathered with him. Ash pushed himself to a sitting position, and any agents remaining in the boxing bay vacated the premises like someone had announced they were giving away free donuts in the canteen. One lone figure remained, heading toward him.

"How's Cael's training going?" Sloane held a hand out and helped Ash to his feet.

"Let's see. He's pissed, and he punched me in the balls. I think it's going rather well." Ash headed for the towel rack and snatched up a towel to wipe the sweat from his face.

"Good." Sloane patted Ash on the back, a big dopey grin on his face. "I want you to train Dex."

"What the fuck?" Ash threw his towel over his shoulder. He'd prefer letting Cael sock him in the nads again. "Are you shitting me?"

"It's important."

Sloane's smile faded, and Ash groaned internally. He hated when his friend got that stupid sad-puppy look on his face.

"He's learned a hell of a lot since he joined, but I need you to teach him what you're teaching Cael. I haven't been cleared to train yet, and you're the close-quarters expert."

"Let me get this straight. You want me to teach your certifiably insane partner my weaknesses. How to take me out."

Sloane shrugged. "You're teaching Cael."

Ash took a seat on the bench, and Sloane joined him.

This argument was pointless. Sloane had already won. The least Ash could do was attempt to put up a fight.

"Cael would never use it against me."

"Really? He just punched you in the balls, man."

"Because I told him to, not because he wanted to." Maybe he hadn't exactly told Cael to do that, but he *had* told Cael to fight him. It had been painful, but it worked.

"You sure about that?" Sloane teased.

"Is this you making me feel better about all this, because I hate to tell you, it ain't working."

Sloane laughed and threw an arm around his shoulders. "Come on. Please. I mean, you've only just started with Cael, and he managed to get away from you. That's impressive."

He was so going to regret this. "Fine. But you owe me. Big time."

"You got it." Sloane held a hand up in promise. "What's up with your boy, anyway? He's been really pissy lately. Angry."

Sloane let out a sigh. He checked the bay to make sure no one was close enough to hear. A few agents had wandered back in, but they were staying as far away from Ash as possible. No doubt Herrera was off telling anyone who would listen how Ash had gone down.

"He's really worried about what's going on with me. I know he's pretending everything's okay, but it's just to keep me from worrying. It's got him on edge. And then there's that whole other mess, you know."

Ash nodded. Sloane was referring to what they'd been told by Shultzon. After Sloane had returned from his therapy session, Dex and Ash had sat down with him and told him what they'd learned. Sloane was adamant Austen wasn't involved, or if he was, he didn't know what he was involved in. Dex had dropped it quickly. Ash guessed he didn't want to add to Sloane's concerns, especially not without proof. Sloane said he'd think about it, but since they had nothing to go on other than Shultzon's suspicions, there wasn't much—if anything—they could do. Sloane said he'd contacted Austen but as yet hadn't heard back. None of them had brought it up.

"It's been a while since we've been on a date, so I'm going to take Dex to Jersey this weekend, watch a movie and get some dinner. Try and get his mind off everything. I think working a case might do him good. He gets restless when he's not keeping busy." Sloane stood and gave Ash's shoulder a squeeze. "Thanks for doing this for me, man. I'm going to submit the request to Sparks. Make it official."

"Sure. Could you put one in for Cael? Work your magic to get it approved?"

"You got it. See you later."

Sloane was off, and Ash remained seated on the bench. He leaned back against the wall, thinking of his next move. It was certain Sparks would approve Sloane's request for Ash to train the brothers in an official capacity. He also knew she would allow it because it was him. Ash's experience and track record meant he held a certain amount of sway, and rather than sending Dex or Cael offsite to train or arranging a THIRDS training specialist, Ash would be permitted to carry out the training as he saw fit. That's if he could convince Cael to continue training with him. His methods might have been unorthodox, but he got results. He'd managed to get Cael really pissed, and that's what the young agent needed for combat. He wasn't lacking in ferocity; he simply needed to learn to reach deep down and draw from it.

Ash stood with a groan. Time to work on his groveling.

SIX

THAT JERK!

Cael climbed into their black Suburban and slammed the passenger side door shut. He was so mad it took him over a half dozen tries before he could click his seat belt into place. All he could think about was Ash yelling at him to get angry. Then he thought about Ash writhing on the floor in pain. Poor Ash. *Unbelievable!* "No," he scolded himself. "You are not allowed to feel guilty after what he did. Nope. No. *Noooo.*"

Rosa eyed him worriedly. "You okay, *gatito?*"

"Ugh!" Cael let out a frustrated grunt. "Ash Keeler is the most frustrating, infuriating, jerkface jerk ever!"

"Wow." Rosa stared at him. "A jerkface *and* a jerk. Must have been bad."

Cael felt his cheeks growing warm from his little outburst. "Just start the car." He folded his arms over his chest, refusing to give it another thought. He was *not* going to feel guilty. Ash had asked for it. Literally. He'd asked Cael to get mad and attack him. So he did. He'd given Ash exactly what he'd asked for.

"What did jerkface do?" Rosa asked as she turned on the ignition and pulled out of their designated parking spot. Cael ignored the amusement in her tone.

"He's training me in CQC."

"Oh?"

Rosa drove out of the subbasement at the rear of the building where the THIRDS garage housed all their tactical vehicles and onto the street. They were heading to NY Presbyterian Hospital. Their first case since returning to duty. Why did it have to be that hospital, of all places? Like they hadn't been there enough recently.

"And it's not going well?"

"I punched him in the balls," Cael muttered, feeling embarrassed now that he'd said it out loud.

Rosa let out a bark of laughter. "I'm sorry." She tried to keep herself from laughing but was failing miserably. "I'm sorry. I don't mean to laugh."

"Liar. You'd do the same if you had the chance."

"You bet I would. Don't think I haven't tried. Fucker's too fast."

"Wasn't fast enough this time around," Cael said with a snort.

Rosa laughed as they drove, their siren and flashing lights announcing their presence and demanding traffic get out of their way as Rosa maneuvered through New York City's busy streets. Cael couldn't help thinking about his training. Ash had said and done what he had to get him angry. Cael knew that. He thought about Ash's crude remark about what "she said," and his frown deepened. It was stupid, but it had really gotten under Cael's skin. It made him think about the women Ash had been with. Why was it so easy for Ash to be with them? All Cael wanted was to understand. Was that too much to ask? Dex had a point.

Why was it a big deal for Ash? Images of him on Ash's lap Thanksgiving night made him want to crawl under a rock and never come out. God, what an idiot he'd been. He'd even taken off his shirt, dry humping Ash like some wolf Therian in heat. It was pathetic. And then to make things worse, Ash had shot him down.

"*Gatito?* Cael."

Rosa prodded Cael's arm, and he gave a start. Shit.

"Sorry, Rosa."

"We're here."

She motioned to the main hospital entrance, and Cael hopped to it. Time to get to work. Berating himself for his poor romantic choices would have to wait until later.

They headed through the glass doors to the reception area and spoke quietly to one of the nurses.

"Agent Cael Maddock from the THIRDS Unit Alpha and Agent Rosa Santiago."

"Yes, of course."

The nurse quickly got to her feet and spoke quietly to her coworker before motioning for them to follow. They followed her through the hospital wings toward the ICU and down another wing containing only offices. At the entrance was a medium-sized reception area with three nurses.

"I'll leave you to it, Agents."

The nurse excused herself, and Cael frowned. He looked over at the nurses by the desk, who were chatting as if nothing was happening. The corridor was empty. No flurry of activity, no agents, no CSIs coming and going. Rosa must have been thinking the same because she turned to him with a questioning look.

Cael shrugged, and they headed over to the nurses' station, showed their badges, and introduced themselves.

One nurse pointed to one of the open offices. Did they know one of their coworkers had just died? Why was everyone so... blasé?

"This is fucking weird," Rosa whispered as they walked into the doctor's office. Cael stilled.

"Where is everyone?" The only occupant was the dead body lying on the floor in the middle of the room.

Hudson and Nina were always the first ones on scene, with a long line of CSIs trailing behind them. They should have arrived long before Cael and Rosa. He tapped his earpiece and asked Lisa, Unit Alpha's receptionist, to patch him through to Hudson. There was no answer from him or Nina. That was odd.

"Agents?"

Cael turned in the direction of the soft voice and found a blond male Human nurse with pale-blue eyes, his mouth covered by a surgical mask. His hospital ID said his name was Jude Russell.

"What can I do for you?" Cael asked.

"I've been instructed to inform you that your team has been momentarily detained. They should arrive shortly."

Cael nodded, waiting for the nurse to leave before turning to Rosa with a frown.

"Why wouldn't Hudson or Nina call us?"

"I don't like this." Rosa walked around the body and crouched down, reading the doctor's ID. "Dr. Ward. Why does that name sound familiar?"

"Shit. Dr. Ward?" Cael crouched down beside Rosa. "This is the doctor that treated Ash when he was shot. He was also Sloane's doctor when he was brought in after the explosion."

"*Carajo.*"

"Yeah." Cael looked the body over. "Male wolf Therian. Looks to be in his mid to late thirties."

Rosa took notes on her tablet, and Cael pulled a pair of examiner's gloves from his pocket. He tugged them on as he studied Ward. "We'll need Hudson to confirm, but from the looks of him, I'd say he hasn't been dead long. About an hour at most."

"I don't see any signs of a homicide." Rosa used her pen to push open the sides of the doctor's coat. "No blood, bruising, or wounds."

Cael very gently placed his hands on the doctor's head, feeling around and under. "No lacerations or bumps. Strange, considering he's on the floor."

"Heart attack?" Rosa asked.

None of this was sitting well with him. He removed his hand from Ward's head when he noticed a tiny purplish-blue blemish behind his earlobe. "I found something." He leaned in for a closer look. "I've got an entry point. He was injected with something." Damn it. Where the hell was Hudson? Cael was about to pull back when he noticed something white under the doctor's desk.

Rosa followed his line of vision. "What is it?"

"I don't know yet." Cael got down on his hands and knees in front of the desk and reached under it, then pulled out a small white prescription bottle. He read the label. "Thelxinomine. I've seen this name before." And recently too. "Can you run it through Themis?"

"Sure. Give me a sec."

Rosa tapped away at her tablet. The search was taking longer than usual.

"Nothing." She shook her head. "That can't be right. I'll run it again."

She tapped away, conducting another search, her frustrated huff telling him the second search had yielded the same results.

"This isn't possible. How can a hospital-prescribed drug not be in Themis?"

Cael couldn't understand it. Every legal and illegal substance known to man and Therian alike was listed in Themis. If the information was out there, Themis could find it.

Nurse Russell returned, lingering in the doorway. "Is there anything I can help with?"

"Perfect timing." Cael showed Russell the prescription bottle. "Can you tell me what this medication is? What it's used for?"

"I'm kind of new here, so I'll have to look that information up. I can bring you the file." Russell took the bottle from him and motioned toward the door. "I'll be back in a sec. Left my tablet at the nurses' station outside."

"Sure."

The nurse left, and Cael looked around the office. Everything was so clean. If Ward had been poisoned, they'd need Hudson and Nina to get the body back to the lab to run some tests. They needed confirmation on time of death and whatever it was the Therian had been injected with. Cael couldn't shake the feeling something was off about all this. Why were they the only ones here? Why did no one seem bothered? They were all so cold. And why the hell hadn't Rosa been able to find any information on the drug?

"Where did that nurse go? I thought he said he left his tablet outside at the nurses' station?" Rosa said, standing to join Cael.

"Let's go find out." Cael left the office with Rosa behind him. The nurses' station was a short distance from Ward's office. This time there was only one nurse behind the desk.

"Excuse me." Cael flashed his badge again. "Have you seen Nurse Russell? We're waiting on some information."

"One second." The Therian nurse picked up the phone, and seconds later, a young Therian female nurse with dark hair appeared.

"Can I help you?"

Cael frowned. "No. Sorry. We're looking for Nurse Jude Russell."

"I'm Nurse Jude Russell," she said, smiling pleasantly.

Cael looked at her ID. It did indeed say Jude Russell. Well, that wasn't confusing at all. What the holy hell was going on around here?

"The nurse we're looking for is a male Human," Cael insisted. "Blond hair and pale-blue eyes."

The two nurses exchanged puzzled glances before female Nurse Russell turned back to him. "I'm sorry, Agent, but I'm the only Jude Russell in this department."

"Okay." Rosa turned to the nurse behind the desk. "Is it possible the Jude we're looking for was from a different department?"

She tapped away at her screen. "I'm sorry, but there's no other registered nurse under that name."

What the hell? They hadn't made up the guy. Cael hurried back to the office with Rosa on his heels. "What the hell is going on?"

"This is seriously fucked, Cael."

Cael rushed inside and came to an abrupt halt. No, *this* was seriously fucked. "Rosa, tell me I'm not going crazy. There was a body on the floor last time we were in here."

Rosa walked past him and stared down at the floor where Dr. Ward had been a moment ago. "What the fuck is going on?"

There was no sign anyone had been in the room, yet the

place had been swept. It was empty. All of Dr. Ward's belongings, everything on his desk, in it, the shelves, anything that wasn't furniture, were gone. They'd yet to hear from Hudson and Nina. Cael spun on his heels and stomped back to the nurses' station, frowning at the male Therian sitting where the female Human nurse had been seconds ago.

"Who are *you*?" Cael asked, trying not to snap at the nurse.

The Therian blinked up at him. "Can I help you, Agent?"

"Where's the nurse who was here a moment ago?"

"She had to go. Emergency."

"Right." He thrust a finger in the direction of Dr. Ward's office. "Maybe you can tell me who the hell went into that office and moved Dr. Ward's body?"

"I'm sorry, who?"

Jesus. Cael pinched the bridge of his nose. This was getting absurd, and he was starting to lose his patience. "Dr. Ward. He was found dead earlier, and we're here to investigate. Someone has moved his body."

"I'm sorry, sir, but there's no doctor by that name here."

Cael gaped at the guy. "Yes, there is. We were just in there with him. Look up a patient. Ash Keeler. Tell me the name of the attending doctor."

The nurse tapped away at his screen. "Here it is. Ash Keeler. THIRDS agent. It says here his attending doctor was Dr. Fredrickson."

"What? No, that's not right. Look up a patient named Sloane Brodie. He was admitted in August."

More tapping. The nurse looked up at him and turned the screen so Cael could see. He pointed to the name in blue letters. *Dr. Fredrickson.*

"This is bullshit," Cael declared. He was about to chew out the nurse when his earpiece beeped. "Cael Maddock," he growled.

"Agent Maddock, this is Lieutenant Sparks. I want you and Agent Santiago in my office immediately."

"Can it wait? We have a situation." It took a hell of a lot of patience not to spit the words out.

"Your job isn't to question my orders, Agent Maddock. Your job is to follow them."

"Yes, Lieutenant." He tapped his earpiece and motioned for Rosa to follow him. "Come on. Sparks wants us in her office." He pulled off his gloves and disposed of them in one of the nurses' biohazard bins.

"Cael, what's going on?" Rosa asked as they hurried out to the parking lot and their Suburban. He climbed into the passenger side as his partner slid in behind the wheel. They fastened their seat belts and soon were on their way back to HQ.

"I don't know. But I intend to ask Sparks. This is all just... wrong. From the moment we stepped foot in there, it was wrong. Something was up with those nurses. And that guy who disappeared with the prescription? Someone went in there after us and swept the place."

They'd had newbies contaminate crime scenes, had to face uncooperative witnesses and all kinds of messed-up things, but this was the first time they'd had a body disappear on them. Not long after, they arrived back at HQ and the subbasement garage. They took the elevator up to Unit Alpha, and Cael couldn't shake the feeling in his gut. If he were in his Therian form, his fur would have been bristling. He went to tap his earpiece to get a hold of Hudson, but instead he headed for his and Rosa's office.

"Where are you going? I thought Sparks wanted us in her office."

"She does. I need to make a quick call." He put his hand to his desk's interface and tapped Hudson's extension into the digital keypad. Hudson answered cheerfully.

"Cael. What can I do for you?"

"Where were you guys?"

"I beg your pardon?"

"You and Nina weren't at the hospital."

"Were we supposed to be?" Hudson asked, sounding puzzled. "We've not had any callouts today."

"You weren't requested at NY Presbyterian?"

"No."

"Okay. Sorry. Must have gotten my intel wrong. Thanks, Hudson."

"No worries. Let me know if you need anything."

"Will do." Cael hung up and arched an eyebrow at Rosa. "That nurse told us they'd been detained. They hadn't even been called out. Let's see what Sparks has to say."

They'd left the office and were walking through the bullpen when he saw Ash sitting at his desk in his and Letty's office. Taking a detour, he knocked on the glass wall. Ash looked up and smiled tentatively.

"Hey. Everything okay?"

"I'm not sure." He walked in with Rosa beside him. "What was the name of the doctor who attended to you at NY Presbyterian Hospital?"

"Dr. Ward."

"I knew it! That bastard." They weren't losing their minds. Ward had been there. Dead.

"Who?"

"Something really fucked-up is going on," Rosa said,

coming to sit on the edge of Ash's desk, talking quietly. She brought Ash up to speed on everything that had happened from the moment they'd arrived at the crime scene, the puzzling game of musical chairs with various nurses, disappearing staff, vanishing bodies, and altered information. "And then Sparks orders us back here."

"Wait, what was the name of the drug you found?"

"Thelxinomine," Cael replied. "Have you heard of it? I swear I've seen it somewhere."

"I know exactly where you saw it." Ash opened his desk drawer and straightened. "What the fuck?" He jumped to his feet, and Cael was immediately at his side.

"What is it?"

"My prescription. It's gone."

"Are you sure you left it in there?" Rosa asked.

"Yes. I took one at lunch and put the bottle in this drawer. And now it's fucking gone."

Ash searched through the rest of his desk drawers, coming up empty every time. Ash's side of the office was impeccable. It would be hard to believe the guy could lose anything there. Letty's side was less organized but still tidy enough not to drive Ash mad. Cael knew what a neat freak Ash could be.

"Where's Letty?" Rosa asked.

"She's with the sarge, taking inventory on the last shipment of ammunition."

"Did you leave your office recently?" Cael looked around the office, not that he'd be able to spot if something was out of place. If Ash hadn't noticed, it was likely whoever had come in and taken the pills had done so discreetly. Someone had to have seen something. They were in the freakin' bullpen, for crying out loud.

Ash narrowed his eyes at his desk, as if doing so might

make the pills reappear. "About twenty minutes ago. I went to the bathroom."

Rosa walked to the door and discreetly peeked outside. "You can get a new one, right?"

"I suppose, but the doctor who prescribed it for me is dead. It was Thelxinomine. Dr. Ward signed off on it. I had two weeks' worth of doses left."

"There's no way this is a coincidence." Cael tapped his earpiece. "Dex?"

"Hey, bro. What's up?"

"Are you around?"

"Yeah, in the office with Sloane."

"Stay there."

"Sure."

The three of them left Ash's office and found Dex sitting behind his desk. His brother quickly tapped his desk, as if they hadn't noticed the brightly lit neon table hockey he'd been playing on his desk's interface. Ash entered his badge number into the security panel and initiated the office's privacy mode. The walls went white, and he turned to Sloane.

"Your doctor at the hospital was Dr. Ward, right?"

Sloane nodded. "Yeah, why?"

"Was he the one who prescribed your meds?"

"Yeah, Thelxinomine. I've still got another few weeks left. What's going on?"

Ash walked over to Sloane's side. "Where's the bottle?"

"In my desk." Sloane opened his drawer and frowned. He tried the other drawers. "At least it *was* in my desk." He looked up at Dex in question. "Have you seen my meds?"

"Not since this morning when you took your last dose, but I saw you put them back in the top right-hand drawer."

Cael turned to Sloane. "Were you and Dex out of your office recently?"

Sloane nodded. "Sparks called us into her office about twenty minutes ago. She wanted to know how I was doing and if Dex was up for some extra training."

"How long did the meeting take?" Cael asked.

Dex shrugged. "Maybe ten minutes at most."

"Guys? What's going on?"

"We'll let you know as soon as we get some answers. Until then, don't let anyone know your prescription has gone missing."

Cael entered his badge number into the security panel, and the office went back to normal. He left with Rosa and Ash in tow. As they left the bullpen and headed for Sparks's office, Ash took hold of Cael's arm and pulled him to one side.

"Before you go in there, connect to my com and leave your line open."

Cael stared at him, his voice low when he spoke in case anyone was close by. "You want to listen in. Why?"

"Trust me. I'll explain later."

"Okay." He had no idea why Ash was asking him, but there had to be a good reason for it. He tapped his earpiece and connected to Ash, then pressed the button in farther until it clicked, putting it on covert mode with no green light to give him away. Ash would be able to hear whatever Cael heard. They walked into Sparks's office.

"Close the door behind you," Sparks said from behind her desk in her usual no-nonsense tone.

Cael obliged, pressing his hand to the security panel. The door closed, and he joined his partner, taking a seat in the empty chair.

"Why the detour?" Sparks asked.

Shit. How the hell did she know? "Sorry. Dex had asked me to pick up some ibuprofen from the hospital while I was there. For Sloane."

"It could have waited."

Cael cleared his throat and tried his best not to fidget under her penetrating stare. "My apologies."

"I apologize as well."

Wait, what now? Cael was flabbergasted. Since when did their lieutenant apologize for anything? Before he could ask, she elaborated.

"You and Agent Santiago weren't supposed to have been called out to NY Presbyterian Hospital. Dispatch was misinformed. They were under the impression you were taking calls. They were meant to have put the call through to another Recon team. That's why Dr. Colbourn and Dr. Bishop weren't on scene when you arrived. The CSIs had already been there and processed the body."

"You mean Dr. Ward."

"I'm afraid that information is classified."

Cael frowned. "It's not classified if we've already seen it. We saw the body. It was Dr. Ward." And since when was a regular homicide classified? The information was most likely already public knowledge.

"You must be confused, Agent Maddock. The wolf Therian brought in was a Dr. Fredrickson. Now if you'll excuse me, I have some important matters to attend to. You may return to your duties."

What the hell? "With all due respect, Lieutenant, what's going on? The body we saw belonged to Dr. Ward, but then the nurse at the station—who wasn't the first nurse we spoke to—told us the guy didn't exist. The information on Agent Keeler and Agent Brodie's files had been altered, and then the bottle—"

"Lieutenant," Ash interrupted. "Damn. I'm sorry. I didn't know you were in a meeting."

Sparks didn't look pleased by the disturbance. "The status on the door hasn't glitched again, has it, Agent Keeler? It does say 'Engaged' in English and not Japanese, correct?"

Ash cringed. "Sorry. I wasn't paying attention. Have a lot on my mind."

Sparks seemed to consider that before giving him a smile. "Understandable. What did you need, Agent Keeler?"

"Am I cleared for authorization on advanced CQC training for Agents Daley and Maddock?"

"Your request has been accepted. I'd like an eighteen-week training schedule submitted to me by the end of the week, detailing what you hope to accomplish and the expected results."

"Yes, ma'am."

Sparks gave him a nod and turned her attention back to Cael and Rosa.

"You're dismissed, Agents."

"But—"

"There's nothing further to discuss. Get back to your training. In light of recent events, we need Destructive Delta to be in top form. I'm expecting to see results, Agent Maddock."

"Yes, ma'am." There was something about the way she said it that had Cael wondering if she was hinting at knowing more than they believed she knew. With Sparks, there was no way to tell. The female Therian was impossible to read. But if she knew about the unsanctioned mission, why hadn't they heard anything about it? Surely they would have heard something from Seb, who'd been permanently assigned the position of team leader for Theta Destructive.

They silently left and headed back to the bullpen. Cael tapped his earpiece and shut it off before leaning into Ash. "What's going on? Why didn't you want me to tell her about the drug?"

"Tell your brother to put in a call to Bradley and ask if we can borrow the second floor of Dekatria before it opens. We're having a team meeting. I want everyone there. This is off the books, so no one says a word. You inform Dex and Sloane. I'll inform the others. Something fucked-up is going on around here, and it's time we get to the bottom of it."

"THANKS FOR LETTING us use your bar."

Ash would never have thought they'd be using Dekatria as a base of operations, but the place was secure enough for them to have a meeting without having to worry someone was listening. Ash was comfortable here, which was saying something. He was always alert and on edge when hanging around someplace new, but he'd quickly acclimated himself to Dekatria. The retro décor didn't even bug him anymore.

"No problem. If you need anything, let me know." Bradley leaned over Ash to pass Cael a soda, his tattooed arm in front of them.

Bradley gave them a cheerful salute and headed toward the door. Ash excused himself to use the bathroom. On the stairs, he caught up to Bradley and took hold of his left arm. Puzzled, Bradley's smile dimmed. Recognition came into his eyes as Ash tightened his grip and turned his arm.

"Tell me this isn't a problem anymore and it's the last

time I'll be bringing it up. I won't let you endanger my team."

Bradley's amber eyes glowed with a familiar fire, his reply grave. "It's not a problem anymore."

Ash nodded. "Does Lou know?"

The anger in Bradley's eyes dimmed. "No. It's in the past."

"The past has a way of catching up with us. Believe me." Ash released his arm. "Tell him. If he really cares, he'll stick around. But he has a right to know."

Bradley nodded. "Thanks."

Ash turned and headed back upstairs, hoping Bradley was right. It made sense now, why the guy was happy to have them in his bar all the time. Who wouldn't want half an army to back them up if an old gang came around to give them trouble? Ash had seen the gang tattoo woven into a new design. Someone had done a great job of covering it up with a tattoo sleeve of new art, but Ash had seen it. The symbol wasn't the only thing he'd noticed. Several of Bradley's tattoos hid a variety of scars. Whatever Bradley had been mixed up in, it had been bad. Poor Lou. The guy was crazy about Bradley. He hoped things worked out for those two. They made a sweet couple. Speaking of sweet...

Ash slid into the booth beside Cael as they waited for Calvin to arrive. Glancing at his team, he saw Rosa was chatting with Letty, while Dex and Sloane were being all close and stupidly cute together. Ash took the opportunity to bump Cael playfully. He leaned in to talk quietly.

"So exactly how much groveling do I have to do to make up for what happened during training?"

Cael looked thoughtful as he sipped his soda, his plump lips especially pouty and wet as he sucked on his straw. If Ash didn't know any better, he'd say Cael was doing it on purpose. Was Cael giving him the silent treatment? No, Cael wouldn't do that. He knew how much Ash hated those sorts of games. Cael was either thinking up ways for Ash to make it up to him, or he was plotting his demise. Both were somewhat worrisome, though not exactly surprising.

"I know I was an asshole," he said, his fingers finding the hem of Cael's T-shirt. He slipped them under the gray cotton and held back a smile at the way Cael's cheeks turned pink. "And you're the last person on this earth I would ever want to be an asshole to. But your safety and well-being mean more to me than what you might think of me for my methods. *You* are what matters most to me, and if I have to piss you off every day to make sure you stay safe, then so be it. Whatever happens during our training, I promise to apologize after every session. To remind you that what you see in there is me doing what I have to do to protect you. So I'm sorry for being an asshole. As a peace offering, I'd like to make you dinner. We can watch a movie, hang out, play video games. Whatever you want. Just like we used to. What do you say?"

Cael looked up at him, his big gray eyes and loving expression stealing Ash's breath away.

"Really?"

"Really. Do you forgive me?"

"Only if you forgive me for punching your boys." He cringed. "I'm so sorry." Cael put his hand to Ash's bicep, his expression worried. "Are you okay? I didn't hurt you too bad, did I?"

"You punched me in the nuts."

Cael burst into laughter, then slapped a hand over his mouth. "I'm sorry," he mumbled. "I didn't mean to laugh." He laughed again, a sweet chuckle that warmed Ash's heart. "I am so sorry."

"No, you're not." Ash pretended to be put off. He laid his arm behind Cael's head on the seat's backrest and poked him in his side, making him squirm.

"Sorry I'm late."

They all turned their attention to Calvin, who looked like he could use some sleep. Something was going on with his teammate. Ash had stopped by Calvin and Hobbs's office after his training with Cael, but neither had been in. He hadn't seen Hobbs all day, which was unusual.

"Where's Hobbs?" Ash asked. He'd specifically told everyone they had to be there.

"He couldn't make it. I can't stay long. He's on his own at home."

Everything fell into place. Jesus, why hadn't Calvin told him Hobbs was having a rough time with his anxiety? It wasn't as if the team didn't know Hobbs. They all understood and supported the guy and had been doing it for years. They knew when to encourage him and when to back off. If Hobbs was at home, it meant he couldn't leave the apartment. This was usually one of those times when Calvin would stay home with his partner. He always did.

"It's been a while," Cael said, worried for his friends.

Calvin sighed and slipped into the booth across from Ash and Cael. There were bags under his eyes, and he looked exhausted. "Sorry I haven't told you guys. It's been a rough couple of weeks. He hasn't had it this bad in a while. Thanksgiving was a fucking disaster."

"I thought you and your mom spent every Thanksgiving with Hobbs and his family?" Cael said.

"We do, and we did again. Man, I wish we hadn't. That morning, when Ethan woke up, I knew it was bad. It took me three hours to get him out of bed. I helped him pick out his clothes, and then his mom called, and he didn't even want to talk to her. She understood. His parents are really supportive and understanding, always have been. They've done everything they could for him and his condition since he was a kid, and the meds were really helping. He still has rough days, but they haven't been nearly as bad as this." Calvin looked like he was on the verge of tears. Dex must have noticed because he sat down beside Calvin and put his arm around him.

"What happened, Cal?"

"Ethan calmed down. I made him some tea, and he seemed okay. I told him if he didn't want to go to his mom's it was no big deal. We could stay in and chill. His mom even offered to drop us off some Thanksgiving dinner. Ethan said it was fine. I know he just didn't want to disappoint his mom. So we went. My mom was already there because she always heads over early to help with the cooking." Calvin took a breath and then continued.

"We all sat around the table, and everything was fine. Ethan was quiet, but he was smiling, so he was doing okay. Then the doorbell rings. Rafe had fucking invited a friend without letting us know ahead of time, some guy Ethan had never met. He panicked, got up so quick he knocked over a bottle of red wine by accident, and that fucking prick Rafe yelled at him." Calvin blinked back his tears. "His brother is fucking hyperventilating in front of him, and he's yelling at him, telling him not to be such a child, that he does it to get attention."

"Hey, it's okay, pal." Dex rubbed his hand over Calvin's back.

Calvin balled his hands into fists on the table, a tear rolling down his cheek. "Rafe is yelling at Ethan, and then that stupid son of a bitch friend of his starts laughing and calls Ethan a spaz. I fucking lost my shit. Tackled him and punched him in the face. Seb pulled me off him, and I would have gone right back to beating the shit out of him if I hadn't seen my mom hugging Ethan. He was sitting on the floor covering his ears and struggling to breathe. Seb helped me get him to his old bedroom. We got him into bed, and Seb left me alone with him. I don't know how long it took, but I stayed up with him, soothing him until he fell asleep." He drew in a shaky breath and let it out slowly before wiping his eyes. "Sorry, I just, I haven't been sleeping well."

"Why didn't you call us?" Dex asked. "You know we would have done whatever we could to help."

"I know, but sometimes he just can't see anyone. It's not because he doesn't want to. He can't. Having someone besides me or Seb there with him could make it worse." He gave Dex a wobbly smile. "But next time, I'll ask him if he's okay with one of you guys coming over. He might like it."

"Has he gone to his doctor to see what's going on with his meds? They seemed to be helping him just fine," Ash said. He didn't like all these different Therian meds floating around, and after years of working, why were Hobbs's meds failing him now?

Calvin shook his head. "We're working our way up to an appointment. I don't get it. They were really helping him until recently. He got a refill of his prescription a couple of weeks ago, but there were no changes to his dose, so I have no idea what's going on."

"Let us know if you or he needs anything," Cael said gently.

"Thanks. So what's this meeting about? And why are we having it at Dekatria?"

Ash turned to Sloane, who sat in one of the retro armchairs. "I think we need to tell them."

Sloane looked uncertain, but he gave Ash the okay.

"Tell us what?" Calvin looked from Ash to Sloane and back. "What's going on?"

"We hadn't said anything yet because we didn't want to worry you guys until we knew more, but Sloane's lost control over his Therian half twice since he was released from the hospital after the explosion."

Rosa gasped and turned to Sloane. "Oh my God, Sloane. What happened?"

"The first time was after I was released from the hospital while Dex was out tracking down Hogan. I attempted to shift, but with the extent of my injuries, it did more harm than good. Dex and I got into an argument the next morning, and I lost it. I shifted. The most terrifying part was my fuzzy memory afterward. I couldn't remember being there. I woke up, and there I was in my Therian form standing over Dex, his pajama pants torn."

"He pushed me down the stairs," Ash added.

Sloane threw a hand up. "Again with that? How many times do I have to say I'm sorry? Because I'm beginning to not be."

Ash shrugged. "Just saying, if you'd been present, you wouldn't have done it."

"No, just tempted," Sloane grumbled. "Anyway, it happened again before Thanksgiving. Luckily this time Dex was ready, and he tranqed me. I couldn't remember anything after I woke up."

Now it was Ash's turn. This was going to be pleasant. "I had a similar feeling in Central Park. When we caught up to Collins. Except I didn't shift. I felt this blinding rage." He held a hand up. "And before you say anything, yes, I'm normally pissed off, but I've never had trouble controlling it. After what happened with Collins, it made me wonder if what's happening to Sloane will also happen to me."

Cael poked Ash in his side, his expression worried. "Wait, what happened with Collins? Seb's report stated Collins swiped one of his agent's guns, took aim at another agent, and was neutralized."

"That's not entirely what happened."

"What?" Cael stared at Ash before his expression turned hurt. He looked around the room. "You all know, don't you? Why am I the only one who doesn't know?"

Ash turned to Cael and took a deep breath. "When I saw the picture Hogan sent of you bloodied and bruised on Collins's phone, I felt this intense white rage go through me. Something I'd never felt before. I wanted to kill Collins. The guy refused to tell us where Hogan had taken you. We had to find another way. Something happened, everything I felt intensified ten times over, and..." God, what would Cael think of him? Ash hadn't wanted him to find out about what he'd done, what he'd been pushed to do. Would Cael think it was part of his nature? That he was more animal than Human? As ruthless and heartless as some believed he was?

"Ash?"

"I let Collins take my gun. When he aimed at Dex, I killed him. I snapped his neck."

Cael's stunned, wide-eyed expression scared the shit out of Ash, and he took Cael's hand in his. "I told everyone I'd do whatever it took to find you. That I'd go through however many of Hogan's goons it took to get you back alive, and I would. I just never believed myself capable of killing like that. I've neutralized threats before, we all know I have, but this was different. I forced his hand. I knew what he wanted to do, and I gave him the means to do it so I could take him out."

"I..."

Cael swallowed hard, and everyone allowed him a

moment to process what he'd learned. Ash expected Cael to push him away, to tell him what he'd done was wrong and that he needed time. Instead, Cael nodded.

"I understand. We can talk about it later if you like, okay?"

He smiled warmly, and Ash let out the breath he hadn't realized he'd been holding.

Relief washed through Ash, and he returned Cael's smile. "Okay. How about you tell them about the case of the disappearing doctor?"

"Right. Rosa and I were called in to investigate the murder of Dr. Ward."

"Wait." Dex held a hand up. "Dr. Ward is dead? Why didn't you mention this earlier?"

"Shit."

Sloane ran a hand over his face, and Ash knew his best friend was piecing it all together. It didn't take much considering the information they had. There was no mistaking it was all connected.

"Why's that name familiar?" Calvin asked, looking pensive.

"He was Sloane's doctor," Cael replied before turning his attention to his brother. "Sorry, we got wrapped up with the whole disappearing meds, bodies, and everything that came after."

"He was also my doctor," Ash added.

Letty looked from Sloane to Ash. "So you're both experiencing similar problems and both happen to have had the same doctor?"

Ash nodded. "Who also prescribed us the same doses of Thelxinomine, a Therian antibiotic meant to help our immune system and fight off infection from our injuries."

Something seemed to dawn on Calvin. "Wait a second. How is Dr. Ward missing if he's dead?"

This was getting fun. His team had no idea what the hell to make of all this. He could see it in their faces. Cael chimed in with an answer.

"Rosa and I showed up at the crime scene like usual. I found a bottle of Thelxinomine under Dr. Ward's desk. The name of the medication seemed familiar, so I asked Rosa to check it out in Themis, except nothing came up, which we all know never happens. So I asked a Human male nurse for more information. The guy left and never came back. When we went to find out what was taking so long, we were introduced to a Therian female nurse with the same name. Apparently, the only nurse working there with that name. When we returned to the crime scene, the body was gone. The scene had been swept. The whole office was empty."

Rosa let out an indelicate snort. "It gets better. Hudson, Nina, and the CSIs should have been there before us, but they weren't. We were told they'd been detained. When Cael spoke to Hudson, he said they were never called out to begin with. Then Ash and Sloane's meds vanished from their desks, where they'd been keeping them while at work."

"Okay." Calvin frowned thoughtfully. "We can rule out freak coincidence. You both had the same doctor, who wound up dead. You were prescribed the same meds, which were at the crime scene and now have mysteriously disappeared. No doc, no evidence, no pills. This is all very fascinating and weird, but I don't understand what your investigation has to do with the rest of us."

"Because it was never our investigation," Rosa said. "Sparks told us the case had already been assigned to another team. That dispatch had made a mistake by giving us the call. When Cael brought up Dr. Ward, Sparks said he was mistaken. That the body brought in was a Dr. Fredrickson, which happened to be the name on file at the hospital as the attending doctor for Sloane and Ash, which we all know is not true. After that, we were dismissed."

Ash met Dex's gaze and gave him a nod. If Calvin was confused now, wait until he heard the rest of it.

"After Sloane lost control of his shift the second time, Ash and I went to see Dr. Shultzon. We had no idea what could be causing it, so we figured we'd ask the one guy who knew more about Therians than anyone. Unfortunately, he didn't have any answers for us, just left us with more questions. He believes the THIRDS is still carrying on with the development of the control drug from the research facility. The one Isaac used on me. One that could be used to control Therians."

Dex paused, and Ash understood his hesitation. Shit, he didn't want to break the news either.

"He also believes a high-ranking THIRDS officer is involved, most likely using specialist agents. He told us someone isn't who they say they are, and we should be mindful of the orders we're given."

Everyone went quiet as they thought about that. There was only one officer who gave them orders who could be involved. No one believed Maddock would have anything to do with this mess. The man would sooner hand in his badge than be involved with a Therian mind-control drug, and Sloane wasn't even a consideration.

Letty jumped to her feet. "*Mierda*. Are you suggesting Sparks is involved?"

"How well do you guys know her?" Dex asked.

Cael shrugged. "As well as anyone in our unit. She's really reserved. But that doesn't mean she's involved in some control-drug conspiracy."

"I hate to say it," Ash pitched in, and he really did hate saying it, but someone had to, "but when you think about it, she's the only logical choice. She was mighty pissed off when she showed up at the research facility after we took Isaac down. What if she knew what was going on, and she was pissed off for another reason? Ward was somehow involved, and he got killed for it. Then Sparks covers it up."

"*If* Ward was involved, which is likely considering what's happened, and he prescribed your meds, which disappeared. Do you think the meds are what's been messing with your feral half?" Calvin asked.

Letty looked startled. "Do you think he gave you the drug, passing it off as meds?"

Sloane shook his head. "The drug's supposed to control Therians. There was no control when I shifted. If it *was* the drug, it's a complete failure. I can't explain why our meds disappeared or what purpose they served, outside of what we were led to believe. Either way, it leaves us with a hell of a lot of unanswered questions."

He let out a sigh, and Ash knew his best friend was feeling guilty for his thoughts about Sparks. Ash felt the same. Maybe they didn't know her all that well despite having worked under her for so long, but she always had their backs, always supported them, gave them more leeway than any officer had to. She was a damned good lieutenant. If they assigned guilt to someone simply based on their abrasive nature, Ash would be responsible for everything wrong with the world.

"I don't know if Sparks is involved, but her recent behavior raises a lot of questions," Sloane admitted. "Any time I've asked about the First Gen Research Facility, she's shot me down. And don't forget Austen showed up with the very same drug when you were moving in on Bautista. Austen reports directly to Sparks. Shultzon said whoever was working on this was using specialist agents."

"You think Austen's in on this too?" Letty asked worriedly.

"God knows I don't want to believe it, but all this has left me unsure of anything. I know the evidence right now is against him, but I believe in him. I don't think he's capable of doing anything like this, and if he is involved, I can't imagine he'd do so willingly. I admit there's a huge amount I don't know about what his job entails, but I trust him to do what's right."

"So what do we do now?" Calvin asked.

Everyone turned their attention to Sloane.

"It'll be interesting to see if I have any episodes now that I'm off the meds. As for the rest, keep your eyes and ears open. I want to hear about anything you might come across that's strange. There isn't a whole lot we can do until we're back in the field. I'm going to try to get a hold of Austen and see if he can shed any light on all this."

Ash frowned. "You really think he'll tell you? What if he's involved?"

"Austen and I go way back. If there's something he wants me to know, he'll find a way of telling me without actually telling me. Until then, watch your backs."

SEVEN

CHRISTMAS EVE WAS TURNING out better than Cael had hoped. It might have to do with the fact he'd gone into it with little expectations other than to have a good time with his friends and family. He'd treat this Christmas like the last one. No pressure, just fun. He'd barely stopped smiling since Ash and Sloane had arrived at the house earlier in the day. They all hung out, drinking eggnog, munching on snacks, and having a great time. In the evening, Cael finished preparing a light dinner while Ash set the table. Sloane distracted Dex to keep him from eating the food before Cael served it. This had involved allowing Dex to tune the kitchen radio to *Retro Radio*. There was air guitar and Ash threatening Dex with grievous bodily harm if he thrust his hips in his direction one more time. Tony watched his favorite Christmas movies in the living room, leaving them to their "shenanigans."

Ash had been hesitant around Cael at first, but he loosened up later in the evening. He'd even kissed Cael's cheek in front of Tony. Cael didn't make a big deal out of it but took it more as a wonderfully pleasant surprise. Every little gesture from Ash was a sweet revelation. Cael and Dex were finishing the dishes when he heard it. He wiped his hands on a hand towel and turned to his brother.

"What was that?"

"What? I didn't hear anything," Dex said, drying his hands.

Cael was positive he'd heard something. "I heard a distinct 'aw.'"

"You did?" Dex listened intently when laughter erupted from the living room. Dex's eyes widened the same moment as Cael's. "He wouldn't."

"This is Dad we're talking about."

"Oh my God, he totally would!"

Dex bolted from the kitchen with Cael on his heels. They ran into the living room, Dex coming to an abrupt halt and nearly forcing Cael to slam into him. Cael peered around his brother with dread. Their dad sat on the large couch flanked by Sloane and Ash, a photo album in his lap.

"And this Halloween they decided they wanted to dress up like Ghostbusters. It was also the year a certain someone decided he was going to take green Jell-O with him while he trick-or-treated. Little did I know it was so he could throw it at the other kids and declare them 'slimed.'"

Everyone's eyes moved to Dex.

"What? Who says it was me? It could have been Cael."

Ash let out a snort. "Yeah, no one believes that. Dweebus."

With a sniff, Dex folded his arms over his chest. "I was going for authenticity."

"Right. Good to know you've been weird all your life."

Cael's eyes dropped to the next album in the lineup. He gasped and swiftly clamped a hand over his mouth. Ash smiled wickedly.

"What?"

Cael shook his head. "Nothing."

Ash narrowed his eyes, and Cael made the mistake of glancing down at the baby-blue album on the coffee table. Ash followed his gaze, and Cael made a dive for it, snatching up the album before Ash could get his hands on it. Cael dashed behind the couch where his dad and Sloane were sitting. *Thanks for not helping, Dex.* Dex took a seat on Sloane's lap, pointing out pictures of himself and his dimples. Ash stood across the coffee table, clearly plotting his next course of action.

"What's in the album?" Ash asked, getting that predatory look in his amber eyes.

Cael held it close to his chest. "Coupon clippings!"

"I don't think so."

"They're his baby pictures," Dex offered cheerfully.

Cael gasped. "Traitor!"

His brother gave a lazy shrug as he turned another page in the photo album. "You told Sloane about me and the vacuum cleaner hose, so now we're even."

"We are *so* not even," Cael scoffed. "I told him that because you called me Chirpy in front of him!"

Their dad let out a bark of laughter. "Oh shit." He looked at Sloane. "Cael told you about the vacuum cleaner?"

"Yep." Sloane grinned broadly, squirming when Dex poked him in the belly. "Hey, it's not *my* fault. I was living in blissful ignorance before then."

Tony reached over and patted Sloane's knee. "You don't know the half of it. During his teenage years, you could bounce a quarter off his socks when laundry time came around."

Everyone burst into laughter, except for Dex, who

appeared unimpressed. "Masturbation and food consumption were the core foundations of my teenage years. It's perfectly healthy."

"I didn't need to know that," Ash muttered, taking a step closer to Cael as if Cael wouldn't notice.

Sloane wriggled his brows at Dex. "Guess some things never change."

"I really didn't need to know *that*," Ash ground out, glaring at Sloane, who brushed him off with a laugh. Ash moved to his right, and Cael did the same, his eyes narrowed at Ash.

"There's no way you're getting your hands on this album, Keeler."

"We'll see about that."

Ash slowly crept toward him, and Cael slowly backed away. Ash paused with a frown.

"Did you leave the milk out?"

Had he? Cael gasped. He was pretty sure he'd put it away after serving up the pie and—Two strong hands took hold of his waist and hoisted him up. Cael yelped and flailed, but he kept a firm grip on the album as Ash tossed him over his shoulder, holding him down by his legs.

"No fair! Put me down!" The big sneak, distracting him like that. Spoiled milk was a very serious offense. Milk was needed for the enjoyment of cookies, and baking, and... more cookies. "Damn it, Ash!"

"Give me the album."

Ash walked around to the love seat and dropped him onto it.

"I'm giving you one more chance. Hand over the package, Agent Maddock, or face the consequences."

"Never! You can't break me." He wrapped his arms tightly around the album, rolling onto his side and away from Ash. There was nothing Ash could do to make him give up his baby album, filled with pictures of him and his bare bottom sticking up in the air. Or the one his dad took of him potty training, or dear God, the pictures of him running around the house naked during his "clothes are stupid" phase.

"All right. You've left me no choice."

Ash lifted Cael's legs and sat down, pulling him onto his lap as he launched a tickle assault. Cael squealed. Oh no! He was horribly ticklish.

"Stop!" Cael cried, holding steadfast on to his album. He squirmed and laughed, tried curling on his side, then his back, but nothing eased the cruelty of Ash's assault. He tickled Cael under his arms, on his sides, his neck, his belly, and his feet. It was ruthless! Cael had tears in his eyes, and his mouth hurt from laughing. Just when he thought he couldn't take any more, the assault stopped. Cael flopped onto his back, sprawled across Ash's lap as he tried to catch his breath. He maintained a firm grip on his baby pictures. And then Ash kissed him.

Ash was kissing him in front of his family and Sloane. Rather than allowing his shock to take over, Cael let himself get swept away by the taste of Ash's soft lips against his own. He returned the kiss, melting against Ash. A soft sigh escaped him, and the album was slipped from his fingers.

"Thank you," Ash murmured, brushing his lips over Cael's before planting a quick kiss and pulling back.

Cael glared at him. "You have no shame."

Ash let out a husky laugh. "And you're just figuring that out?"

Cael sat up, falling into the gap between Ash's legs when he spread them. He might as well take it like an agent. Ash opened the album and "aw"d. The first page had a six-month-old Cael looking up at the camera with huge gray eyes and a confused expression. Not exactly unusual for babies that age. He was also naked, with his bottom in the air and part of him covered by a fluffy cheetah-print blanket.

"I think I might die of how adorable this is," Ash said. "This sort of cute should be illegal." He grinned at Cael and kissed the tip of his nose. "You should be illegal."

"Shut it," Cael griped.

He had no choice but to sit there—on Ash's lap—while Ash looked at his baby pictures. At least he was enjoying one of those things. He ignored the chuckles from his family. Ash continued to look through Cael's album, making silly cute noises and pointing out pictures. There were hundreds of photos of Cael in his Human baby form and then later when he was a little older and his first shift happened, in his cheetah Therian form with his cheetah fuzz sticking up all over. There were pictures of him chirping, of him with bows in his fur thanks to his jerkface big brother, and of him hiding in a bucket while he played hide-and-seek with Dex.

Usually a Therian's first shift happened during puberty, but there were always exceptions, and some shifted sooner. Cael had been an early shifter, so he'd still had his cheetah fuzz. Luckily he didn't have it for too long.

Cael perked up, and a sly smile came onto his face. Why should he suffer alone in this baby picture hell? "Sloane," Cael called out sweetly.

Sloane looked up. "Hm?"

"That yellow-and-baby-blue album with the little lion on it is Dex's baby album."

Dex gasped. He made a dive for it, but in true Dex fashion, he lost his balance and hit the carpet instead. With a smile, Sloane plucked the album from the table. "Thanks, Cael."

With a groan, Dex sat up. He kicked at Sloane's foot.

"Ow. Why are you assaulting me?"

"You could have saved me, you big dork. Instead you went for the album?"

Sloane blinked at him. "But if I grabbed you, then I wouldn't have the album."

Dex prodded their dad's leg. "And what's your excuse?"

Their dad didn't even bother looking up from the album in his hand. "It's not my job to kiss your ouchies anymore." He jabbed a thumb in Sloane's direction. "That's his job now."

"So you let me fall?" Dex whined.

"If I caught you every single time you fell, you'd never learn how to get yourself up."

Dex gaped at their dad while Cael snickered.

"Ha! You just got schooled by Dad."

"Be quiet, Chirpy."

"Stop calling me that!"

Cael jumped to his feet, grabbed one of the couch's throw pillows, and launched it at Dex, who was getting to his feet. His brother swatted it away, and it smacked Ash in the face. There was a collective gasp from everyone.

Ash looked down at the pillow in his lap, then up at Dex.

"Hit the deck!" Dex leapt over the coffee table, rolled, and disappeared behind the armchair. Cael slowly backed away as Ash stood, gently put the album on the table, and took hold of the pillow he'd been smacked with. Cael dove behind the love seat. His brother was a dead man.

"Don't break my pillow," Tony muttered, unfazed by whatever was about to transpire. Cael crawled to the edge of the love seat and peeked out. His dad continued flipping through the pages of the photo album in his lap.

"Sloane, save me!" Dex used the furniture for cover as Ash stalked him. At least Dex had one advantage over Ash. Having grown up in this house, Dex was familiar with every nook and cranny.

"Sloane? There's no Sloane here," Sloane replied. "Apparently just a big dork."

Dex popped his head up from behind an armchair. "Have you no sympathy for my impending demise?"

Sloane opened Dex's baby album and chuckled. "Aw, look at you! You look like a little burrito."

Dex looked uninspired. "It's called swaddling."

Cael watched as Ash got ready to pounce. His brother had to know he was there.

"Whatever it's called," Sloane said, "it makes you look like a burrito. An adorable baby burrito." He turned the page. "Oh, now this is precious. Dexter Justice Daley in sheriff footie pajamas."

Ash froze, pillow raised high above his head. "Hold the phone." He arched an eyebrow at Sloane. "What did you say?"

Tony closed the album in his lap. "Look at the time. I think I'll head up to bed." He placed the album on the table and stood. "You break it, you buy it."

With that Tony headed upstairs. Cael slowly crawled over the armrest of the love seat, grabbed a throw pillow, and sat with his knees drawn up to watch the chaos. Man, he wished he had some popcorn.

"What?" Sloane asked. He looked down at the album when it seemed to dawn on him. "Oh shit."

Ash turned to Dex, a wide grin spreading at the horrified expression on his face. "Your middle name is Justice?"

Dex shook his head at Sloane. "Why would you do this to me? I thought you loved me."

"I'm sorry," Sloane squawked. "It slipped out!"

Ash erupted into full-blown laughter. "That's the funniest shit I've ever heard!" He doubled over, laughing so hard he was soon in tears.

"It's not that funny," Dex grumbled, dropping down onto the couch beside Sloane, who drew him into his embrace and attempted to soothe Dex's epic pouting.

Cael shook his head. He was related to crazy people. Ash was on his knees and holding on to his side as he laughed. Apparently, he was also in love with a crazy person. Sloane kissed Dex's cheek, then his jaw, and whispered something in his ear. Dex appeared to consider whatever it was Sloane had said to him. The lewd smile he gave Sloane had Cael cringing. Ugh, they were going to have sex.

"Good night," Dex declared. He stood and pulled Sloane with him. "Ash, you're a douchebag." With that he marched off, Sloane in tow. Cael waited as Ash continued to laugh. He couldn't even reply to Dex's insult.

Maybe Cael should change into his pajamas while the fiercest Therian Defense agent he knew rolled around on the floor laughing like a five-year-old.

"Is this going to take long? Because I might go upstairs and change."

Ash wiped his eyes, his laughter easing up. "Man, I have enough material for at least a year. This is fucking brilliant. Best. Christmas. Ever."

"It doesn't take much, does it?" Cael asked, amused by how happy Ash looked. Like a little kid who'd been given a big red fire engine for Christmas.

"To annoy the living daylights out of your brother? No, it doesn't. This is payback for every time he's called me

Simba, for that fucking puppet, for every smartass remark." He rubbed his hands together gleefully. "I am going to have a fucking ball with this."

Cael chuckled and got up. "I'm going to go change." A thought occurred to him. "I haven't shown you my room, have I?" Ash had seen his apartment bedroom plenty of times when he crashed at Cael's, but Cael had never taken him up to his old bedroom.

Ash shook his head and got up off the floor. "Can I see it?"

"Sure."

Cael beamed at him. He motioned toward the stairs, and Ash accompanied him. Upstairs there were several doors. He pointed to the door at the far end of the hall, away from the others.

"That's Dad's room. The room closest to his is mine, across the hall's the bathroom, and the first room here is Dex's."

There was faint moaning coming from Dex's room.

"You've got to be shitting me," Ash grumbled, grabbing Cael's wrist and hurrying toward Cael's bedroom. He walked in and closed the door behind them. "How can you sleep with them in the next room sexing each other up? I had to sleep in your dad's freakin' office Thanksgiving night."

Cael winced. "Sorry, should have told you about the headphones."

"Headphones? You were wearing headphones?"

Cael took a seat on the edge of his bed. "Yeah. So was Dad. That's why we didn't hear anything. Dex warned us."

"That fucker. He didn't warn *me*."

Cael couldn't help his laugh. "Sorry." He so wasn't sorry. "I have a spare set you can borrow if you need it."

Ash flopped down across from him. "I shouldn't have to sleep with headphones. I can't believe your dad lets your brother get away with it. It's not like anyone's asking him to refrain from having sex for the rest of his life. It's one fucking night."

"You've known Dex over a year now. When has he ever not gotten away with something? If Dad told Dex no, he'd come up with an elaborate scheme to do it anyway, and believe me, the alternative would most likely be worse." Cael fell back onto the bed. "Those two are like freakin' bunnies. All the damn time." He turned his head to observe Ash, who was taking in the room around him.

Like Dex's bedroom, their dad had kept Cael's room how he'd left it when he'd moved out. Unlike Dex, who moved out when he went to college after buying his own house, Cael had stayed home. It wasn't like he had to go far to get to school. His bedroom furniture, bedding, and carpet were varying shades of gray. A dark gray bookshelf on the far wall contained all his old textbooks and all the books his dad had read to him since he was little. A few toys from his childhood, along with some gadgets, were arranged here and there. Boxes filled with all his baby belongings were stacked neatly in his closet, along with his toys, and later his Little League equipment. Their dad didn't believe in throwing their childhood belongings away, especially since he'd taught his boys how to appreciate what they had from an early age.

"Who's this?" Ash got up, walked to the bookshelf, and picked up Cael's favorite stuffed toy from his childhood.

"Oh, that's Brave Heart Lion." Man, he'd loved that thing. Still did.

Ash ran his hand over the fuzzy brown mane, a big smile on his face. "He's cute."

"I've had him since I was a baby. He was my favorite growing up. Had him with me everywhere I went." Cael chuckled at the memory. There was nowhere he'd gone without Brave Heart. When Dex wasn't around, Brave Heart kept him from feeling scared.

"That's adorable."

"Well, he used to be Dex's favorite. It was his."

Ash put Brave Heart down. "Less adorable." He walked back to the bed and resumed his spot, flopping back next to Cael.

"My dad said when he brought me home Dex insisted I have Brave Heart because I needed him more than he did. I took him everywhere. When I was unsure or scared and Dex couldn't be with me, Dex would say that Brave Heart would help me be strong and brave. I believed him." He couldn't help his smile.

"Must've been something."

"What's that?" Cael hadn't expected the almost wistful tone in Ash's voice. He couldn't begin to imagine what Ash's childhood must have been like. Cael had been lucky. If Tony hadn't adopted him, who knew what would have become of him. With all the conflict and intolerance going on, he would have been another Therian child lost in a world that didn't want him.

"Growing up here," Ash replied quietly, drawing Cael's attention. "Your dad's an amazing guy. Your brother..."

Cael couldn't help his smile. "My brother...?"

"Isn't always a jackass," Ash admitted. He actually looked like it pained him to say the words, and it made Cael chuckle.

"If you tell him I said so I'll deny it till my dying breath."

"Don't worry." He gave Ash a wink. "Your secret's safe with me."

Ash lay down on the bed so his head was next to Cael's but upside down. "There were days back then, when I didn't think I would make it out of there."

"The facility?" Cael asked gently.

Ash nodded somberly. "A part of me didn't want to, didn't believe I deserved to, but I did. For Sloane. He needed me. After years of being alone, of feeling like I deserved everything that was happening to me in there, I met someone who needed me to protect him." He swallowed hard and closed his eyes. "I'd failed my brother. I wasn't going to fail my best friend."

Cael nodded his understanding when it struck him. "Wait. You have a brother?" How was it possible he hadn't known? Why wouldn't Ash have told him? Or even mentioned him? Cael was so confused.

"Had. He's dead."

Cael swallowed past the lump in his throat, watching Ash's eyes grow glassy. He rolled onto his side toward Ash. "I'm so sorry to hear that. Were you close?" Ash flinched at his words. "Ash?"

"Arlo and I did everything together. When we were kids, I..." Ash drew in a deep breath and let it out slowly. "I was figuring myself out. There was a boy. I really liked him. One day he told me to meet him behind the bleachers for some fooling around. It was during the riots. I was supposed to have walked home with Arlo. Instead I sent him ahead so I could kiss Davie." A tear escaped and rolled down Ash's cheek. He quickly wiped it away. "Arlo was beaten to death on the way home."

"Oh, Ash." Cael put his hand to Ash's shoulder. "I'm so sorry."

"To make things worse, when I got home, with everything going on, I shifted for the first time. It was too much for my parents, and they called Animal Control. I was caged up and carted away before Dr. Shultzon took me in. He's the reason Arlo's information never made it into Themis."

Cael couldn't believe it. He wasn't so naïve that he wasn't aware of how cruel the world could be, but he never understood how parents could discard their Therian children so easily. How could Ash's parents send him away when he needed them the most?

"Arlo was my twin. I used to tease him that I was the oldest because I was born first."

Cael's eyes went wide. "Your twin?"

"Losing a sibling is difficult enough, but when that sibling is your twin, it's a whole other level of loss. Like a part of you is missing. Arlo's death still haunts me. In my dreams, when I'm awake. That anger and anguish has become a part of me. It's made me who I am, and I don't know that I can change."

"Why would you want to change?" Cael tenderly stroked Ash's jaw. "If you want to change who you are, then you do that, but you do it because it feels right to *you*. If you don't want to change, the hell with everyone else. I know what's underneath that gruff exterior. I fell in love with you for who you are, Ash. Every cursing, foul-mouthed, grumpy inch of you."

Ash turned his face toward Cael, his expression troubled. "Why?"

How could Ash not see it? "You mean why would I fall for someone who's so sweet and wonderful to me? Who drives me crazy in the most amazing ways? Who takes care of me, protects me, stands up for me, who respects me and makes me incredibly happy? Why would I fall for this unpredictable unstoppable force of awesome who's sexy and fierce? Why would I fall for that guy?"

Ash's smile reached his eyes. "I love that about you. The way you look for the good in everyone. You see me the way I want to see myself."

"And you can, Ash. One day at a time. I wish you'd let me be there with you while you find your way." Cael took Ash's hand in his. "I'm not expecting you to change your online status to 'in my first relationship with a dude.' I just want you to give us a chance."

"That's the problem, Cael. I don't want a chance with you."

Cael's heart sank. "Oh."

"No. You don't understand." Ash covered Cael's hand with his own and leaned into his touch. "I've never felt this way about anyone. I tried to stop feeling how I do about you. Haven't been remotely successful since the day we met."

Cael smiled at the memory. "You mean the day I pulled my smooth moves on you, bumped into you, and spilled your hot coffee all over you?"

Ash chuckled. "Yeah. That day. The moment I saw you, that was it for me."

"So why don't you want to give us a chance?"

"Because I don't want a chance. I want a whole lot more. I want everything with you for as long as I can get it. I'm terrified of messing up."

"You? King of the jungle? Ash Keeler isn't afraid of anything," Cael teased.

Ash turned his face and kissed Cael's palm. "That might have been true. Once."

The butterflies in Cael's stomach were fluttering wildly.

"You know the saying, ''tis better to have loved and lost than never to have loved at all.'"

"Someone should have Tasered Tennyson in the balls for that one. That jackass."

Cael laughed, his heart going out to Ash. Everything fell into place. Ash had always been reserved when it came to his past, but Cael did his best to be understanding. He figured Ash would confide in him when he was ready. Never would he have imagined the pain and heartache that he'd suffered. Cael's heart broke after finding out about Ash and the facility, though it put a lot into perspective and gave him a clearer understanding as to why Ash was the way he was. And now Cael's heart was breaking all over again for the Therian he loved. He ran his fingers through Ash's hair, ready to offer as little or as much comfort as Ash needed.

"What if I mess it all up?" Ash said quietly, staring at the ceiling.

"What if I do?"

"That's not going to happen."

"I'm not perfect, Ash."

"Nearly."

Cael smiled, touched by Ash's never faltering esteem for him. "The charming Mr. Keeler."

"Stop it." Ash looked away, embarrassed.

"Neither of us is perfect. Relationships are hard work, and everyone comes into it with their own baggage. Granted, some more than others, but if you really care about someone, you do what you can to make it work. Look at Sloane and my brother. How much have they been through together, and that's only the beginning. Yet each time they come through the other side and their relationship is stronger for it."

"Yeah, but Sloane's not an asshole. No one would look

at Dex and wonder why the hell he's with Sloane. Your own brother can't understand what you see in me."

"That's not true."

"Oh?" Ash sat up, kicked off his shoes, and came around the other side of the bed so he could lie down next to Cael. He propped himself on his elbows and smiled. "You know something I don't?"

"You two might not get along all the time, but he understands. He respects you, and although he'd never admit it to you, he thinks you'll treat me right."

Ash's eyes widened. "Daley thinks that?"

"Yeah." Cael felt his eyelids growing heavy, and he wondered when he'd gotten so sleepy. He closed his eyes for a moment before startling himself awake.

"It's okay," Ash murmured, his words laced with sleep. His eyes were closed and his breath steady. Had they both fallen asleep? "I should probably go downstairs." Ash didn't move, and Cael was glad.

"Stay," Cael whispered, afraid if he spoke any louder, Ash would leave. He held his breath as he waited for Ash's reply. It was only one word, but it was the most wonderful word Cael had ever heard.

"Yes."

With a smile, Cael closed his eyes. There was a chance Ash might get up in the middle of the night and leave, but Cael hoped not. What he wouldn't give to wake up in Ash's arms. For now this would have to do. His heart soared at having Ash sleeping here beside him. With a contented sigh, Cael drifted off to sleep.

ASH WOKE up in the middle of the night with a low groan. He rubbed his eyes to orientate himself. That's right, he was in Cael's bedroom. *Shit.* He was in *Cael's* bedroom. In Cael's bed. He lay perfectly still, listening to the sound of Cael's soft breathing. Had he turned off the lights or had Cael? He vaguely remembered dreaming about taking Cael to bed and turning off the lights. Wait, it hadn't been a dream. He remembered now.

Sometime after falling asleep, he woke up, got up, and turned off the lights. He'd planned on going downstairs and leaving Cael asleep, but not without straightening him out on the bed first so he wasn't sleeping with half his legs hanging off the side. Quietly and carefully, he'd picked Cael up and laid him down on the sheets, but when he turned to leave, Cael had mumbled something and said his name. Ash had no idea what Cael had said, but when Cael smiled in his sleep after saying his name, Ash knew he wouldn't be going anywhere. And here he was.

Ash never would've believed a man could be beautiful, but Cael was—in every way imaginable. When the hell had his future become so uncertain? His life had been simple. His friends, his team, the job. Now he was starting down a path that scared the ever-living fuck out of him.

All his life, he'd stumbled along the way, putting on a tough façade, pushing away anyone who tried to get too close. He told himself he did it to keep from hurting some-one, but now as he lay here watching Cael sleep—the one person he'd let in—he discovered the truth he'd been fighting for so long. He wasn't afraid of hurting anyone. He was afraid they'd hurt *him*. Cael had his heart. There was no denying it. Ash had presented Cael with the most vulnerable part of him. Was he overthinking their relation-ship? Next to Sloane, Cael had been his closest friend.

Their relationship had changed, but their friendship was still there. The only difference now was that he could act on all those desires that had secretly consumed him for so long. "You're so beautiful," he said quietly, reaching out, then pulling back. He shouldn't start something he couldn't finish. It wouldn't be fair to either of them. *Fucking hell.* Everything he'd ever wanted was right in front of him. All he had to do was reach out...

Cael let out a soft sigh and rolled toward him, snuggling against his pillow. Hesitantly, Ash placed his hand to Cael's head, loving the feel of his feathery hair. Without the gel, it fell over his brow, making him appear even sweeter. "I must have done something right for you to love me."

Cael's eyes blinked open, and he smiled. That smile would be Ash's undoing. Not allowing himself any time to reconsider, Ash pressed his lips against Cael's. He was warm, and his scent invaded every inch of Ash, reaching down into his soul and lighting him up from the inside out. Cael parted his lips, and Ash slipped his tongue inside, his whole world spinning off its axis. He pulled Cael hard against him, deepening his kiss in the hope that his head would finally embrace the want in his heart. There was nothing he craved more than to be the guy Cael believed he was.

Cael returned his kiss, his fingers gently clutching at Ash's bicep. Needing to taste more of him, Ash moved his lips to Cael's jaw, sucking, nipping, and licking. Every sensation was new, frightening, and thrilling. He wrapped his leg around Cael's and pressed himself against him, his blood boiling beneath his skin. Cael let out a soft moan, and it went straight to Ash's dick. He ran his tongue up Cael's jawline, the slightly rough texture of Cael's stubble a new and strange sensation. He had to have more. A little voice in the back of his head kept telling him to stop, to pull back, but Ash did his best to ignore it and follow the overwhelming desire spreading through him like wildfire.

Ash ran his hand over Cael's torso to his back and under his T-shirt. He slipped his hand underneath the cotton fabric, his fingers meeting soft, warm skin and firm muscle. With a shaky breath, he pulled back, his eyes meeting Cael's in the darkness. Cael licked his kiss-swollen lips, his cheeks flushed.

"I need to see you," Ash breathed.

The lust in Cael's eyes was a thing of beauty, and Ash rolled over Cael, straddling his legs and taking hold of the hem of his T-shirt. He didn't question what he was doing. All he could think about was Cael. He'd waited so damn long for this. He'd dreamed about Cael and gotten himself off thinking about him.

After pulling the shirt off, Ash tossed it to one side. He shimmied back and unbuttoned Cael's jeans, then took hold of the waistband along with Cael's boxer briefs underneath. He paused to make sure it was okay. Cael nodded, his cheeks flushed pink in the darkness. Holding his breath, Ash removed what was left of Cael's clothes. He'd seen Cael naked before at work, in the showers. This was completely different. Cael lay beneath him, stretched out like an offering.

"You're so beautiful." Ash bent forward and put his hands to Cael's neck almost reverently. Was he worthy enough to touch something so precious? Ash wanted to caress and taste every line, curve, and dip. Wanted to feel their bodies pressed together, hear their mingled breaths. He wanted to draw gasps and pleas from those plump pink lips. His desire scared the shit out of him, but he reminded himself this was Cael. Cael who loved him despite all his faults. Who defended him, stood up for him, believed in him. He ran his fingers down Cael's neck to his collarbone, down his chest and the sinewy firm muscles. His fingers ghosted one of Cael's nipples, and the sweet gasp Cael let out as he arched his back, exposing his neck, had Ash on the brink of losing his calm.

He continued to explore Cael's torso, running his hands down Cael's abs to his strong thighs sprinkled with fair hair. Between his legs, Cael's pink-tipped cock jutted up from his neatly trimmed groin. Holy fuck, Cael trimmed. Ash released a groan, the saliva building up in his mouth at the thought of tasting Cael. What would it feel like to have Cael's dick in his mouth? His own cock strained painfully against his jeans at the thought, and Ash carefully wrapped a hand around Cael's dick, riveted by the whimper that met his ear. God, he loved that sound. Ash removed his own T-shirt, dropping it to one side before leaning down to kiss Cael's lips again. There was so much he wanted to do, yet he didn't know where to start or how far to take things. As if sensing his troubled thoughts, Cael cupped his face.

"It's okay. We have all the time in the world."

Cael gently pushed at Ash's shoulder, and Ash followed his lead, lying back on the bed. He swallowed hard, sweat beaded across his brow as Cael got on his knees and unfastened Ash's jeans. He took care pulling them off before dropping them off the side of the bed. Maybe he shouldn't be doing this. Fuck. What was wrong with him? He opened his mouth to say something, but no words made it past his lips the moment Cael's hand wrapped around his girth.

"Don't worry. You're safe with me," Cael purred. "It's just you and me."

Ash felt his face burning as Cael began to stroke him, his other hand fondling Ash's balls. It was strange yet so damn good. He was so hard, and every inch of his skin felt as if it was on fire. Somewhere in his brain, he told himself he shouldn't feel this way. It was wrong. As he fought his own thoughts and guilt, a wet mouth closed over his cock, and he almost jumped off the bed.

"Oh fuck!"

Ash clutched at the sheets, his back arching up off the bed and his toes curling. Oh God, this was better than anything he'd imagined. He forced his eyes open and looked down at Cael, his body shuddering at the sight of Cael's lips around his dick. It was mesmerizing watching himself slide in and out of that amazing mouth. Ash let his head fall back. Fuck this. Fuck that. Fuck everything. The only thing he knew right now was the feel of Cael sucking his cock, moaning around it, caressing his thighs, making Ash feel desired in a way he'd never felt with anyone.

Cael licked, nipped, and sucked, his tongue pressing against his slit. "Oh fuck, Cael." Ash slipped his fingers into Cael's hair, holding on tight, his bottom lip between his teeth to keep himself from making too much noise, but right now he didn't give a shit about anything. All that mattered was the amazing man between his legs driving him out of his fucking mind. He was embarrassed to discover he wasn't going to last long.

"Cael," Ash gasped in warning, but Cael only doubled his efforts. "Oh fuck. Fuck. Cael," Ash growled, his voice strained as his muscles tightened and orgasm barreled through him. Oh God, Cael was swallowing. Ash threw a hand out and clutched the sheets so fiercely his knuckles hurt. A low strangled cry escaped him as he emptied himself into Cael's mouth, leaving him out of breath. He lay there, staring at the ceiling, basking in the afterglow of what Cael had done to him.

Cael lay between Ash's legs, his cheek resting against Ash's stomach. He smiled warmly at Ash, his fingers tracing the contours of Ash's abs.

"You okay?" Cael asked softly.

"That was... Wow." He ran a hand over Cael's head and nodded. "Shit. That was fucking amazing."

Cael moved up and lay beside him, his warm bare skin pressed against Ash's. Should he have been freaking out that he'd been given a blow job by another guy? He frowned at the thought. It wasn't just any guy. It was Cael. The idea didn't freak him out. In fact, having had Cael's amazing mouth on him had him craving more. Ash turned on his side and kissed Cael, his hand slipping down Cael's body until it reached the hard cock between his legs.

"Are you sure?" Cael asked in a hushed tone, as if he was afraid to speak louder in case he spooked Ash.

Ash replied by stroking Cael and bringing their mouths together. When the voice in his head tried to speak up, Ash filled his senses with Cael. He drew on every unsteady breath, every whimper and moan Cael released. Using Cael's precome to lube him up, Ash gently pulled and stroked. He thought about what had always felt good for him, listened to the cues Cael gave him, changed things up in the hopes of pleasing Cael. Ash's lips demanded more of Cael, and he deepened their kiss to a frenzy of desperate sucking and dueling tongues. He reveled in the way Cael squirmed and gasped, in how he clung to Ash, nails digging into his skin as he thrust into Ash's hand, frantic for release.

"Ash, please. Faster."

Ash obliged, pumping Cael's hard dick. He slipped his leg between Cael's, bringing their bodies closer together. He bit down gently on Cael's neck and sucked until he'd left a small blemish. "That's it, sweetheart. Come for me. I want to see your beautiful face when you come."

Cael's gasp was swiftly followed by a quick succession of swear words and moans as he came. His movements grew erratic as he released himself, his plump lips parted in ecstasy. He thrust against Ash's hand until he let out a hiss at his own sensitivity. Ash couldn't take his eyes off Cael's mouth, how his lips were still parted as he tried to catch his breath. Unable to resist the temptation, Ash ran his thumb over Cael's bottom lip before leaning in to kiss him. They kissed for what seemed like ages, until sleep came for them.

Ash pulled Cael into his embrace, unwilling to think of anything other than the amazing younger man in his arms. He couldn't think of a time when he'd felt more at peace or happier than right here, right now. There had to be a way for him to hold on to this, because as Cael fell asleep in his arms, Ash knew letting him slip away would be the greatest tragedy of all.

EIGHT

It was hard to believe another year was about to end. The team decided to take Bradley up on his offer of ringing in the New Year at Dekatria. The place was packed, but then so were most places on New Year's Eve. Since they weren't officially taking any cases, they were assigned to work the day shift, leaving them free in the evening to celebrate. They'd all shared cabs over, knowing they'd be drinking, except maybe for Sloane, who wasn't taking any chances considering his recent problems with shifting.

Cael had hoped what happened Christmas Eve was the start of something for him and Ash, but things were still slow going between them, and Ash had yet to bring up anything official. On the one hand, Ash had grown more comfortable showing Cael affection in front of his family and Sloane. Christmas Day had been wonderful, with Ash hanging around the house with him, teasing him, kissing him in front of whoever was around. They'd watched movies, had Christmas dinner, exchanged gifts, laughed, and eaten some more. Whenever Cael sat down, Ash had pulled him close against him and in some cases playfully grabbed him as he walked by and pulled him onto his lap. Dex, Sloane, and Tony had been surprised, but they quickly moved on as if nothing out of the ordinary was happening.

They'd arrived at Dekatria a few hours ago. Cael had danced with Rosa and her girlfriend, while Letty busted some serious moves with Dimples the firefighter. Man, they really needed to learn the guy's name. Ash had been sweet but maintained his distance. This was the first time they'd been out in a social setting since their night together Christmas Eve. They'd been drinking and chatting by one of the pillar tables when they heard it.

"Oh my God! Ash?"

"Yeah?" Ash turned in time to catch a blur of glittering, shrieking sequins that launched itself into his arms. Apparently, there was a busty brunette underneath all those sequins.

Cael stood stunned as the woman smeared her bright pink lipstick all over Ash's mouth. Seeming to get a grasp on the situation, Ash swiftly placed her on her feet and wiped the lipstick from his mouth.

"Jesus, what the fuck, Hanna?"

Hanna giggled and slapped his arm playfully. "You used to love it when I jumped on you. Of course, we were both naked at the time. I tried calling you, but you never answered my calls." She pressed herself up against him and ran a finger down his arm, a pout on her face. "Where have you been? I missed you. We used to have so much fun together."

"I've been a little busy." Ash moved her hand off his arm and took a step to the side, looking incredibly uncomfortable. That made two of them. Hanna was either oblivious to Ash's less than subtle gestures or was purposefully ignoring them. Cael took another sip of his vodka and lemonade.

"Are you busy tonight?" she purred, drawing circles on his chest with her finger.

Ash frowned at her. "Yes. I'm here with my team."

"What's the matter? You would have had me up against the bathroom stall by now."

Oh, come on. Really? Cael cleared his throat, and Hanna blinked at him as if noticing him for the first time, which was likely the case. Did the woman go around sexually accosting all her exes? Why would she assume Ash was willing and able?

"Well, aren't you adorable." She turned her attention back to Ash with a wide smile. "Who's your little friend?"

Ash ran a hand over his hair. "Um, this is Agent Cael Maddock. He's on my team."

Wow. Not even friend. He'd been relegated to teammate. Cael managed to summon a smile. "Hi." He didn't bother extending a hand, seeing as how Hanna was back to fondling Ash, and Ash was doing absolutely fuck all about it. Despite the music thumping through the place, Cael would guess Ash could hear his teeth grinding because he once again removed Hanna from his person.

"Look, Hanna, I'm with someone."

Cael's pulse picked up speed, and the butterflies in his stomach went crazy. His cheeks grew warm, and he bit his bottom lip. Was Ash actually going to say it?

Hanna gasped, her hand flying to her mouth. "Oh my God. I'm *so* sorry. I'm such an idiot. Of course you have a girlfriend. I shouldn't have assumed. So who's the lucky lady?"

Ash's gaze dropped to his feet, and he shoved his hands into his pockets. "Um... no one you know."

The remark hit Cael harder than a slap in the face. He'd

never felt more vulnerable, wounded, and mortified, despite being the only one privy to Ash's brush-off.

"Why so secretive?" Hanna prodded. "Come on, tell me all about her."

"Hanna—"

"Go on, Ash," Cael replied through his teeth. "Tell her all about your girlfriend." He threw back what was left of his vodka and lemonade before putting his glass down. "Excuse me." He walked off, ignoring Ash's attempts to call him back.

He should have known. A part of him had expected it, yet having it happen had been more painful than he could have imagined. He hadn't expected Ash to introduce him as his boyfriend, but to let Hanna assume he was in a relationship with a woman? Screw that. And screw Ash Keeler.

Cael pushed his way through the crowd until he reached the bar. Bradley's smile faded when he saw him. "Everything okay?"

"I need something that'll get me shit-faced."

Bradley looked uncertain, and there was a good chance he might tell Dex, but Cael didn't care. Why was everyone always babying him? "Is that okay with you?" he growled.

"Yeah, sorry. I'll get you that drink."

Seconds later, Bradley returned with one of his foggy "specials," the kind he was always putting together for Sloane. Cael was on his second when Ash made an appearance.

"Cael, please. I'm sorry."

"Okay." If that's what Ash wanted to hear, that's what he would say.

Bradley placed another "special" in front of him, and Cael picked it up, only to have Ash take hold of the glass, his hand over Cael's. The pain in his heart intensified.

"It's fine," Cael managed to get out. "Do you mind?"

Ash rubbed his thumb over Cael's hand. "I know I hurt you."

Fuck no. He did *not* get to do that. Not this time. Cael met Ash's gaze. "Yes, you did, Ash. And it's starting to become a really bad habit of yours."

Ash flinched. "What else was I supposed to say?"

A humorless laugh escaped Cael despite the tear that rolled down his cheek. "You're right. What else could you possibly have said? After all, it's not like you have someone who's so crazy in love with you that they'd endure one cruel stab to the heart after another, all in the hopes that one day you might feel the same. That you might think they're important enough to really fucking try to push through the fear and the pain. I *love* you."

Ash had opened his mouth to reply when some guy got within earshot. The discomfort in Ash's expression, the way he withdrew, had Cael resigning himself to the fact Ash might never be comfortable in his own skin, much less in an out relationship with Cael.

"Don't worry, Ash. We both know I'll keep waiting like a lovesick idiot." He moved Ash's hand off his and swallowed down the contents of his glass in two gulps, feeling it burning down his throat. Leaving the glass at the bar, he turned and headed for the dance floor. The countdown would be starting soon. Maybe he should call a cab and get the hell out of here. Tonight had started out amazing, and now it couldn't get any worse. He should have known. He didn't know what felt worse, not being with Ash or living off the tiny morsels of affection Ash fed him when he was feeling bold. How long could he carry on like this?

Forget midnight. He was going home. The last thing he felt like doing now was celebrating. He had turned for the coatroom when he ran into something hard. "Sorry. Excuse me."

"Well, look who it is."

It wasn't possible.

The deep, familiar voice paralyzed Cael, leaving him numb and cold. *Please, don't do this to me.* He forced himself to look up, the name slipping past his lips barely a whisper. "Fuller."

"Surprised to see me?" Fuller's hard amber gaze had the same effect on Cael it always had. It pinned him to the spot and filled him with dread. Fuller didn't look all that different from the last time Cael had seen him. He was still rugged, though his face was more haggard, and he looked meaner, if that was possible. His dark hair was shaved close to his head, and he was dressed casually. It had been a long time since Cael had been plagued by nightmares of Fuller showing up.

"What are you doing here?" Cael asked, taking a step away from him.

Fuller pouted. "Aw, don't be like that, kitty cat."

"Don't call me that." He hated that pet name, especially since Fuller had used it derisively, laughing at him, telling him he was nothing but an oversized kitten with spots that should be playing with yarn rather than trying to be part of an organization he had no business being in. "I thought you moved to Nevada?"

"I did. And now I'm back."

"In New York?" Cael prayed it wasn't true.

"Obviously. I'm right here in front of you, silly. Come on, Cael. Use that little brain God gave you."

Cael glared at him. "What do you want?"

"A drink. Maybe catch up for old time's sake."

He raised his hand, and Cael flinched. He took a step

back, hating himself for it. Fuller's laugh curdled his blood. He remembered that laugh. Remembered the way Fuller had made him feel so small and insignificant, so worthless.

"You haven't forgotten me. I'm touched."

Cael felt sick to his stomach. Fuller reached out, and Cael slapped his hand away with a hiss.

"Don't touch me." How dare he! After everything Fuller had put him through, he thought he could just show up and, what? Pick up where they left off?

"Sorry." He held his hands up in front of him. "I wanted to talk, that's all."

"I have nothing to say to you."

Cael tried to go around him, but Fuller blocked his path. His gaze raked over Cael, making him feel naked and exposed.

"Oh, come on. We had good times, didn't we? Remember when we used to fool around? When you'd get down on your knees and beg me to let you suck my dick."

Cael gaped at him. What the *hell*? He had to get out of here. His chest felt tight, and the room was starting to close in on him. "I need to go." Cael shoved through the crowd looking for Dex, but he couldn't see him. He really wished Dex were here right now. His brother would know what to do. His brother would probably plant one right in Fuller's face. Cael wished he were anywhere but here right now. There were too many people. Everyone was so much bigger. He was trapped. Surrounded by people and noise, movement, and the shadows were creeping closer.

"*I* remember," Fuller said from somewhere behind him. "I remember how much you liked to beg."

Oh God, he couldn't breathe. Cael stumbled outside into the cold air and almost slipped on the snow-covered sidewalk. He was shaking, his teeth chattering from the cold and the fear threatening to cripple him. He wrapped his arms around himself and walked to the street to hail a cab. His lungs burned, and he felt like such a fucking asshole for the tears in his eyes. A steel-like grip snatched hold of his arm and jerked him back against a hard body.

"Where are you going?" Fuller asked smugly. "I'm not done reminiscing. I gotta admit, you look good. Less scrawny than you were when we were together. Might even be a better fuck."

"P-p-please." He was so cold, so tired, and all he wanted was to be away from here.

"Music to my ears. Beg me some more."

Fuller squeezed harder, and Cael cried out. Everything he thought he'd put behind him, that he'd buried deep down came bubbling up. He didn't want to go back there. He didn't want to feel helpless and scared. This wasn't him. He was a different person now, wasn't he? Why couldn't he stand up to Fuller?

"Let go of me!"

Cael pulled back a fist and swung at Fuller, who moved his face just in time, Cael's knuckles only grazing his jawline.

"You little prick."

Fuller smacked Cael across the cheek with the back of his hand, splitting his lip. Cael would have gone hurtling into the parked car across from him if Fuller hadn't been holding on to him so tightly.

"You son of a bitch! Get your fucking hands off him!"

Fuller stumbled back as Ash shoved him away from Cael. He snarled at Ash, who wrapped Cael up in his embrace.

"Who the fuck are *you*?"

Ash placed himself between Cael and Fuller. "His boyfriend."

Fuller looked Ash over and shook his head with a laugh. "Oh shit. Well, how about that. Guess some things never change. Watch out for this one. He'll ask for it rough, then send you to prison for it."

Cael wheezed, and Ash took a step toward Fuller. "Don Fuller?"

"Ah, so he's bitched to you about me. Isn't that sweet."

"You piece of shit!" Ash moved fast, throwing a punch that snapped Fuller's head to one side and knocked him into a parked car. "You're such a fucking tough guy, how about you hit *me*."

Ash grabbed a fistful of Fuller's hair and snapped his head down as he brought his knee up, the crack resonating above the noise of the gathering crowd. Fuller hit the icy sidewalk with a litany of curses, the blood from his broken nose turning the snow beneath him red. He pushed himself to his feet and rolled his shoulders, his near black eyes filled with a familiar fury Cael recognized too well.

Ash motioned for Fuller to advance. "Come on. Hit me. Give me another reason to lay you out."

"I'd say he's not worth it, but I don't back down from a fight," Fuller said, spitting out bloodied saliva.

"He's worth more than you'll ever be."

"Wow. You've got it bad, my friend." Fuller shrugged and wiped at his nose. "He's a good fuck, but not that good."

Cael wrapped his arms tighter around himself, his whole body racked with shivers. The darkness was starting to close in, his vision growing blurry as he wheezed. He couldn't breathe. He dropped to his knees and tried to get air into his lungs. *Oh God, oh God, oh God...* "Ash..."

"Cael!" Ash hurriedly removed his coat and threw it around Cael's shoulders. "Cael, talk to me." He tamped down his panic as Cael shook in his arms, his lips turning a purplish color and his eyes glazing over. "Tell me what you need. I'm here. You're safe with me. You're always safe with me."

Cael clutched him, squeezing him and gasping for air. "I can't..."

"Breathe. Come on." Ash breathed in deep through his nose and let it out through his mouth, urging Cael to do the same. "That's it, angel. Breathe. That's it. Breathe with me. In and out. It's okay. You're okay. I'm here. Nothing and no one's going to touch you. I won't let them."

Cael let out a strangled noise, but he was breathing along with Ash. He craned his neck to see past Ash, looking for Fuller. Glancing over his shoulder, Ash was grateful to find Fuller was gone. Right now, Cael was what mattered. He turned his attention back to Cael and placed a hand to his cheek.

"Look at me. Sweetheart, look at me."

Cael did, tears in his eyes.

"You're safe with me. I won't let anything happen to you. You believe me, right?"

A whispered "Yes" escaped, and Ash wanted to pull him close, but Cael was still struggling to breathe and compose himself. Instead he rubbed his thumb tenderly over Cael's cheek. "Tell me what you need from me."

"Home," Cael let out shakily. "I want to go home."

"Okay. Let's go." He helped Cael to his feet and tentatively moved Cael closer against him, relieved when Cael allowed it. Then he pulled the coat's hood over Cael's head to shield him from the cold and the crowd gathered on the sidewalk behind them. Cael snuggled closer.

"Is he okay?" someone called out.

"Yeah, thanks," Ash said, hailing a cab as it drew near. He helped Cael inside, gave the driver Cael's address, and pulled Cael close to him. Pushing back the hood, he kissed the top of Cael's head. "It's okay, angel. It's okay." Ash's heart was pounding, and he felt Cael's trembling down to his soul. *What the hell was Fuller doing here?* He put that thought aside and concentrated on Cael. Soon they were standing outside Cael's apartment door. Cael fished his keys out of his jeans pocket and handed them to Ash, who opened the door and led him inside, then closed the door behind them. Without a word, Cael kicked off his shoes and made straight for the living room. He left Ash's coat on the armchair, climbed up onto the plush gray couch, clutched one of the throw pillows to his chest, and drew his knees up. Minutes went by as Cael stared down at the fluffy pillow before burying his face against it and crying softly. It broke Ash's heart.

Leaving his shoes on the mat by the door, Ash walked to the kitchen. He filled the kettle with water and set it to boil before opening a cabinet door and removing Cael's favorite black mug with the words *Talk nerdy to me* in white letters stamped across it. He opened the drawer where Cael stored his boxes of tea and plucked out a chamomile one. A few minutes later, he was crouched down in front of Cael and holding the cup of tea out to him.

"Chamomile with a little bit of lemon and honey, just the way you like it."

"Thank you." Cael slowly took the cup from him, his bottom lip quivering. He let out a heart-wrenching sigh. "I'm sorry."

"There's no reason for you to apologize. You haven't done anything wrong."

"I'm such an idiot. Overreacting like that. Making you take me home."

"Hey. You had every right to feel the way you did. And you're not an idiot. You're the smartest guy I know. If you want to talk about it, I'm all ears. You know I'd never ever think of you as anything less than amazing, because you are."

Cael shook his head. "I'm weak and pathetic."

Ash hated to hear Cael talk about himself that way, especially since it wasn't Cael talking but that son of a bitch, Fuller. "You're strong. I know at times you might not feel it, but you are. Where would our team be without you? Where would *I* be without you?"

Cael smiled. "Back at the bar... I thought maybe I heard you say you were my boyfriend."

Ash returned Cael's smile. "You heard right. I'd like to be. If you still want me. I know it won't be easy, and I still have a long way to go, but maybe you can help me? Help me be as strong and brave as you are."

"Yes." Cael put his tea down on the coffee table next to the couch before he threw himself into Ash's arms. "Thank you."

Ash held him close and ran a hand over Cael's head. "No. Thank *you*. For showing me what it's like to be loved."

He held on to Cael and moved to the couch, taking Cael with him so he sat in Ash's lap, cradled in his arms. Cael snuggled close, and Ash held him, soothing him, offering what comfort he could for as long as Cael needed it. Sometime later, Cael spoke up quietly.

"How do you know Fuller?"

"That day your dad came to Dekatria, we were upstairs talking, and he told me."

"What?" Cael pulled back, his expression hurt. "When were you going to tell me? I can't believe this."

"Cael—"

"Did my dad tell you how Fuller used to knock me around? How he'd push me to do things to him and then make me feel like a filthy piece of shit for doing it? For two years I believed every word that came out of his mouth. I lied to my family and defended him. He made me feel like I was worthless, like no one in their right mind would ever love me because I was weak and useless. And maybe I am because everyone seems to think I can't do anything for myself. They treat me like a child. My dad, my brother... you. I haven't seen Fuller in years, and he shows up out of the blue, and I..." Cael wiped a runaway tear from his cheek. "I fall apart. What kind of THIRDS agent does that?"

"The kind who's been through a hell of a lot," Ash said gently. "We might be agents, but that doesn't mean we're not vulnerable. You got blindsided by that asshole. I should have told you your dad brought Fuller up, but you need to understand something. Your brother, your dad, and I don't think of you as a kid. We think of you as someone we love with everything we've got, who we can't stand to see get hurt or worse. And the truth of it is, it's not just about you."

"What do you mean?"

"We all know what it's like to lose family, to lose people we care about. The thought of losing you... I can't. I'll do whatever it takes to protect you, even if it makes you hate me for it. I love you."

Cael's smile stole Ash's breath away.

"You do?"

Ash nodded. "I do. I love you, Cael. I've been fighting it a long time, and I can't anymore. More importantly, I don't want to." He swallowed hard and met Cael's gaze. "I'll try harder. I don't want to hurt you. When I do, it kills me. I'll deal with my shit, I promise, but in the meantime, I want you to be with me." He laced their fingers together. "I'll admit, I don't know what the fuck I'm doing, but as long as I'm doing it with you, I know I'll be okay."

"Ash..."

"If you tell your brother about how sappy I sound, I will seriously have to retaliate. Like, tell him you have his iPod."

Cael's jaw dropped, but his eyes were filled with amusement. "You'd narc on me to my brother?"

"If it means keeping him off my back about not being an asshole, then I might. Probably not, but I feel like I need to have some kind of leverage. Who the fuck am I kidding? You know you have me wrapped around your little finger. God, is this what it's like for Sloane and your brother?" No wonder Sloane was always giving in to Dex. How the hell could Ash say no to anything his amazing man asked of him?

"Sort of. Unlike Dex, I promise not to abuse my power."

A mischievous smile came onto Cael's face. Damn, he was beautiful.

"Too much."

"You little sneak." Ash poked Cael playfully in the ribs, making him squirm.

"Stop!" Cael squealed.

The door slammed open, and a familiar voice shouted out, "Hands where I can see them!"

Ash slowly put his hands up, and Cael joined him, his eyes wide.

"Shit," Dex muttered, Sloane cringing behind him.

"Did you just kick my front door in?" Cael crawled off Ash and scrambled to his feet, his hands going to his head at the sight of his splintered wooden doorframe. "You kicked in my door!"

He spun to his brother, who returned his gun to his off-duty holster.

"Um, happy New Year?"

"What the hell, man?"

"Dude, you disappeared from the bar without saying a word, left your coat behind, and then Bradley says you weren't looking so good, and after you left some guys got into an epic fistfight outside. There's blood in the fucking snow and you don't pick up your damn phone and—"

Cael looked away, his voice soft. "It was Fuller."

"What?" Dex had Cael in his arms in seconds. He ran a hand over Cael's hair and looked him over. "Are you okay? Did he hurt you?" He put his thumb to Cael's lip and the small cut left behind from Fuller's slap. "That motherfucker! He did this, didn't he?"

Dex released Cael and started pacing. Ash had never seen him so livid.

"I'm going to find that asshole and put the fear of God in him. The fucking nerve of that prick showing up and—"

"Dex, I'm fine." Cael took hold of his brother's shoulders to stop him from pacing. "Ash was there. He broke Fuller's nose. That's the blood you saw."

Dex turned to Ash and gave him a nod in thanks before turning back to Cael. "How are you, really?"

Ash caught Sloane's eye and motioned over to the balcony. He grabbed his coat and slipped into it, letting Cael know he was stepping out with Sloane so he and his brother could talk. After sliding the door closed behind Sloane, Ash walked to the handrail and leaned against it.

"Who's Fuller?" Sloane asked, joining him. "And why did Dex look like he was about to take someone out when Cael said his name?

"Probably because he's tempted to. Don Fuller is Cael's ex. A real asshole." Ash told Sloane as much as he needed to know about the situation without infringing on Cael's privacy.

Sloane stared at him. "Shit. I had no idea."

"Yeah. They've kept it close to their chests. Guess there's still a lot we don't know about the Daley-Maddock family. Maddock told me the day he came to talk to us at Dekatria. He was worried. At the time, I wished he hadn't told me, but now? Cael had a panic attack."

"Fuck. It's probably a good thing Dex wasn't there. God knows what he would have done to Fuller. What the hell's he doing back in New York?"

"I don't know, but I find it pretty fucking convenient that he happened to show up at Dekatria. I ran a check through Themis the moment we were called back on duty to make sure the bastard was still in Carson City and he was. I was supposed to receive a notification if he crossed state lines. How the hell he made it here without Themis picking up on it is bugging me. Either way, I'm not letting that son of a bitch near Cael again. He's done enough damage." Ash went quiet for a moment before addressing a different issue. "Are you free sometime this weekend for a chat? Without your shadow."

Sloane chuckled. "Sure. Anytime."

"Okay. I'll call you, see when I can drop by."

"Everything okay?" Sloane asked worriedly.

Ash wasn't the most skilled at opening up, but Sloane was his best friend. There was no one he trusted more. Whatever happened in life, he knew Sloane would always have his back, just like he'd have Sloane's. If he was going to really make a go of this, he wanted to do it right. Also, Sloane had experience in being wrapped around his boyfriend's finger.

"Yeah, I might need some advice. I've, uh, I've never been in a committed relationship before."

Sloane's jaw went slack, and Ash felt his face burning up. He rubbed his hand over the back of his neck. "Don't make a big deal out of it."

"Like official?"

Ash nodded. "Seeing Fuller hurting him... My feral half was clawing to get out, to tear Fuller apart for laying a hand on Cael. I had to protect him. It was stupid, letting my fear stop me from being with someone I feel so deeply for. Nothing's changed, yet everything's changed." He sighed and shoved his hands into his pockets. "I'm still so fucked-up inside and terrified of being out in the open about it, but at least now I can face that fear with him at my side."

"Congratulations, man. That's great."

Sloane pulled him into a hug, and Ash groaned, pretending to be put off. His friend was so happy for him. Ash could see it in Sloane's eyes. Like he'd been wanting this for Ash almost as much as Ash had wanted it for himself.

"Thanks."

Ash peeked through the glass doors to find Cael standing by the broken door with Dex as they talked. Dex looked worried, despite Cael clearly attempting to reassure his big brother. Ash was with Dex on this one. He had no doubt Dex was going to be keeping an eye on his brother. He'd probably look into why Fuller was here. Giving the brothers more time to talk, Ash went back to chatting with Sloane. In the back of his mind, he couldn't shake the feeling that he'd be seeing Fuller again real soon.

———————

CAEL WAS EXHAUSTED. And now he had a broken door.

"I'm sorry. I'll replace it." Dex fiddled with the split frame. Cael supposed he should be grateful his brother was the one who'd kicked at his door and not Sloane. Damn thing would have been torn off its hinges.

As much as Cael wanted to be mad at his big brother for busting his door down, he couldn't be. Dex had believed Cael was in trouble. He did wish his brother could save the day with a little less property damage involved. It drove their dad just as crazy.

"It's okay," Cael said, fastening the bottom deadlock. Luckily he never used that one or the chain lock. "You still need to fix it, though."

"I'll get someone over tonight."

"Dex, it's"— Cael checked his watch—"one in the morning. On New Year's Day. Unless you intend to hand over your first born as payment, it can wait."

"Okay."

Dex's brows drew together, and Cael nodded to the couch. He knew that look. His brother was worried about him. The last thing Cael wanted was to worry Dex. His brother had enough on his mind as it was.

Cael dropped down onto his comfy couch, pulled his legs up, and folded his arms over his knees. "I had a panic attack."

"Are you okay? Do you need anything?"

Cael shook his head, a smile coming onto his face at the memory. "Ash helped me."

"Ash?"

"Yeah. He was great. Asked me what I needed, helped me focus on breathing, made me feel safe. He helped calm me. Even made me my favorite tea."

"Wow."

Cael couldn't help the big dopey grin that came onto his face, his cheeks feeling hot. "We're officially dating."

Dex gaped at him. "Shut the front door!"

"I can't. My dorky brother broke it," Cael said, giving him a push. His excitement bubbled up, and he grabbed his brother's arm. "Can you believe it?" He bounced in his seat, and Dex grabbed Cael's arm, bouncing along with him.

"I'm so happy for you!"

"Oh my God, we're like teenage girls!" Cael squealed, still bouncing.

"I don't care! Oh my God, Ash is your boyfriend. That's... I can't even. I don't... I'm..." The sliding glass door to the balcony slid open, and Dex stopped bouncing. "Play it cool. They're coming back in."

"We can hear you, dumbass." Ash closed the door behind Sloane and walked into the living room. "Therian hearing."

Dex turned back to Cael with a frown. "You sure you don't want to maybe date a cactus? Less prickly."

Cael laughed and hugged his brother, and after reassuring Dex for the bajillionth time that he was okay, was going to be okay, would call if he wasn't okay, Dex and Sloane said their good-byes and left. By then it was nearly three in the morning.

"I need a shower," Ash muttered. "You mind if I use yours and crash here?"

Cael smiled. "Of course not. Just leave the water running when you finish. I could use one too."

He took his empty teacup to the kitchen, noting how Ash quietly followed. Cael didn't utter a word as he placed the teacup in the sink and proceeded to wash it. Ash slipped his arms around Cael's waist and delivered a kiss to Cael's temple, their bodies pressed together.

"How about if you join me? You know, conserve water, ozone, environment, and all that hippie shit."

Cael chuckled and turned in Ash's arms. "Well, when you put it that way, how can I resist?"

"All right," Ash sighed, his eyes alight with amusement. "How about, will you join me in the shower because I'll miss you if you're not there with me?"

"Now that's more like it."

Cael laughed as he grabbed Ash's hand and pulled him upstairs with him, both of them shedding clothes along the way. By the time they reached the bathroom, they were both naked and all over each other, kissing, touching, fingers digging and stroking. Ash bumped into the doorframe on the way in, and Cael giggled against Ash's lips. The big goof.

Somehow they managed to get the water turned on and at a temperature that wouldn't freeze their boy bits off. They stepped into the bathtub, and Ash took hold of the soap. Gently he pulled Cael in front of him and lathered him up, delivering kisses as he did. His hands didn't miss a spot as he soaped Cael up. Lost in Ash's ministrations, Cael closed his eyes, feeling Ash washing his hair before leading Cael under the showerhead to rinse him off. What had started as a frenzy of hands and lips had become a sweet expression of affection. They washed each other, offering tender kisses and slow, lingering caresses.

Once they were done, Ash helped Cael out of the tub, and they dried each other before Ash swept Cael off his feet, making him laugh. He carried Cael into the bedroom and laid him in the middle of the bed before crawling over him, lowering himself onto his elbows so as not to put all his weight on Cael. Cael spread his legs so Ash could fit against him. How he loved the feel of Ash on him. Despite Ash's size and strength, Cael had always felt safe with him.

"Thank you for looking out for me," Cael offered softly, his fingers running through Ash's wet hair.

"Always." He brushed his lips over Cael's, the heat from Ash's body sending the most delicious shiver through him.

Cael tentatively thrust his hips up, his hard erection pressing against Ash's stomach, and Ash released a groan, his hips grinding gently down. The scent of soap and Ash invaded Cael's senses, and he let out a whimper. His skin was ablaze, his insides twisting. He tried his best to let Ash take the lead, to not push, but it was killing him. He was desperate to feel Ash inside him, had wanted this for so long.

"Please," Cael whispered, his body writhing with need. If something didn't happen, he was going to lose his mind.

"Lube and condoms?"

Cael's heart was ready to burst out of his chest. He pointed to the nightstand on his left, and Ash didn't waste any time, returning with the bottle of lube and a condom packet before Cael's skin cooled from his absence. Cael felt his face burning up, and when he dropped his gaze to Ash's hands, he realized he wasn't the only one about to go off like a firecracker. Ash's hands shook as he tried to open the condom packet. Cael sat up, his hand coming to rest on Ash's.

"Are you sure?"

Ash met his gaze, fire burning in his amber eyes. "I've never been surer of anything in my life." He kissed Cael and placed the condom in Cael's hand, murmuring against his lips, "Put it on me."

Cael smiled and took the condom from him. He tore the foil packet open as Ash sat back on his heels, his tanned skin smooth and his thick cock jutting up against his stomach. Cael took a moment to admire the stunning Therian before him. Ash was all sculpted muscle, from his expansive chest and six-pack down to his strong thighs and legs. His large hands rested on his thighs. Cael loved Ash's hands. Ash was handsome, rugged, intimidating, and at times mean-looking, but Cael saw the gentle, loving soul within the warrior's frame.

Having looked his fill, Cael rolled the condom on Ash, loving the way Ash sucked in a sharp breath and closed his eyes. Cael picked up the lube and applied a generous amount to Ash's cock, his eyes on Ash's face as he stroked him and squeezed him ever so gently. Not able to hold out any longer, Cael lay on his back and took one of his pillows to place under him, his body trembling with anticipation.

Ash knelt between Cael's open legs and took hold of the lube, a blush coming onto his cheeks as he poured some on his fingers. His eyes locked on Cael's as he lifted one of Cael's legs to his shoulder, his finger entering Cael. Cael moaned, his fingers closing around fistfuls of the sheets, his back arched at the sweet invasion. Ash took his time prepping Cael, their eyes never looking away. When he was done, Ash lined himself up and pushed the tip in. Cael let out a desperate whimper. Slowly, Ash pushed in little by little. It was driving Cael crazy.

Cael sucked in his breath as Ash began to move, rocking gently against him. Ash swore under his breath and closed his eyes, his head falling back as he moved in and out of Cael. He turned his head and kissed Cael's leg and ran a hand down it before opening his eyes and meeting Cael's gaze once more.

"You're so beautiful," Ash breathed.

He released Cael's leg and bent over him, holding Cael close to him. He kissed Cael slow and deep, matching his thrusts. Cael shivered at the delicious pleasure, and he wrapped his arms tightly around Ash. He didn't know what was going on in Ash's head at the moment, whether this was all very strange for him. Cael did his best to make sure Ash was lost in them and nothing else. Ash went slowly, as if he were savoring every second. They explored each other, touched, and tasted. It was absolute torture. Cael never thought it could feel this amazing. Ash stretched him wide, but it was nothing Cael couldn't handle. Ash's skin was flushed, his brow beaded with sweat as he moved against Cael.

Cael wrapped his legs around Ash and hung on to him for dear life while Ash pushed in deep and pulled out, their bodies moving together as one. Ash's movements picked up speed, his breath growing more ragged. He pushed himself back onto his knees and hooked his arms under Cael's legs, his hips smacking against Cael's ass. With a groan, Cael took hold of his cock, stroking himself.

"Fuck." Ash's movements grew more frantic as he watched Cael touching himself.

Loving the way Ash licked his lips as he watched Cael, Cael pumped his cock faster, his free hand going to his own nipple to rub and pull at it.

"Oh God. Yes." Ash's breath was unsteady as he thrust into Cael again and again. "I want to see you come."

Cael nodded. He ran a hand over his chest and down to his abs as he jerked himself off, the sweet pressure building. The feel of Ash inside him, his eyes on Cael, had him close to the edge of ecstasy in no time. "I'm going to come," Cael warned, his muscles tightening as his orgasm slammed into him, come squirting out across his chest.

"Oh fuck," Ash moaned, a pained expression on his face as Cael came, forcing him to clench around Ash. "Oh fuck." Ash held on to Cael's legs as he fucked him, his hips losing all rhythm as his orgasm hit. He thrust hard and deep, surprising Cael, who let out a strangled cry. Ash pushed himself in, pumped himself a few more times, rotating his hips on the last plunge as his body shuddered and he folded over Cael. He lost track of how long they remained in each other's embrace. Cael had been drifting off when he felt Ash stir and slip out of him with a low hiss. Ash pulled back and removed the condom. He tied it up and kissed Cael before getting up and heading to the bathroom.

Ash returned a few minutes later with some wet wipes Cael kept in the same drawer as the condom and lube. Cael smiled bashfully as Ash wiped the drying come off Cael's chest. He tossed the wipes into the small wastebasket nearby, and Cael took the opportunity to climb under the covers. Despite the heat being on, it was getting chilly. He held the covers back, and with a chuckle, Ash climbed in and pulled him close, nuzzling his face against Cael's hair.

"You always smell so good," Ash murmured against his hair.

Cael looked up at him, searching his eyes for any sign he regretted what he'd done, but Ash just kissed him and wrapped his leg around him so they were pressed together. Ash closed his eyes and let out a contended sigh.

"I like this."

Ash's words made Cael's heart flutter. "What's that?"

"Lying here with you, having you in my arms, making love to you. It feels right. Like we've always been together."

Cael took Ash's hand in his and held it to his lips for a kiss. "I like the sound of that."

"I'm sorry it took me so long."

Cael shook his head and planted a kiss on Ash's chest. "That doesn't matter. What matters is that you're here now." He felt Ash's breath steady, felt his chest rise and fall beneath his hand. Ash was here now, and Cael hoped it's where he would always remain.

NINE

IT WAS TIME TO GO.

Ash lay in bed for a moment, a smile spreading across his face at the memories of the amazing night he'd had with Cael. It was like nothing he'd imagined and by far the best sex he'd ever had. Fuck, if he wasn't careful, he was going to get hard thinking about it. From here on out, it was going to be tough to keep his hands off Cael. Just looking at him made Ash want to pounce. Then he remembered why he had to go, and the smile fell from his face. He silently slipped out of bed and began picking his clothes up off the floor to dress.

"You're leaving?"

Cael's sleepy voice brought him to a halt. He turned, unable to help his smile at the sight of Cael sitting up in bed looking adorable, his tousled hair sticking up every which way. Cael yawned, his drowsy, silver Therian eyes all but glowing in the dim light.

"I'm sorry. I didn't mean to wake you. I have to go." Ash pulled on his jeans and was buttoning them up before grabbing his socks when he heard the disappointment in Cael's reply.

"Oh."

Shit. Cael thought something else. "It's not you. I—"

"It's okay."

Cael drew his knees up and wrapped his arms around them. Nope. This wasn't how things were going to be after the amazing time they'd had last night. Ash quickly finished buckling his belt and went to Cael's bedside. He sat and took Cael's hand in his.

"It's not what you think. I'm not regretting what happened. I'm still soaring from that. It was the most amazing thing I've ever experienced. That's why I didn't want to wake you. After last night, I wanted you to keep that feeling." A lump formed in his throat, and he pushed past it. Shouldn't he have gotten used to this feeling by now? No matter how many times he'd gone, it still hurt like hell.

"What's wrong?" Cael asked, cupping Ash's cheek. With a sigh, Ash leaned into the touch.

"Every New Year's Day, I visit Arlo's grave."

Cael was quiet, pensive, before speaking up. "Can I come with you?"

Ash searched Cael's eyes, finding nothing but love and warmth in them. "I won't be very good company." And he wasn't exactly an enthralling entertainer on the best of days.

"You're always there for me. Let me be there for you."

Ash swallowed hard. He'd never taken anyone to Arlo's grave. Not even Sloane. It was a burden he'd always placed on his shoulders and his alone. Mostly, he never wanted anyone to see his heartache. "You really want to?"

Cael nodded, his sincerity unquestionable.

"Okay. I'd like that."

An hour later, they were in Ash's new truck heading for Brooklyn. It was the first time he'd taken the black truck out since driving it off the lot a couple of days after Christmas. Fucking taxicabs had been bleeding him dry, and since he was off the meds—on account of them being stolen—he went back to driving. Ash headed to Holy Cross Cemetery in Brooklyn, passing through Park Slope on the way there like he always did. He stopped at a red light and said, "This is the neighborhood I grew up in."

Cael looked out his window. "Do your parents still live here?"

"No. They moved away after Shultzon took custody of me. I don't even know where they are now. I set up an alert in Themis to let me know if they pass away, but I don't want to know where they are." It would be too tempting for him to show up on their doorstep, and no one needed that kind of drama. He certainly didn't. It's not as though they would welcome him. If they'd wanted him in their lives, they would have called. He wasn't exactly hard to track down considering he worked for the THIRDS. His parents probably didn't even know if he was alive. His father certainly wouldn't care.

Cael didn't ask him any more questions, and Ash was grateful. When he felt like he could share something, he did. He parked off Brooklyn Avenue and turned off the engine. Cael handed him the bouquet of flowers, and Ash took them from him with a kiss.

"It means a lot to me, you being here."

Cael smiled that beautiful smile of his. "I'm always here for you, Ash."

With a wink, Ash got out of the car. He came around and closed Cael's door for him after he hopped out. Ash activated the alarm, and they headed for the entrance, his nerves turning what little he had in his stomach to lead. Every year it was the same. That sinking feeling in the pit of his stomach and the emptiness in his heart he could never fill. Would things be different now that Cael was here with him? His visits had never been long. Usually he came, placed the flowers on the ground in front of Arlo's tombstone, said a small prayer, and left. Ash walked along the empty path flanked by trees, grass, and graves, lost in his own thoughts. The temperature was in the midthirties, and the wind was bitter, or maybe it felt that way because of where he was, but at least it wasn't cloudy or rainy. Ash appreciated how Cael didn't try to fill the silence with conversation, simply offered his quiet strength. They finally reached the grassy pitch where Arlo's tombstone was. Every year the marble tombstone seemed to get smaller, and it struck him that it was simply how long he'd been coming here, his body growing, his legs getting longer, his chest broader. To think he'd been such a scrawny little kid once upon a time.

What the hell was he doing here? This had to be the stupidest thing he'd ever done. His chest felt constricted, and it was getting hard to breathe. A warm hand slipped into his, and he took a deep breath. His eyes moved down to Cael, who gave him a warm smile.

"Tell me something about him."

Ash inhaled deeply and let it out slowly. He thought back to when he and Arlo had been kids. Inseparable. "He loved to ice skate," Ash said, his voice rough with emotions he thought he'd have moved on from by now. "When there was a thunderstorm, I'd climb into his bed and tell him it was to keep him safe, when really, I was the one who was scared." He chuckled at the memory. "I used to do that a lot. Act like the big tough guy, when all I wanted was to have him there with me. I missed him so much when he wasn't there." His voice broke, and he blinked back his tears. He had to hold it together.

"Who are you, and what are you doing here?"

Ash turned, his chest tightening at the sight of the elegantly dressed couple in black hats and winter coats. The world around him was reduced to a blur of color and mumbled sounds.

"Ash?"

"Mom..."

Ash's heart squeezed in his chest as his mom took a step toward him, only to have his father throw an arm out to stop her. The look of remorse on her face crushed what remained of Ash's heart into tiny pieces. Was it possible she didn't hate him? That she'd forgiven him after all these years?

"I'm surprised you bother to visit him," his father ground out through his teeth.

"I've visited him every year for twenty years," Ash said quietly. He shouldn't feel like the insecure, frightened child he'd been. His father no longer had a hold on him. Ash had every right to be angry. Angry for what they'd done to him. He could be angry if he wanted to, but what was the point? It wouldn't undo everything that had been done. It wouldn't bring Arlo back. There was no doubt his father hated him as much now as he had then. Ash could see it in his piercing amber eyes. It was hypocritical of his father to loathe him for being a Therian, when the same "contamination" that ran through Ash's veins was in his. The unstable mutation in his father had been incomplete, and unlike many Pre-First Gen Therians, his father couldn't shift. It made it easy for him to deny being infected at all. The mutation had cost him an arm due to an injury he'd sustained during the war.

His arm's weakened tissue hadn't stood a chance, but the rest of him remained very much Human. His father looked him over and sneered.

"Do you really think that by coming here, you'll be absolved for what you did?"

"It wasn't my fault," Ash replied, doing his best to believe it. Twenty years, and the only changes in his father were the silver strands in his auburn hair and the wrinkles around his eyes and mouth. He was still large, strong, and imposing. The resemblance between them was easy to see, and Ash hated it.

"Then why do you come every New Year's Day to punish yourself for facing another year without your brother? That's why you come here. Not to remember him or feel connected to him, but to punish yourself for letting him die."

"That's outrageous!" Cael turned to Ash, who couldn't bring himself to deny his father's words. "Ash?"

"You should have been with him that day. At least then I'd have the memory of two good boys and not of a dead son and the abomination his brother became."

Cael gasped, his hold tight on Ash's arm. "How can you be so callous to your own son?"

"He's not my son," Ash's father spat out. "He's an animal. A filthy beast that should be locked away in a zoo."

Ash flinched at the words, berating himself for his cowardice. What good was all his ferocity when he couldn't stand up to one man? Why did he continue to punish himself? Why did this one Human have the power to paralyze him? Cael stepped between Ash and his father, taking Ash aback. His sweet cheetah Therian bristled, his arm back behind him as if shielding Ash from his father's onslaught.

"What happened to Arlo was tragic, but instead of being there for Ash, who was very much alive, you threw him away. You blamed him for Arlo's death, but it wasn't his fault. If he'd been there that day, he most likely would have been killed as well. He was just a child, for heaven's sake! He needed you. You were supposed to protect him, not throw him away!"

"I don't know who the hell you are, but you stay out of this you little Therian—"

"Hey," Ash growled, his voice as fierce as his Therian roar, bringing his father to a standstill. "Say what you want to me, but you watch what you say to him. I won't let you treat him the way you've treated me. All these years I blamed myself for Arlo's death. I told myself I'd failed him. That I'd failed you. But the truth is, you failed *me*. Your job was to love me. To keep me safe. Instead you called Animal Control to take me away. Your own son! In your eyes, I was as dead as Arlo. I'm very much alive, and I've been blessed with a new family. One who loves me no matter how fucked-up and miserable I may be. I have great friends and the love of a man who proves that I'm not the monster you made me out to be." Ash slipped his arms around Cael and held him close.

"Thanks to Cael, I've learned that everything I believed about myself was wrong. I deserve to be loved and live a full, happy life. I'm an agent for the THIRDS, and what I do matters. I protect my city, both Therians and Humans, and fight so that one day assholes like you are the minority, and your bigoted, hateful, ignorant voice will fade away. Most importantly, I've grown up to be a good, decent man who is *nothing* like you."

His father blustered and huffed, opening his mouth to rebut, but no coherent words escaped. His faced turned crimson, his nostrils flaring before he turned away, snapping at his wife, "Come along, Vivian."

"One minute."

"Vivian, now," his father fumed.

She clasped her hands together. "Please, Richard. Just one minute."

"Fine. I'll be in the car. If you're not there in five minutes, you can take a cab."

Ash stood stunned, watching his father stalk off through the grass until he'd disappeared. He turned to his mother, his voice quiet. "How can you let him talk to you like that?"

"Look at you. Look how big you are," she said, smiling warmly.

The back of Ash's eyes stung. He remembered that smile, remembered when she'd squeeze him tight and kiss the top of his head. They'd bake together in the kitchen, and Arlo would end up eating most of the chocolate chips meant to go in the dough. His mom was as pretty now as she had been then. Her hair was silver, and her blue eyes didn't sparkle the way he remembered, but she was still elegant and beautiful.

Tears welled in her eyes, and Ash wanted to go to her, but she was already taking a step away from him.

"And so handsome." She composed herself and smiled again. "I caught you on the news a few months ago. You looked so dashing in your uniform." Her gaze moved to Cael. "Is this your boyfriend?"

Ash beamed proudly. "Yes. Mom, this is Cael Maddock. Cael, this is my mother, Vivian Keeler."

Cael gave her a nod. "Ma'am."

"You look so sweet together." She took Cael's hand in hers. "Look after him. He's a good boy. He deserves to be happy."

"Mom...?"

She stepped up to him and patted his arm, her hand lingering on his own gloved one before she pulled away. "I'm sorry. I have to go. It was wonderful to see you. Be safe."

She hurried off, and Ash stood watching her go until she'd disappeared beyond a group of trees. He didn't know how long he'd been standing there, staring off into the distance.

"Ash?"

Ash's vision blurred from the tears in his eyes. No matter how hard he tried to fight it, he was too exhausted. After all this time... His knees felt shaky, and he had to sit down. He let himself drop to the grass in front of Arlo's grave, leaned his elbows on his knees, and covered his face with his hands. Everything he'd been holding back over the whole of his life bubbled up and erupted like a geyser.

A strangled cry tore through him, and he let the tears fall. He cried for the death of his brother, torn from his life too soon. He cried for his stolen and fucked-up childhood. For every godforsaken piece of shit that got away with hurting someone. For Cael and what he'd suffered at the hands of that asshole. For his mother living under his bastard father's thumb. His mother... Had she wanted to see him before today? When had she stopped hating him? Did she still blame him? He had no idea how much he'd missed her until now.

He felt a hand on his back gently rubbing circles, and Cael's scent enveloped him like a warm blanket. Ash wrapped his arms around Cael, allowing himself to take comfort in the man he loved. Cael had stood up for him, fearlessly defended him. He pulled back and cupped Cael's face.

"Thank you for all that you are. For your gentleness, your fierceness, your smarts, your beauty, your charm, but mostly, thank you for trusting me with your heart."

"Did you mean what you said to your father?" Cael asked softly, removing a small packet of tissues from his coat pocket. He pulled one out and very tenderly wiped Ash's face.

"I meant every word."

Cael smiled and kissed his lips. "Good. I've always believed in you. I'm so happy that now you believe in yourself. You are a wonderful man, Ash. Never let anyone make you feel less than that."

Ash stood, bringing Cael along with him. He pulled him close and kissed him. How had he gotten so lucky? He couldn't imagine his life without Cael. Without his sweet face and warm smile, his infectious laughter and charming quirks. Ash gave him a squeeze, his hand going to the back of Cael's head, and he hugged him. It had taken him so long to see what was right in front of him. He had no intention of letting go.

SHIT! Austen tapped the security code into the panel on the small bulletproof case and opened it. Inside, snuggled securely in their padding, lay six large blue vials and, next to the vials, a Therian jet injector. This was it. Holy fuck, this was it.

"You have to go! They'll be here any minute."

Agent Boyle pulled a Glock from under his white lab coat, and Austen stared at him.

"Are you insane? You can't take on an army. Wait for the extraction team."

"There's no time. Don't worry about me. You have to get the package to Sparks."

"Goddamn it." He knew this was going to happen. Regardless of his feelings on the matter, Boyle was right. Austen swiftly removed the small hooligan kit from his back, opened the hidden padded pocket beneath the det cord compartment, and stuck the case inside before zipping everything back up and returning it to his back. He clicked all the straps into place and removed his own gun from his thigh rig.

"Boyle—"

Shooting erupted down the hall, and a small explosion shook the walls. They'd gotten through the locked fire door.

"Go!"

Boyle opened the door and slipped out into a blaze of gunfire, the door locking behind him before Austen could utter another word. He heard Boyle scream, and it jolted Austen into action. He couldn't let Boyle's sacrifice be in vain. The package had to be delivered.

Austen looked around the room. The vent was out of the question. He'd be a sitting duck. There was a window above the filing cabinet just about big enough for his slender frame to slip through. Time to get to work. He pulled on his tac gloves with knuckle reinforcement and smiled. Now came the fun part. Leaping onto the stationary chair by the desk, he used it as a springboard to hop onto the top of the cabinet. Shielding his face with one arm, he pulled back his right fist and punched through the window's glass. The glass shattered, and he hurriedly punched at the larger shards left in the frame so he could get through without getting cut up. He popped his head out, hearing the sirens going off in the facility.

Assessing the surrounding area, it was immediately

clear the only way was up. The building's smooth surface was clear of anything he could use to climb down, and even if there had been something, the wall surrounding the building was lined with barbed wire. The roof ledge was three floors up. Fun times. He pulled himself back inside, hearing the shouts outside the room getting closer. They were looking for him. Quickly, he unhooked his hooligan kit and removed the grappling gun with rappelling rope. He clicked, locked, and secured all the pieces before securing his kit back in place. Getting on his back, he pushed his upper body through the window, aimed, and fired. The hook whizzed through the air, soared over, and sank, latching on to the roof's ledge.

"That's my girl." Securing the rope around his gloved hands, he pushed himself through the window just as a loud thud resounded against the heavy door. They'd be breaching any moment. He swung out and came back against the building, his boots hitting the smooth brick. Not wasting a single moment, he climbed the side of the building, one hand after the other, one step at a time. The sound of gunfire echoed through the otherwise quiet evening air, but no one would be calling it in. Next to the research facility, there was nothing around but empty warehouses used for equally shady dealings. Which meant if he was caught, no one would hear him scream. That was the price he paid for doing the job he did. He gritted his teeth and moved as fast as he could without compromising his safety.

"He's heading for the roof!" someone yelled from the window below.

A bullet hit the brick wall to Austen's right, and he cursed under his breath. He breathed in through his nose and out through his mouth, his breath visible in the cold night air. Upon reaching the top, he pulled himself over, gathered up his shit at breakneck speed, and shoved it through the side zip in his bag. He took a few seconds to assess the area around him. Several of the rooftops were connected. Thank you, New York City. Austen bolted for the end of the roof, hearing a door slam open somewhere behind him. Gunfire erupted, and Austen dove behind a cooling unit.

"Come out with your hands up!"

"Sure," Austen yelled, snatching a flashbang from his pocket. He pulled the pin, rolled out, and chucked it at the group of armed men before making a break for it. The bang was accompanied by a flash of blinding light and plenty of cursing, shouting, and grunting. Austen's boot hit the roof's ledge, and he leapt across to the other building, hitting the floor in a roll and carrying on as if he'd never stopped. Two roofs ahead, he spotted an iron ladder hanging off the side. He sped onward, ignoring the shouts, threats, and gunfire behind him. Approaching the ladder, he jumped on the ledge, turned, and hurried down, the armed men fast on his heels. Reaching the end of the line, he hopped down and landed on the roof of a car parked between the buildings.

"Stop!"

Why did they always say that? Like Austen was going to decide *You know what? I think I'll do that.* Bunch of idiots. Taking off at full speed, he knew there was no hope the Human guards would catch him. The Therian ones might catch up, but from the quick glance he'd managed, they were all large classifications. Austen grinned as he sped through a congested parking lot filled with truck trailers and shipment containers. Everything was packed together, allowing him plenty of darkness to play in. The Humans would never hear him or see him. It was the Therian gunmen he had to be careful of. Austen paused and sniffed the air. They were getting closer. Across the lot was a large wooded area. The trees were mostly dried up, but it was dense enough to provide cover, especially at this time of night.

Listening for the sounds of approaching guards, Austen stealthily used the containers to conceal himself as he made his way closer to the exit. Someone quietly gave orders, but Austen heard them fine. They were spreading out. He pulled his black beanie from his pocket, secured it on his head, and readied himself. *Here we go.* He picked up a couple of rocks, edged toward the end of the container, and hurled them over the next container. The rocks hit, and orders were given. Austen made a break for the woods.

"Over there!"

By the time the order was given, Austen was running at his full cheetah Therian speed. Although he wasn't as fast in his Human form, he was still damn fast, and thanks to his Therian vision, he maneuvered through the trees easily. Making it out onto the other side, he came across an underpass. He jumped the fence, crossed the underpass, and kept running. Using the darkness as cover, he slipped in and out between buildings, climbing fire escapes, crawling through windows, and using the New York City landscape as his personal playground. He stayed high, knowing those goons would stay low, trying to follow his scent through the streets and alleys.

A block away, there was an old abandoned school. He tore at one of the boarded-up windows and climbed through. Heading upstairs past debris-filled classrooms, he picked the crumbling auditorium. If anyone tried to get the drop on him, it would give him several escape options. Jumping onto the stage, he tapped his earpiece. "I'm coming in with the package."

"Agent Payne, this is unacceptable!" Sparks stated angrily.

"I'm being hunted down. Do you really think I give two shits if it's acceptable to you?" He was getting real tired of being dicked around. "I'm coming in, so if you want your goddamn package, you better have someone there to receive it!"

"It's too soon."

"Too fucking bad! This shit just blew up in our faces. We need to make this disappear, and we need to do it now!" He wanted to offload this thing as quickly as possible.

"Where's Boyle?" she asked.

"Boyle's dead. Or captured. Who the fuck knows. Point is, he's gone."

There was a long pause before she spoke again. "Get the package to the drop-off point. I'll arrange a transport."

Austen froze. "The usual suspects?"

"There's no one I trust more to get the job done without question."

"*Without question?* All those guys do is ask fucking questions!" He paused. "If word gets out..." And there was no doubt in his mind it would. Destructive Delta would have a target painted on their backs.

"They can handle it."

"Cut them a break, man. They've had buildings falling on them, been exploded, shot, kidnapped, beaten, and now you're throwing them into a fucking volcano?" This was fucked-up.

"Don't worry about them. I'll make sure they have backup."

Great. More marshmallows to roast. "I don't like this."

"Perhaps I need to remind you who you work for."

Austen narrowed his eyes, his voice clipped. "How do you sleep at night?"

"Extremely well."

"They're your agents." Austen paced. "At least bench Sloane. The guy's only just recovered."

"Your concern is sweet but invalid. He's their team leader. Besides, benching him would arouse suspicion."

"You—"

"Get the package to the drop-off point. You have half an hour."

The line went dead, and Austen kicked the wall behind him. Motherfucking son of a bitch! He was so pissed off he wanted to punch something. Getting himself together, he did what he always did. His job. He couldn't let emotions cloud his judgment. Right now the package was what mattered. He wished more than anything he could inform Sloane. His friend had left several messages for him, and there was only so long he could ignore Sloane, but the less he and the rest of the team knew, the better it was for everyone. Especially Dex. The guy was in possession of a terrible conscience. Austen headed for the streets. Whatever Sparks said, Austen knew this was bad. He hoped Destructive Delta would make it out of this.

IT WAS time to see what his students had learned.

Ash had been training Dex and Cael every day for two weeks. He'd shown no mercy to either of them, no special treatment. They'd both bitched and moaned, but Ash didn't care. He could hardly teach them in a few months what he'd learned over the course of twenty years, but he could prepare them. A good deal of experience would come while they were out in the field facing real-life situations. So far, he'd lost count of how many times he'd taken them down. They were getting up in what they believed were their weaknesses. Dex being Human, Cael being a small Felid. He needed them to see their so-called weaknesses were actually their strengths.

"All right. We're going to go with the assumption the threat you're facing will be at least my height, size, weight, and strength. Despite being smaller, you can use a Therian's size and strength against them. You'll be lighter on your feet, faster, and more agile and flexible. Let's say you've assessed the threat. You're faced with Hogan."

Cael flinched, but Ash continued. Hogan was a sore point for the brothers, which was why he used him. They'd both come up against the tiger Therian, had both sustained injuries and felt true fear. Now they knew what they were facing.

"I'm Hogan. I'm standing in front of you. I have every intention of killing you. You're unarmed. How are you going to take me down before I snap your neck?"

"Find a weapon?" Cael suggested.

Ash shrugged. "Sure. In this kind of situation, anything and everything becomes a weapon. Except there's nothing you can use."

"Well, then," Dex said, hands planted on his hips, "I'm kind of fucked, aren't I?"

"That's why you're here. The answer is, you fight dirty. You use whatever means necessary to stay alive. You need to be able to perform under impaired visibility and extreme fatigue, both mentally and physically. When in our Therian forms, our Human sides may be neurologically present, but our feral instincts are at their most animalistic. We fight to survive. When in our Human forms, or for those who are Human, you rely on your training to do what needs to be done. Remember, go for vulnerable areas. Neck, liver, kidney, groin, eyes. Use your elbows. Go for the face." He took a stance and motioned for them to advance. "All right. Come on."

"Which one?" Cael asked.

"Both."

Dex arched an eyebrow at him. "My, my. Aren't we full of ourselves."

Ash shrugged. "If I'm wrong, I'm the one who ends up bruised." Which he wouldn't. Now Dex on the other hand... Ash was looking forward to this. There was nothing that put a smile on his face like slamming Dexter Justice Daley into the mat. It was almost therapeutic.

"I don't know," Dex teased. "Can your ego take it?"

"Don't worry about my ego," Ash replied smugly. "Worry about your face when it hits the mat."

Dex flipped him the finger, and Ash chuckled. He held back a smile, watching the brothers murmur to each other. Finally. They were getting it. He tightened his fists and readied himself. He took a deep breath and released it slowly. Combined, the brothers only weighed fifty-five pounds more than he did. Ash could bench eight times that. If his lessons took, Dex and Cael would use his size against him.

This just might hurt.

The brothers bumped fists, and both took off at a run toward him. Ash readied himself, studying them both in an attempt to anticipate who would strike first and how. As expected, Dex moved in first, pulling back a fist as he neared. Ash went for a left hook, smiling when he realized he'd made his first mistake. Dex tended to go high, looking to land a punch to the face. This time he chose the unexpected route.

Dex dropped to his knees—missing Ash's fist—and used the momentum to slide on his knees. Not wasting his own momentum, Ash twisted his torso to catch Cael coming at him from his right. His little cheetah Therian showed no hesitation or mercy, using Ash's bulky frame as leverage. He grabbed hold of Ash's arm and used Ash's bent knee as a springboard to jump and swing a leg around Ash's neck. With a growl, Ash snatched a fistful of Cael's uniform to throw him off when he felt the blow to the back of his leg.

Ash came crashing down onto one knee and was propelled forward by Cael using all his weight to bring Ash down with the help of Dex, who punched the back of his other knee before slamming into him from behind.

Fuck! Ash hit the floor hard, teeth gritted as Cael's legs wrapped tightly around his neck, his hand grabbing a fistful of Ash's hair. A zip tie tugged at his now bound wrists. Cael petted his hair and leaned in with a breathless whisper.

"Tied up looks good on you, Keeler."

"Oh shit." Ash laughed as he was released.

He rolled onto his side and sat up, shaking his head at the whoops from their fellow agents who'd gathered around. Dex and Cael gave each other a high five before Dex crouched down beside him.

"How's that ego doing? Want me to get you an ice pack?"

"Fuck off." He looked from one smug brother to the other. "You boys forgot the most important part of the lesson."

"And what's that?" Dex said, standing and folding his arms over his chest.

"When you take down your opponent, make sure they stay down."

He twisted his body, spun on his side, and swiped his leg under them, knocking them both off their feet and onto their asses. The two groaned, and Ash couldn't help his grin as he got to his feet.

"Other than that, nicely done."

The two cheered, and Ash shook his head at them. He bent forward and thrust his wrists down over his ass. Nothing happened. Feeling the ties with his fingers, he glowered at Dex.

"You're supposed to be using regular zip ties for training. These are Therian-strength zip ties."

Dex blinked innocently at him. "Are those Therian-strength? Must have gotten them mixed up."

"Right." Ash didn't buy it for a second. "Get them off."

Dex patted his tac pants. "I think I might... Aw, damn. Sorry. I must have left my knife in my other pants."

"You little bastard," Ash growled, taking a step toward him.

Dex bolted for the bay doors, calling out behind him. "I'm going to grab it now! Wait here for me!"

"He's not coming back," Ash sighed and turned to Cael, who patted his arm.

"I'm still here."

Ash smiled sweetly. "Then that's all I need."

Cael wasn't fooled. He returned Ash's smile.

"You want me to untie you."

"Gee, that would be real swell."

Cael seemed to think about it. A wicked gleam came into his eyes. "I don't know. Maybe I need to hear you say it first."

Cael headed for the doors, and Ash quickly followed with a frown on his face.

"Hear what?"

"How badass we were."

Ash peered at him. "That depends. Do I have to include your brother?"

"Yep." Cael made his way through Sparta toward the elevators with Ash close behind. He ignored all the amused looks and snickers from his fellow agents as he walked past them with his wrists bound behind his back.

"Damn." Ash stepped into the elevator next to Cael. There were a couple of other agents in there, both desperately trying to hold back their laughter.

"What? You ain't never seen a zip tie before?" He cursed under his breath.

The elevator pinged, and Ash followed Cael out, turning to walk backward so he could glare at the agents, who burst into laughter as the doors closed.

"I know who you are!" He spun around and caught up to Cael in Unit Alpha's bullpen. "Aw, come on, Cael. Seriously? You're gonna parade me around like this?"

"All you have to do is say it."

"Hey, Keeler," Taylor called out. "That's a good look for you."

"You know what's a good look for *you*, Taylor? My fist in your face. Shut the fuck up." Ash turned and ran in front of Cael, cutting him off, his words quiet. "Come on, darling."

Cael's smile never left his face. "Aw, listen to you. Sweet talker. Of course I'll get them off. When you say it."

"I can't," Ash whined. He actually fucking whined. "It'll kill me. I really think it might make me keel over. I can't." Compliment Dex? Unthinkable.

Cael stopped outside his and Rosa's office. "I guess you'll have to get out of it yourself."

He patted Ash's arm, ready to step around him. Ash let his head hang. He mumbled the words, gritting his teeth when Cael put a hand to his ear.

"I didn't quite catch that."

"Fine," Ash ground out. "That was badass. You and Dex were a couple of badasses. Okay?" He looked over Cael's head at their fellow agents pretending not to eavesdrop on what was going on. Bunch of nosy bastards. "You can all stop pretending. Cael and Dex floored me, okay? Probably because that's what I'm fucking training them to do, so you can all get those stupid smiles off your faces."

There was a snicker, and Ash's brows rose. "You wanna get in the ring with me, Herrera?"

Herrera looked like he was about to shit himself. "What? No."

"Good. Then shut the fuck up and go find a fern to piss on."

The room erupted into laughter, and Ash turned his attention back to Cael. "You and Dex were badass. There. I said it."

"Wooh!" Dex popped out from who the fuck knew where, arms thrown up in the air. He did a victory dance and motioned around the floor. "You all heard that. Ash Keeler said I was a badass."

"What the fuck?" Ash gaped at him. "Where the fuck did you come from?"

His jaw all but hit the floor when Dex casually put a hand up and Cael high-fived him.

"I was getting some Cheesy Doodles when I heard your little announcement."

"Unbelievable." Ash shook his head, his frown aimed at Cael. "Are you happy now?"

"I am." He reached into one of his pockets and pulled out his utility knife.

In one swipe, Ash's wrists were free. He rubbed them and ignored Dex dancing around as he popped cheese snacks into his mouth. Where was Zach when you needed him? That would put a stop to Dex's crunching.

"Come on, big guy. Let's hit the showers."

Cael patted Ash's chest and walked off. Ash followed, but not before shoving Dex. He grinned when Dex fell into Taylor, his cheese snacks soaring through the air and hitting the carpet.

"My Cheesy Doodles!" Dex dropped to his hands and knees. "Noooooo! They were so young. So delicious."

Cael shook his head in amusement. "You couldn't help yourself, could you?" he told Ash.

"I need balance in my life." Ash grinned and walked into the empty locker room. They opened their lockers and started undressing. It occurred to Ash this was the first time the locker room was empty during their shower. He removed his T-shirt and chucked it into the laundry bin. Sitting on the bench, he undid his boot laces and glanced up to ask Cael what he wanted to do for dinner when he found Cael naked, his back to Ash and his plump round ass cheeks at eye level. *Fuck.*

Getting himself together, he unlaced his boots and cleared his throat. "So, uh, what do you want to do for dinner?"

"I was thinking of ordering takeout. Tonight's the premiere of that new comic book TV show I told you about. Want to crash at mine?"

"Sure." Ash smiled and placed his boots inside his

locker. He loved cozy nights in with Cael. There was never any pressure to go out clubbing or to a bar. Most wouldn't believe him if he told them, but he was actually kind of a homebody. A little TV, good food, and the company of his sweetheart, and he was content. Chucking his socks into the laundry bin and putting his pants away, he grabbed his toiletry bag and closed his locker door. He followed Cael into the showers, picking up a large towel along the way. Inside it was nice and quiet. Since they weren't on call, they got to shower before the evening rush.

Ash stepped into the stall beside Cael and turned the shower on. He did his best to concentrate on showering and not on Cael lathering himself up in the stall beside him. Ash stood under the showerhead and washed his hair, soaped himself up, and rinsed. He wiped the excess water from his face, and when he stepped out from under the showerhead, he found Cael leaning on the thick glass partition grinning at him.

"Don't mind me," he said, waving a hand in dismissal. "I'm just perving on you."

Ash held back a laugh. "Here I am trying to be good, and you're being wicked."

"It's hard not to," Cael said with a lazy shrug. "Plus there's no one here."

A mischievous look came into his eyes, and he crooked a finger, calling Ash to lean down. What was the little minx up to? With a wicked grin, Cael stood on his toes and licked Ash from his chin to his lip. He took Ash's bottom lip between his teeth and sucked it into his mouth before pulling back.

"I'm going to need you to take me home and fuck me, Agent Keeler."

Ash promptly shut off the water and grabbed his toiletry bag. "Let's go."

With a chuckle, Cael followed his lead, grabbed his bag, and got out. He threw his towel over his shoulder, his ass out in the open for Ash to gawk at as he sauntered away from him.

"Come along, Keeler. Pun totally intended, by the way."

Man, Ash was screwed. And he loved it.

By the time they got inside Cael's apartment and to his bedroom, they'd left a trail of clothing behind. Shirts landed on furniture, socks on lamps, and pants on the stairs. They kissed fervently as they undressed each other. Ash dropped onto the bed with Cael, mindful of his weight.

"I want you to fuck me hard. Don't hold back," Cael murmured against Ash's lips, his fingers grabbing fistfuls of Ash's hair as he rutted against him.

"I don't want to hurt you, sweetheart."

"You won't," Cael assured him, arching his back. He took Ash's earlobe between his teeth before sucking it into his mouth. He licked down Ash's jawline and nipped at his chin.

"Cael." Fuck, Cael was doing everything he could to drive Ash crazy, but he didn't want to hurt him. Their first time had been slow and sweet, an exploration of something new and wonderful for both of them. At the time, all Ash could think about was how he was inside Cael. How after years of secretly dreaming, he was making love to the beautiful young Therian.

"You won't hurt me."

"You sound very sure," Ash replied as he planted kisses down Cael's exposed neck. His hand closed around it. He loved the feel of Cael beneath him, loved how soft and warm he was, while at the same time strong and firm. Cael might be sweet and shy, but he was a formidable agent. He was sharp-witted and sharp-tongued with a host of impressive talents, while at the same time always humble and concerned for those around him.

"Because I'm sure."

Something in Cael's tone caught Ash's attention, and he pulled back to look down and study him. "What aren't you telling me? How do you know?"

Cael's cheeks flushed pink. "Well, I, um, I've been practicing."

"Practicing?" What exactly did that entail? Ash's curiosity was piqued.

"Yeah, um, I've kind of been thinking about this for a long time, and well, I wanted to really feel you, so I..." He motioned toward the left nightstand.

Hesitantly, Ash leaned over and opened the drawer. *Oh dear God.* "Is that what I think it is?" He studied the large tan-colored object.

"It's a dildo."

"Wow." Ash tilted his head to one side. "Am I that big?"

Cael wriggled beneath him. "I estimated."

"Thanks for not underestimating," Ash said with a chuckle.

"You probably think I'm some kind of weird sex stalker or something."

"What? No." Ash closed the drawer and moved Cael's hands away from his face. "I think you're hot and sexy, and the thought that you fucked yourself with that while thinking of me? Fuck. I don't think I've ever been so turned on." He thought about it and nodded. "Yeah, totally fucking hot."

"Really?"

Cael searched his expression, undoubtedly looking for

signs he might be saying that so Cael wouldn't feel bad, but nope. Ash was definitely turned on as fuck. He took Cael's hand and placed it on his painfully hard cock.

"You tell me." He gave Cael a wicked smile. "How do you want it?"

Cael ran his tongue over his bottom lip. He turned himself onto his stomach and looked at Ash from over his shoulder, his gray eyes clouded with lust. Ash swallowed hard and nodded. He grabbed a pillow, and Cael lifted his hips so Ash could slip it under him. He reached into the nightstand on his right where he knew Cael kept the lube and condoms. Sitting back on his heels, he tore at the condom packet and rolled the condom over his cock. He was about to uncap the lube when Cael lowered his head onto his folded arms and arched his back, his ass in the air.

"Fuck." Ash had never seen a more beautiful sight. Tossing the lube onto the mattress beside him, Ash put his hands on Cael's ass cheeks, drawing a moan from him. He ran his hands up Cael's back, then down to his ass again. Cael spread his knees, and Ash couldn't stop wondering what Cael tasted like.

"Ash..." Cael pleaded.

Ash thought about Cael lying on this bed pushing that large dildo inside him as he fucked himself to thoughts of Ash. His feral half roared inside him, demanding he claim the sensual offering before him. Ash had never felt anything as fierce as this. His fingers dug into Cael's cheeks, and he lowered himself onto his stomach. He hooked his arms under Cael's thighs and pulled Cael toward him, the sweet gasp that escaped Cael fueling Ash's scorching desire. He ran his tongue between Cael's ass cheeks, hearing Cael curse and whimper. One taste, and Ash was lost. He made a meal of Cael's ass, licking, nipping, and sticking his tongue inside him.

"Oh God," Cael groaned, thrusting his hips against the pillow in a desperate attempt to relieve some of the pressure.

Ash coveted the taste of him, devoured him, savored him. When Cael couldn't take any more, Ash pulled back. He poured lube onto his hand and stroked himself while using the fingers of his free hand to prep Cael. It didn't take long, and Ash lined himself up behind Cael, rubbing Cael's ass cheeks before he parted them. He pushed the head of his cock into Cael's tight hole, hissing at the delicious pressure. Cael moaned and arched his back.

"Please, Ash. I need you to fuck me."

The desperation in Cael's voice and the way he writhed with need before Ash had him burying himself to the root. Cael pushed himself back, and Ash groaned. His resolve was slowly slipping.

"Damn it, Ash. Fuck me!"

Ash folded himself over Cael and pulled partially out before snapping his hips against Cael's ass, making Cael cry out. Ash snapped his hips again. The sound of his skin smacking against Cael's coupled with Cael's pleas for more drove Ash over the edge. He pumped himself into Cael, pushing in deep and fucking him hard. With a grunt, he wrapped an arm around Cael's neck, his hand covering Cael's mouth.

"That's it, sweetheart. Fuck yeah."

Cael covered Ash's hand with his, their fingers lacing together. Cael held on tight, his cries and moans muffled by Ash's hand as he pounded Cael's ass, his larger body covering his younger lover and his weight pressing him into the mattress that moved beneath them. The headboard slammed against the wall as Ash drove himself deep into Cael over and over. He rotated his hips, his breath coming out ragged as the pressure built inside him.

"Fuck."

Cael moaned, soft high-pitched sounds that grew faster and louder. Ash could feel the pressure building. He released Cael and got on his knees, his fingers digging into Cael's hips as he fucked him.

"Oh God, yes, please. Ash," Cael moaned, his breath coming out in pants.

"I'm going to come. Oh fuck."

Ash thrust into Cael hard, his hips losing their rhythm as he chased after his orgasm. Cael pulled off him and turned to take hold of Ash's cock. He rolled the condom off and sucked Ash's cock into his mouth while bringing himself closer to his own impending orgasm. It was all Ash needed. He gently took hold of Cael's head and thrust into his mouth, his release almost causing him to double over. His body shuddered as he came inside Cael, intensified by the sounds Cael made as he came. Cael continued to suck him off until Ash hissed and gently pulled out. The two of them flopped down onto the bed next to each other, trying to catch their breaths.

With a smile on his face, Ash turned and pulled Cael to him, kissing his temple. "Thank you. That was incredible."

Cael chuckled. "You're welcome."

As Ash held Cael against him, he stroked Cael's chest, still unable to believe after all this time, Cael was here in his arms. "I love you."

"I love you too," Cael said softly.

As they floated toward sleep, a thought occurred to Ash. "Cael?"

"Hm?"

He felt his face burn up, but he asked anyway. "One of these days, will you, um, show me how you uh... you know..."

"Fuck myself with the dildo?" Cael asked nonchalantly.

"Yes. That. Thank you."

"You bet."

"Great." God, he felt like such an idiot. How was it he was the one feeling like some inexperienced virgin while Cael was throwing around words like... dildo? What a fucking horrible word. Then again a lot of words associated with sex sounded unappealing to him, though he was sure the act—especially if it involved Cael—would be anything but.

The steady rise and fall of Cael's chest beneath his hand told him Cael had fallen asleep. Ash lay awake as long as he could to enjoy the feel of Cael's naked body against his. Soon they'd be back on call, facing threats and Therians out to do them harm. Instinctively, his arms tightened around Cael. He buried his face in Cael's hair and inhaled deeply. It was fine. Everything would be fine. They'd been to hell and back. At least now he had Cael waiting for him on the other side.

TEN

Cᴀᴇʟ ᴡᴀs sᴛɪʀʀᴇᴅ awake by a strange yet familiar sound. With a groan, he rolled over and snuggled closer to Ash, who was muttering incoherently and cursing whatever noise was determined to wake them up. The annoying sound was persistent, like an alarm. Cael rubbed his drowsy eyes in an attempt to wake up.

"Shit." He crawled away from Ash, rousing him from sleep.

"What? What is it?" Ash asked, sitting up.

"Do you hear that? It's an emergency call." They both scrambled off the bed looking for their phones, and Cael remembered they'd dropped their pants on the stairs. The alarm they were hearing was reserved for Sparks and used only in an emergency. Cael had heard it on very few occasions during his time at the THIRDS. He found his phone in his discarded jeans pocket and tapped the security screen, the reader accepting his fingerprint before flashing blue, then red. Sparks's message cut through the silence.

All members of Destructive Delta, Beta Ambush, and Theta Destructive are to report to the address enclosed at the end of this message immediately. Arrive in your BearCats with full tactical equipment and be prepared for a threat level red transport. You'll receive full instructions upon your arrival. Discretion is imperative.

Ash's words mirrored Cael's sentiments. "What the fuck?"

"I don't know, but we'd better move."

They jumped to it, getting dressed as quickly as they could before running out of the apartment. Cael checked the address on his phone. It was a parking garage on West Thirty-Third Street. Why would Sparks want them to meet in a parking garage?

When they arrived at HQ, the rest of their team was there in the armory getting dressed and gearing up. Cael pulled his extra uniform from his weapons locker, noticing how everyone seemed to be lost in their own thoughts. They were probably wondering the same thing as him. This wasn't a regular callout.

"Sloane, what's going on?"

"I don't know."

Sloane looked troubled, and that wasn't good. Why would Sparks not inform Sloane? Cael finished getting dressed beside Ash, straightening one of the straps of Ash's tactical vest, when he heard familiar voices. Seb entered their armory, followed by his team. He was dressed in full gear, looking large and imposing, as always. He gave Cael a wink before walking past him to speak quietly to Hobbs, who was looking anxious. Calvin wasn't kidding. Hobbs looked like he hadn't slept in days. His shoulders were slumped, and he stayed as close to Calvin as possible. Seb let his head rest against his little brother's, whispering something to Hobbs, who nodded and even managed a small smile.

Calvin closed his locker and turned to Seb. "Any idea what this is all about?"

"Yeah," Dex pitched in. "And why are we meeting offsite?"

Seb released his brother and shook his head, his expression no less troubled or confused than the rest of them. "I know as much about all this as you guys. We better head out."

They all finished suiting up and grabbing their gear before hurrying out of the armory and heading for their BearCats. Sloane, Seb, and Taylor did a quick recon before splitting up and leading their teams to their respective trucks. Hobbs climbed in behind the wheel with Calvin riding shotgun as usual. Cael sat behind his surveillance console when it struck him.

"Where's the sarge?"

Everyone stilled.

"I'll find out," Sloane said, typing away at his smartphone as everyone took a seat on the bench and buckled up.

Cael fastened his seat belt as the BearCat roared to life when Sloane announced Sarge wasn't coming.

"He's not been called in on this."

Sloane put his phone away, and Cael noticed Ash and Dex exchange glances. What were they thinking? Clearly they weren't happy about it, and Cael was with them on that. Why would their sergeant not get called in for this emergency? Sloane told Hobbs to get them moving, and the three BearCats drove out of the garage and into the night. This whole thing wasn't sitting well with Cael, and judging by the looks on his teammates' faces, they felt the same. Everyone seemed to be lost in their own thoughts as they headed for the address Sparks had relayed. It didn't take long to get there, especially at this time of night. Cael checked his watch. Damn, it was almost four in the morning.

The BearCat turned and drove up an incline, the light dimming around them. Cael figured they'd reached the parking garage. There was a faint beep, like the setting of a car alarm. Most likely the signal. Hobbs drove a couple more feet before their truck came to a stop. Well, this was it. They were about to find out what was going on. Hobbs turned off the engine and joined them in the back, followed by Calvin.

"All right, team. Let's see what this is about." Sloane stood and opened the back door, peering out before opening the door wider and hopping down. He motioned for the rest of the team to follow. Ash jumped down, and Cael was right behind him, sticking close to him as the headlights from the approaching two BearCats neared. The trucks came to a halt, the lights remaining on as the teams climbed out.

The parking lot was eerily quiet, but then it should have been at this time of night. Scanning the area, Cael noticed there were security cameras. They were pointing away, with no lights or anything signaling they were recording. Ahead of them, Sparks and a small team of Therian agents Cael had never seen before approached them. The agents were dressed in black suits, shirts, and ties, and one of them was carrying a medium-sized armored case.

"Thank you all for your promptness. This case is to be delivered to the Teterboro Airport, where a small team of Therian agents will be waiting beside a private unmarked plane. I'll be monitoring your navigation systems. I can't stress enough how crucial this mission is. It's also highly classified. I expect you all to report in the moment the drop is made. Understood?"

Everyone nodded and replied with affirmatives. Sparks

gave the signal, and the agent holding the case handed it over to Ash, who frowned but accepted it.

"Destructive Delta, you keep the package secure. Theta Destructive, Beta Ambush, your job is to make sure Destructive Delta delivers the package at all costs." With that she turned and headed for the black Suburban parked a few feet away.

None of them knew what the hell was going on, but each team leader gathered their team and headed back to their respective truck. Ash climbed into the BearCat, the package in his hands. He took the lone seat across from the bench, where their sergeant usually sat, and buckled himself in, using the extra safety harness as well. The rest of the team silently took their seats on the bench and buckled up as the truck's doors closed. The engine roared to life, and Hobbs waited until Theta Destructive's truck had driven past before following, with Beta Ambush taking up the rear. The trucks left the parking garage, traveling up West Thirty-Third Street.

THERE WAS silence as they headed toward Ninth Avenue. Of course, the silence didn't last for long. It never did when Dex was around.

"Okay, since no one else is going to say it, I will. That's the fucking drug, isn't it? We're transporting the drug."

"We don't know that," Sloane stated calmly.

"What else can it be? We're transporting a mysterious armored case to a private airfield at four o'clock in the morning, our sergeant's not been informed of this, and we have two other teams providing backup with enough firepower to take on a small army. Sparks, Ward, the drugs? It has to be."

"This isn't the first transport we've done," Ash offered, "and we don't exactly keep regular hours."

None of them wanted to believe Sparks was involved with the control drug. That after years of being with the THIRDS, being their lieutenant, she could be behind an unsanctioned op. And for what purpose? She was a Therian. Why would she get involved in something that would control her own kind? The agents with her had also been Therian. It made no sense.

Dex looked to Sloane. "Tell me you're not thinking the same thing."

Everyone turned their attention to their team leader. If Sloane believed it, so would the rest of them. They all waited, hoping Sloane could offer them something to argue Sparks's innocence.

"Fuck." Sloane leaned his elbows on his knees and ran his fingers through his hair.

"What if it is the drug, Sloane?" Rosa said. "Are we just going to hand it over to God knows who? It'll disappear."

"And what do you propose we do?" Ash griped. "No wonder she didn't call Maddock in on this. He would have fucking blown his shit."

"We could take it back to HQ," Dex pitched in.

Sloane shook his head. "If Sparks is involved, she could easily get to it. She has high-level security clearance. She'll be able to get into areas we can't."

"We could hide it."

Ash scoffed at Dex. "Where are we going to hide an illegal unsanctioned mind-control drug, genius?"

"Fuck you, Simba," Dex snapped. "At least I'm making suggestions."

"Stupid suggestions. *Justice.*"

Sloane sat back and put a hand out. "All right, that's enough. Just let me think for a second."

"Aren't there contingency plans for this sort of thing?" Dex asked Sloane, though his glare was still pinned on Ash, who couldn't resist having a dig at Dex.

These two were going to drive them all nuts. How did they always get themselves into these situations? They needed a real vacation, one as far away from New York City as possible.

"You mean for the 'your lieutenant is involved in a conspiracy, please drop off all illegal substances at point B' situation?"

Dex appeared unimpressed. "And here I thought your sleeping with my brother might actually make you less of an asshole."

"Dex!" Cael gasped, unable to believe his brother had blurted that out in front of everyone. He wished he could crawl under a rock. His brother must love the taste of boot because he was always sticking his foot in his mouth. For crying out loud!

Rosa thrust a finger at Ash. "I knew it! *Pendejo*. You said nothing was going on between you two."

"Well, I lied," Ash replied sweetly. "Cael and I are dating, okay? You and your girlfriend will have to find a way to get over the loss."

"Screw you," Rosa huffed, her arms crossed over her chest.

"Sorry, that position's *ocupado*."

Cael groaned before Sloane finally lost his shit. "Will you all just *shut the fuck up?*"

The entire truck went silent.

"We have an extremely grave situation on our hands and little time in which to resolve it, and you're fucking

bitching about who's dating who? Unless you have a solu-
tion, I don't want to hear a peep out of any of you. Un-fuck-
ing-believable."

The speakers on the surveillance console turned on
with a beep, and Cael frowned. "What the hell?" He hadn't
turned anything on.

"Destructive Delta, come in!"

"Austen?" How the hell did he patch himself into the
console, and why wasn't he calling them through their
earpieces? The urgency in Austen's tone had Cael's
instincts on high alert. Something was going on.

"Brace for impact!"

"Harness!" Sloane shouted. No one questioned Sloane's
orders. They all strapped into their harnesses within
seconds. "Austen, what's going on?"

"Hijack! I repeat, you're about to get—"

Cael's head shot up in time to see the headlights of a
colossal Mack truck speeding right for them before it hit.

The world fell into silence.

His body jerked fiercely, a sharp pain jolting through
his neck and limbs. There was a burst of noise and chaos
before nothingness consumed him.

EVERYTHING HURT.

Cael groaned at the pounding in his head. He blinked a
few times and forced his eyes open after a great deal of
effort, his vision blurred. Rubbing his eyes, he tried again.
Around him he heard groans, and someone sucked in a
sharp breath. *What happened?* Carefully, he pushed
himself to his feet, the floor clanking beneath him. What
the hell? He dropped his gaze, frowning at the weapons

cage beneath his boots. Hadn't he been strapped into his chair? Something brushed the top of his head, and he looked up, a choked gasp escaping him. Rosa hung from the ceiling unconscious, a thin line of blood trailing down the side of her face. No, wait. It wasn't the ceiling. The BearCat was on its side. It all came back to him. They'd been rammed.

Cael took in the damage around him. Oh God, his team. Rosa was unconscious. Letty was groaning and coming around, a nasty bruise on her forehead. Ash was cutting through his harness, and Dex was—Where the hell was his brother?

"Sloane, wake up!"

Cael turned, his eyes widening at Dex on his knees next to Sloane, who was out and on the floor, his torn straps hanging from the truck's wall. The impact had been enough to dislodge the bench's backrest and Sloane's harness. Cael carefully climbed off the cage and went to Sloane's side. He felt for a pulse, hanging his head in relief when he felt the steady beat. "He's just out. His pulse is steady."

The sound of machine-gun fire erupted outside, and Ash handed the armored case to Cael. "Hold this for me. Dex, help me get the girls down."

Dex removed the tactical knife from his thigh rig and helped Ash cut Rosa and Letty out of their harnesses. Outside a small explosion rocked the truck, and everyone stilled.

"Shit. We're under attack." Dex tried to look out one of the ballistic windows now above them, but he had no luck. All they could see was sky and smoke.

"Shit. Everyone, move your asses," Ash ordered, hurrying to free the girls. Together he and Dex lowered them to the floor, Letty now fully awake and trying to get

Rosa to come around. Sloane groaned, and Dex went to his side, helping him sit up.

"What the hell?"

"We were rammed," Dex said, looking up past Cael and cursing under his breath.

They all followed his gaze, finding Hobbs standing there, his eyes glassy as he held Calvin limp in his arms, a small trickle of blood coming out of Calvin's ear. *Oh no. No.* Cael went to Calvin's side and felt for a pulse. It was weak, but it was there.

"He needs a hospital," Cael said, turning toward his team when he heard Seb's voice coming in through their earpieces.

"Destructive Delta, come in!"

A chorus of gunfire resounded around them, and Ash entered his security code into the weapons cage, removed tranq rifles, and passed them out. He tapped his earpiece. "Seb! What the fuck is going on out there?"

"It's a hijacking. We're under heavy fire. I make roughly forty armed hostiles. My team and I are coming to get you out of there. Taylor's backing us up. Wait for my signal. You can't stay in there. They're coming for the package."

"Shit." Sloane stood and grabbed his helmet off the floor, securing it on his head before picking up an MP5 machine gun from the weapons cage and one of the ballistic shields from the floor. "Everyone gear up. We gotta get to a secure location." He turned to Hobbs, who was worriedly looking down at Calvin in his arms. In the distance, they heard sirens.

"Hobbs, give Calvin to Rosa and Letty. We need you."

Hobbs looked uncertain, his troubled gaze going down to Calvin in his arms. Letty stepped to him and put her hand to his arm.

"We'll take care of him. Rosa's going to look him over, okay?"

Hobbs nodded and laid Calvin gently on the floor, leaving him to Rosa and Letty, who quickly checked him over. Rosa went to work administering first aid, telling Letty they needed to get Calvin to an ambulance.

Ash turned to Cael, his expression determined and scaring the hell out of Cael. He knew what was coming, and he didn't want to hear it.

"Whatever the hell is going on, it's all about this." He pointed to the case before putting his gloved hand to Cael's cheek. "No matter what happens, you get this case out of here. You hear me? You get it out and somewhere secure."

Cael shook his head. "I can't leave you."

"You have to. Whatever's in there is important enough for them to kill for. We can't let them have it." He slid his hand down behind Cael's neck. "We'll get through this."

He kissed Cael briefly but passionately before pulling back. With a wink, he picked up a helmet and handed it to Cael, who secured it on his head as Dex did the same. They all geared up, with Dex, Cael, and the girls the only ones not picking up shields.

"All right," Sloane came in over their earpieces. "Dex, you and Cael get that to a secure location, and once you do, you call the sarge. Letty, Rosa, you take Calvin and the three of you get somewhere safe. Get him to an ambulance. The three of us will help Seb and the others cover you. Got it?"

Dex readied his rifle. He took hold of Sloane's chin, pulled him down, and kissed him. "You be safe."

With a nod, Sloane hit the com button on his vest. "Seb, we're ready. We've got one man down and need to get him to an ambulance. Dex and Cael have the package. We'll cover them so they can get the hell out of here."

"Copy that."

"Here we go!"

Sloane opened the back doors, and everyone rushed out of the truck. It was like they'd entered a war zone. There was smoke and debris everywhere, bullets flying, and flash bangs going off. There were masked men and Therians shooting at THIRDS agents from behind parked cars and the Mack truck that had been used to ram the BearCat.

Sloane, Ash, and Hobbs used their shields to form a protective barrier around their five smaller members, deflecting fire and shooting as they all quickly worked in unison to get behind the truck for cover. Seb and three other members of his team hurried over, shields in hand.

"I've tried calling dispatch, and no one is answering. What the fuck is going on?"

"I don't know," Sloane replied, firing at the hijackers. Cael couldn't see past his teammates' shields. The circle grew bigger, with Seb and the other agents joining. Horns honked, people screamed, and Ash broke formation.

"Take cover!"

Cael managed to get a glimpse of a tactical vehicle heading their way before Ash grabbed him around the waist and hoisted him off his feet. With the case in one hand, Cael snatched his Glock from his thigh rig and shot at the asshole aiming at Ash, hitting him in the vest twice and knocking the guy off his feet. Cael and Dex were pushed together behind a parked car as the arriving tactical vehicle that had been looking to run them over came skidding to a halt, armed men emerging from its back doors, one of them about Ash's height with a mask on his face.

"Hand over the case!"

His voice sounded familiar, but he was using some kind of scrambler or enhancer.

Sloane tapped his com. "Rosa, Letty, where are you?"

"Taylor got us to an ambulance. We're leaving Calvin and—"

"No," Sloane ordered. "You stick with him. Find out what the hell is going on with dispatch and get us some backup."

"We can't leave you guys out there."

"That's an order, Santiago!"

"Copy that."

"Where's Hobbs?" Sloane said, looking around. He tapped his com. "Hobbs? What's your twenty?"

"Take him!"

Cael edged toward the end of the car, looking over Sloane's shoulder in time to see Hobbs taking down three armed men as he protected his brother, who lay unconscious at his feet.

Seb!

Hobbs's shield was on the ground out of his reach, but he didn't let that stop him from raising hell and protecting Seb. He let out a fierce roar as the Human gunmen approached with rifles in hand. One launched at Hobbs, and Hobbs lifted the guy off his feet. He flung him at two of the other armed men. Around them, Seb's team was trying to get to them, but they were being kept busy by the rest of the hijackers, along with Taylor's team, who was clearing the area of the panicking and screaming citizens.

"Fucking tranq him!" the large masked Therian shouted while someone took aim.

Cael opened his mouth to warn Hobbs when a gloved hand clamped over it. Ash kept him quiet, and they watched in horror as a dart hit Hobbs in the leg, another in the arm. Hobbs crumpled to the ground beside his brother. Whatever they were using, it wasn't standard issue. Cael had never seen a tiger Therian go down that quickly.

Oh God. Hobbs.

Cael moved Ash's hand away from his mouth, his voice hoarse. "We can't let them take him!"

"We're outnumbered," Sloane said, grabbing a magazine from his vest and reloading his rifle. "We need to keep that case safe."

It took seven Humans to move an unconscious Hobbs. They left Seb behind. Why would they take Hobbs and leave Seb? Ash interrupted his thoughts and turned to him.

"You and Dex need to make a run for it. We'll cover you."

Cael had no time to respond. Ash grabbed hold of his vest and hauled him to his feet along with Dex. He released them, snatched his shield up, and along with Sloane came out from behind the car. Ash roared and charged the group of men heading for them. He and Sloane worked together, covering each other's backs and using their shields to slam into the Human hijackers. The men went flying. Cael had never seen anything like it. The hijackers doubled in number, and Cael gasped when Ash was shot in the leg with a tranq.

"Ash!"

"Run!" Ash shouted, dropping onto one knee. Sloane backed up against him, helping him up with one arm when Sloane's shield clattered to the ground. A tranq hit Sloane's arm. Another hit Ash in the same spot, then in the other leg. He crumpled to the asphalt with Sloane landing on top of him.

The large Therian walked toward them. "Take them!"

"No." Cael shook his head when Dex grabbed Cael's vest and pulled.

"We have to go!"

Cael and Dex sped down Ninth Avenue and into the commercial building site on the corner of Ninth and West Thirty-First Street. Their boots kicked up dirt and splashed through mud puddles as they dodged the bullets whizzing around them. They sprinted in between containers, through massive tubes, and jumped over cinder blocks. Shots rang out all around them, but they couldn't stop. Cael led the way, knowing Dex could follow the reflecting letters of his name on the back of his vest. The Therians would be able to see him regardless of the letters, and hopefully the Human gunmen would knock themselves out against something, the assholes.

Cael knew exactly where they were, and he thanked the city's never-ending construction for the first time in his life. He knew where they could hide, rest for a while until they could get a hold of someone to come get them. But first they had to lose these bastards.

"Dex! Leapfrog!" Cael called out behind him, holding out the case at his side and slowing enough for Dex to overtake him. Dex snatched the case and ran, skidding when he came to the chain-link fence at the end and getting on his hands and knees. Cael picked up speed, leapt on his brother's back and his tac vest, snagged a hold of the fencing, and climbed. They'd done this hundreds of times as kids in the park. Cael landed on the other side, catching the case that Dex tossed over before he climbed the fence. Dex was as adept at climbing as any Therian. He'd spent his childhood getting into mischief by climbing whatever he could reach.

They took off, the hijackers forced to climb or break through the fence, giving them enough of a lead. Cael ran across Tenth Avenue into the 10 Hudson Yards office tower currently under construction. It was a maze of steel girders, cranes, equipment, coverings, tubes, mixers, wiring, and shrouded with enough floors, rooms, and darkness for them to hide in. They ducked through some scaffolding, and Cael clipped the case to his tac vest before he started to climb, Dex close behind. They climbed up the scaffolding and into the building, careful to avoid falling into any unfinished areas. Cael could hear the shouts of the men down below as they tried to find their way. Cael took Dex's hand so they could venture farther into the darkness, where the Human hijackers would have trouble chasing them even with their flashlights. They climbed up and up, until Cael heard nothing but the faint sounds of the city. When they finally thought it was safe, he bent over to catch his breath, his heart pounding fiercely. It was dark all around them, save for the rays of moonlight shining through the small gaps in the plastic coverings.

Dex gasped a lungful of air as he paced. "Fuck." He ran his hands through his hair. "*Fuck.*"

Cael didn't have to ask Dex what he was thinking. His brother was worried about Sloane, same as Cael was worried about Ash. "Why do you think they took them?" Cael asked.

"I don't know, but that wasn't by accident," Dex said, taking a seat on a cinder block to catch his breath. "They purposefully shot at them, and that one guy, he shouted at his men to take them. They were under orders to take them." He leaned his elbows on his knees, his head falling into his hands. "This is so fucked."

Cael couldn't agree more. Normally the whole of their organization would have been out there by now making it rain fire and brimstone, getting everyone to safety. The hijackers would have been down and out. Even if dispatch was incommunicado, there was no way they wouldn't have heard of a damn hijacking in the middle of the city involving tactical vehicles and a Mack truck.

Something stirred in the shadows, and Cael removed his Glock and aimed at the figure heading toward them.

"THIRDS! Hands up or I'll shoot!"

"Easy there, pal." Austen emerged, his hands held up in front of him.

"Austen?" Dex stood, his fists at his sides. "What the fuck are you doing here?"

Austen kept his distance, his hands still held up. "I'm here to take that off your hands."

He nodded toward the case, and Dex put himself between Austen and Cael. Cael swiftly unclipped the case from his vest and held on tight.

Dex was having none of it. "Fuck you. We were hijacked, and you want us to hand this over to you?"

Austen frowned at him. "I was the one who warned you about the hijack, dumbass."

"That means fuck all," Dex snapped. "You could be working with them and did that so we'd trust you. So we'd give you the case if you asked for it. Well, it's not going to happen."

"I'm not working with them," Austen insisted, taking a step toward them.

Dex had his gun out and aimed at Austen's vest in a heartbeat.

"Whatever. We're not giving you anything. We're waiting for backup."

"Backup's not coming."

"What?" Cael couldn't believe that. There was no way the THIRDS wouldn't send teams out. Their agents were down, the streets were in chaos with armed men running around, and who knew how many were hurt.

"The THIRDS have been notified of a traffic accident. Your team leaders have reported in that everything is under control. The situation has been contained. The area has been cleared and swept."

Cael gaped at him. "That's bullshit. Two of our team leaders are down."

"It's been cleared," Austen assured them. "The hijackers are gone. Our operatives have taken care of everything."

"*Your* operatives?" Dex shook his head, a look of disbelief on his face. "It's Sparks, isn't it? She set us up."

Oh God, it was true. Cael couldn't believe it. They'd been set up. Who knew what connections Sparks had used to contain the situation.

"Set up? What the hell are you talking about?" Austen stared at them, stunned.

"Sparks," Dex repeated angrily, his gun still in his hand. "She gave us these orders. Worked out the routes, everything. I didn't want to believe it, but... *Fuck!*"

"Where the hell have you been getting your intel?"

Dex told Austen everything, from what they'd learned from Shultzon to Ward and the meds. Cael held firmly on to the case. He didn't know if they could trust Austen. He wanted to, he really did. They needed all the help they could get on this.

"Shit." Austen shook his head, his lips pressed into a thin line.

"You knew?" Dex took a step toward Austen.

"Yeah, I knew."

Dex raised his gun again, aiming at Austen. "So you *are* working with her."

"I am. But it's not what you think."

"Jesus Christ, Austen! Did you see what happened back there? We're being hunted."

Dex threw a hand up, and Cael felt his gut twist. This couldn't be happening. Granted, there was a lot they didn't know about Austen and what he did, but could he really betray all of them like this?

"Dex," Austen warned.

"God knows what they're going to do to Sloane, and you're telling me you're working for the person responsible?"

"Dex."

"How could you do that to us?"

Austen's expression hardened. "Would you shut the fuck up for two fucking seconds!"

Dex promptly shut his mouth.

"Yes, I'm working with Sparks. No, she's not who everyone thinks she is. And I swear on my fuzzy sacks if this gets out, I will beat the shit out of both of you. I don't care who your boyfriends are."

Cael opened his mouth to reply but thought better of it. Now was not the time. How Austen knew Ash was his boyfriend wasn't really important right now.

"Sparks is a Tin Man."

Dex frowned. "Like, *Wizard of Oz* Tin Man?"

"Yes and no. It's just a nickname, 'cause the Tin Man had no heart, and well, TIN operatives aren't known for being warm and cuddly. Anyway, Sparks is part of TIN— Therian Intelligence Network. Sort of the Therian version of the CIA. They exist, but technically they don't. We SSAs work for them. Back in the '90s when the THIRDS opened their doors, Sparks was planted in the THIRDS to make sure everything remained on the up and up. The THIRDS had the potential to wield a shit ton of power, and with the military to fund them and back them up, it made them a force to be reckoned with. Where there's that kind of power, you'll find those looking to either abuse it or exploit it. Someone in the Branch of Therian Defense has decided to fund a little side project using the THIRDS as a scapegoat. That is the project." Austen craned his neck to point at the case in Cael's hands.

"What is it?"

"The drug you have in your hand is called Peitharchia7. It has the ability to suppress the Human side of a Therian. It also enhances the feral side, making the Therian susceptible to suggestion and, more importantly, commands."

"Fuck. I was right," Dex groaned, returning his Glock to his thigh rig.

"And some asshat in the government wants to use it to control Therian soldiers. Take away the Human consciousness but leave the Human body. We all know it's against Geneva Convention protocols for Therian soldiers to fight in Therian form. This gives them a way around that. It also means that intel will be hard as fuck to extract, because once that shit wears off, the Therian soldier won't remember jack. Hard to get intel from someone who has no memory of what he's done."

"Is it the same drug Isaac injected Dex with?" Cael asked, taking a seat on the cinder block his brother had vacated, the case secured between his knees.

Austen shook his head. "That was a watered-down version. The shit you've got there is far more potent. It will fuck a Human up. It's so dangerous, it has to be used with a preliminary drug."

"Hold up. There's another drug?"

Just as Dex said the words, it struck Cael. "Thelxinomine."

Austen nodded. "You guessed it. Peitharchia7 won't work on its own. It would potentially kill the Therian soldier or fuck his head up badly, rendering him unfit for duty. The Therian needs to be prepped first with a preliminary drug that will—with enough doses—short-circuit the Human side of the brain, leaving the feral half in control and susceptible to Peitharchia7, which will allow them to be controlled."

"Is the Thelxinomine in here as well?" Cael asked, looking down at the case.

"No. Sparks had me hunt down that shit and swipe it. I just collected the last of it."

"From where?" Cael peered at Austen. He had an idea of what Austen was about to say.

"Your boyfriends' desks."

"This gets better and better," Dex groaned. "So Sloane and Ash were on the preliminary drug. Was Ward prescribing that shit to Therians as a painkiller?"

"To specific Therians. Therians who made ideal candidates for the program. What better place to find Therian soldiers than the THIRDS? I'm guessing plucking Therian soldiers already enlisted would draw too much attention, and obviously they couldn't just walk up to their chosen candidates and be like, 'Hey, you wanna be the first test subject of this new unsanctioned military-grade mind-control drug that could potentially fuck you up?'"

Cael processed everything they'd learned from Austen. He still had so many unanswered questions, and his thoughts kept going to Ash. He prayed Ash was all right. A lump formed in his throat at the thought of him being taken.

He looked up at Austen. "That's why they took Sloane and the others. To use them for this program."

"Yeah. Defense agents are the easy choice. Your boys are First Gen. Perfectly healthy Therians. Strong Alphas. Ideal soldiers."

Dex frowned. "Hobbs wasn't on Thelxinomine. Was he?"

Austen shoved his hands into his pockets, his expression sympathetic. "Your boy Hobbs takes meds for his anxiety. They were switched out three weeks ago when he went for a refill of his prescription. I swiped his a week ago, but that shit had already worked its way into his system, which is why he's been experiencing severe setbacks." This time it was Austen who looked puzzled. "To be honest, I would have expected Seb to be on the list. He's Pre-First Gen and takes a shit ton of Therian medication, but he's fucking huge and strong as a brick shithouse. There was ample opportunity to switch out one of his meds, but for some reason he wasn't targeted. Granted, any Therians older than Sloane and Ash were born before all the medical research, so they'd be a mixed bag. There's no telling what could go wrong."

Cael cocked his head to one side, studying Austen, his stance and mannerisms. *You have got to be kidding me.* "The male nurse who made off with the drugs I found in Ward's office? That was *you!*"

Austen wriggled his eyebrows. "Yes, it was. A little hair dye, some contacts, and a dash of makeup to cover up my classification." He tapped the tattoo on his neck marking him as a cheetah Therian. "It's all part of the magic."

"And Ward's body disappearing? Was that all part of the *magic* too?" Cael asked irritably.

"No. That was my associates."

"Why did Sparks pull us off the case?"

"She didn't want to put you in danger."

Cael threw his arms up, motioning around them. "Yeah, okay. She didn't really have a choice. We had to move the drug out before it disappeared. We lost an operative getting it out of the facility. Ten years, man. We've been after this shit for ten years. When it was time to move out, Sparks picked the three teams she trusted most."

"If Sparks is on our side," Dex said, "then who's been working on the control drug?"

Austen arched an eyebrow at him. "I'll let that percolate in your head for a moment."

Dex and Cael came to the same conclusion simultaneously. They both looked at each other, with Dex being the first to vocalize their thoughts.

"Shultzon."

"Somebody give the boy a teddy bear. Yes, Shultzon. He was the one working from the First Gen Research Facility that had supposedly closed down. That day you boys took down Pearce and Sparks showed up, she wasn't pissed because she'd been kept in the dark about the facility. She was pissed Shultzon managed to clear out the lab of anything that might incriminate him. He took his show on the road. TIN had an agent undercover with Shultzon for ten years, waiting for the guy to finish the drug and present it to his superiors. Shultzon is the puppet. TIN wants the puppet master. You can bet your ass this isn't the only unsanctioned project going on."

"That son of a bitch," Dex ground out angrily as he started to pace. "Now I hate him even more. What he did wasn't enough? I should have trusted my gut, but I kept thinking it was me being overprotective. That fucker."

"Hey, calm down." Cael stood and pulled his brother in

close. "It's okay. We'll get them back." He felt Austen's arms around him. "What are you doing?"

"Oh, I'm sorry. You're having a broment. I thought it was a group hug. My bad."

He pulled away, and Cael released Dex.

"Dude, you're weird."

"Says the guy related to *that* dude." Austen pointed a finger at Dex.

Cael picked up the case. "If TIN has the power to cover all this shit up, why didn't they move the drug themselves? Why get the THIRDS to do it?

"The facility Shultzon was using belongs to the THIRDS. One of hundreds across the country. His project was buried under a shit ton of fake legitimate research projects. If Shultzon got wind that TIN was moving in, he'd blow the whole thing wide open and expose TIN. They couldn't have that. We're talking national security."

"So the THIRDS take the fall. Is that it?" Dex let out a snort of disgust.

"That's the way the Cheesy Doodle crumbles, Daley. There's an order to things, and if someone's gotta take one for the team, it's gonna be the little guy."

"So now what?" Cael could have sworn he heard something.

"Now, you duck."

Neither of them questioned Austen's casual order. They ducked, an arrow flying over their heads before they heard a scream and a gurgling sound. Standing, they turned to find a Human gunman lying on the floor in a pool of blood with an arrow sticking out of his heart.

"Guess there was a straggler," Austen murmured.

"What the fuck?"

Dex took Cael's arm, pulling him close as they both

gaped at Sparks as she emerged from the shadows dressed in a formfitting black leather jacket, pants, high-heeled boots, and in her hand, a high-tech bow.

"Holy shit!" Dex turned to Cael. "Dude, did Sparks just shank that guy with an arrow?" He turned back to Sparks. "What the fuck is going on?"

"Good job, Austen."

Austen gave her a two fingers salute. "Ma'am."

"Are you two all right?" Sparks asked, collapsing the bow and clipping it to her thigh rig.

Cael was having trouble finding his words. His brain had ceased functioning.

"Yes. Sort of. No."

Apparently, so had his brother's brain.

"I take it Austen has filled you in?" She motioned for them to follow, and after some hesitation, they did. Cael held the case tight in his hand as they followed Sparks through the barely lit floor.

"What's Shultzon going to do with Sloane, Ash, and Hobbs?" Cael asked her.

"He's going to use the drug on them. The hijackers are mercenaries for hire. Shultzon ordered them to retrieve specific agents. Selected candidates for the program. They were supposed to have been retrieved at a later date in a far more inconspicuous way, but Shultzon was left with no choice. Considering Shultzon's history with Sloane and Ash, along with their record at the THIRDS as top agents, I'm not surprised he chose them. He knows them inside and out. Knows what their bodies can take, what they respond to."

"But... we have the drug," Dex said.

Sparks stopped and turned to them.

"That's correct, Agent Daley. And any moment,

Shultzon is going to be calling you. He's going to tell you where to take the drug. If you don't deliver the drug to the location and follow his instructions, he's going to put a bullet in your boyfriend's head."

Dex let out a shaky laugh. "With all due respect, Lieutenant, Sloane and I aren't—"

"Can it, Agent Daley. I work for Therian Intelligence. You really think I'm not going to know when my agents are in a relationship? I know everything. Whole damn team is sleeping with each other. Rosa and Letty are the only ones not breaking protocol. I mean, there's a lot of sleeping around going on in Unit Alpha, but you guys take the cake."

"When you say everything..." Dex prompted.

Sparks narrowed her eyes at him. "I mean *everything*. Your relationship with Sloane, the fact he's moving in with you, when you decided to play Batman and orchestrated an unsanctioned mission including Sebastian Hobbs and the rest of your team. I know about your naps during assembly, the gummy bears in your desk's top right-hand drawer, along with the Cheesy Doodles, the Peanut M&M's, the pretzels, plantain chips, and I seriously hope you listen to Agent Brodie about changing your diet." She turned and started walking again.

"Okay, about the unsanctioned mission," Dex said, catching up to her long-legged strides. "I forced Seb into it. Please, I'll take whatever disciplinary measures you see fit, but don't penalize him."

"I have no intention of disciplining Agent Sebastian Hobbs. He's an exceptional team leader with the potential to do great things. Now's not really the time for this. We're all going to sit down and have a little chat when this is over. Shultzon is going to call and demand you deliver the drug, or he's going to kill Sloane."

"So what do I say?"

"You say what your heart is desperate to say. Say 'Where do you want me to deliver it?' And then you're going to take it there."

"But it'll clearly be a trap."

"Of course it will be. Shultzon has no intention of handing over your teammates or losing the drug. He plans to use it on them and get them transported. Lucky for us, Shultzon is paranoid, and let's face it, not all there. He didn't commit the formula to solid medium in hope of keeping it safe. It's all in his head. There's no time for him to recreate the drug, which is why he needs the supply we have." Sparks stopped beside the construction elevator. She opened the steel door and motioned for them to step inside. They did as asked, and she closed the door behind them. "Agent Maddock, I hope you're ready for what you're about to face."

"Yes, ma'am." Cael didn't know what part he had to play in whatever was coming, only that he needed to do everything within his power to get Ash and the rest of their team out of there safely. Whatever Sparks wanted from him, he'd do it.

"Good, because your ex-boyfriend will be there."

Cael's heart plummeted. "Excuse me?"

"Don Fuller." Sparks turned to him, her expression void of any emotion. "He's the mercenary Shultzon hired to grab your teammates. Why do you think he showed up at Deka-tria? He wanted to see what he was up against. I trust you won't let that impede your performance."

Cael felt Dex squeeze his arm reassuringly. Fuller was a mercenary? How... *What?* Cael was having trouble processing this information.

"Agent Maddock, Don Fuller was never cut out to be a

THIRDS agent, and his connections while in prison allowed him to become a gun for hire. Now before you start blaming yourself for his debut into the world of mercenaries, Don Fuller would have ended up with a gun in his hand one way or another. We have the psych evals to prove it. You, however, *are* a THIRDS agent, and as a THIRDS agent, it's your job to bring Therians like Fuller to justice. It's up to him how he ends up there." Her steel-blue eyes studied him, her jawline set. "What's it going to be, Agent Maddock? Are you going to show him the formidable agent you've become, or are you going to once again allow him control over you?"

Cael clenched his jaw. That son of a bitch. Cael could see that bastard's smug face, reveling in Cael's heartache and suffering at losing Ash. He knew Fuller. Knew he'd laugh at Cael and tell him how pathetic he was, how he couldn't save his own boyfriend. How he was weak. Cael felt his anger rising. He met Sparks's gaze, the words coming from his mouth all but spat out. "I'm going to take him down if it's the last thing I do."

Sparks smiled in approval. "Good. Hold on to your socks, boys. This ride's about to get a little crazy."

ELEVEN

WHERE THE HELL WAS HE?

Ash groaned and rubbed his face. His arms felt heavy and sluggish. Why was he having trouble remembering?

"Looks like Sleeping Beauty's waking up."

That voice... Ash's eyes flew open, and he kicked out, his boots hitting metal bars. He tried to get up, but his body felt heavy, and a wave of dizziness washed over him. Throwing a hand out, his fingers touched cold steel.

"What the fuck?" A familiar terror washed over him. He was in a cage. He scrambled back and forced himself onto shaky legs. His world spun, his vision blurred, and his stomach threatened to empty itself, but he pushed that all back as he thrust his palms hard against the roof. He kicked at the bars, his panic growing. *He was in a fucking cage.* It was tall enough for him to stand up in, yet he felt like he was suffocating. Oh God, he remembered the last time he'd been in a cage.

"Hey there."

Ash's head shot up, and he snarled. "Fuller."

Fuller motioned to the cage around him. "Bring back any memories?"

Ash launched himself at the bars, throwing an arm out in the hopes of ripping Fuller to pieces. "I'm going to tear you apart with my bare hands, you motherfucker!"

Fuller threw his head back and laughed. "Oh shit. You're a funny guy. I can see why Cael likes you."

A lewd smile came onto Fuller's face, and it made Ash sick to his stomach.

"When you've been reduced to nothing but a circus attraction, jumping through hoops at the command of your new master, I'll be there to console Cael. Poor thing. He'll be absolutely devastated, vulnerable, in need of someone with a firm hand."

"You touch him, and I'll fucking kill you!"

Fuller's smug grin never left his face. "It's like looking in a mirror."

Ash tried to control his anger, but it was difficult when there was nothing he wanted more than to beat the ever-living shit out of the Therian before him. "Fuck you, asshole. I'm nothing like you."

"You keep telling yourself that."

"Stop antagonizing him."

Ash froze. "Shultzon?"

Shultzon walked into the room and stopped outside of Ash's cage out of arm's reach, a warm smile on his face. "Hello, Ash. Look at you. It's like when we first met."

The back of Ash's eyes stung, but he quickly blinked the tears away and recovered from the blow. "How could you?"

"You say that like I've betrayed you," Shultzon said, sounding hurt. "Can't you see? You boys have been chosen. I've been so impressed with how far you've come, with everything you've achieved, there was no question who I wanted for this project."

"Project?" Wait, *boys?* Ash looked to his left, his gut clenching when he saw Hobbs out cold on the floor of the cage next to him. He turned to his right and shook his head. *Sloane.* Ash rushed to the end of his cage, his fingers gripping the bars tight. He slid down to his knees and tried to reach through the bars into Sloane's cage. "Sloane! Come on, buddy, wake up!"

"Congratulations, son," Shultzon declared. "You're about to become the next step in Therian soldier evolution."

Ash had no idea what the hell Shultzon was talking about, and he didn't care. What he did know was that he and his friends were locked up like animals while Shultzon prepared to do God knew what to them. Ash couldn't let them get away with this. He needed to think of a way out of here. Shultzon went off with Fuller in tow, scrolling through a tablet. While they were busy, Ash checked his pockets, not surprised to find they'd taken everything off him, leaving him in his tac pants, black undershirt, socks, and boots. Wait... He discreetly glanced down. They'd left his belt on. Fuckwits. Ash held back a grin. Now all he had to do was wait for the opportunity to make his move. He took in everything around him. From the large lab filled with equipment similar to the one in the research facility to the same chair Shultzon used to strap him and Sloane to when they were kids.

Shultzon stopped in front of Hobbs's cage and frowned. "This isn't Sebastian Hobbs."

Fuller crouched down to study Hobbs. "You said Agent Hobbs. This is Agent Hobbs."

"You idiot!" Shultzon fumed. "This is Ethan, the younger Hobbs! I wanted Sebastian, the middle sibling!"

"How many fucking Hobbses are there? You never said anything about there being more than one. Besides, they're both tiger Therian Defense agents. What fucking difference does it make?"

Shultzon looked stricken. "Wait. Is this the Hobbs you had Ward give the medication to?"

"Like I said, I didn't know there was more than one fucking Hobbs. What does it matter?"

Shultzon threw his hands up in frustration, looking like he was about to throttle Fuller. "It matters because the older Hobbs is a stronger specimen. His disabilities are physical and easily controlled. I need soldiers with a strong mind as well as physical strength for Peitharchia7 to achieve optimum performance. This Hobbs is broken," Shultzon spat out. "Absolutely useless." He tapped his head. "His disabilities are psychological."

That son of a bitch. If Ash got his hands on him, he was going to show him broken.

"So what do you want me to do with him?" Fuller asked.

"Just leave him. I'll figure something out. Bring Sloane Brodie. Put him in the chair. I want him prepped and ready to go the moment they arrive with the drug."

What? No. Ash dropped down in front of his bars next to Sloane's cage and kicked at them with both feet. "Sloane, wake up!" He kicked repeatedly, his boots forcing the bars to vibrate and clatter. "Sloane!"

Fuller tapped his earpiece and called in three men. They opened Sloane's cage, grabbed him, and dragged him out.

"No. No!" Ash threw his arm out between the iron bars, his hand managing to grip the tips of Sloane's fingers. "Sloane, wake up!"

"Ash..." Sloane groaned, struggling to rouse himself. The men lifted him and carried him toward the chair.

"Don't you fucking touch him!" Ash screamed, slamming himself against the bars. The cage remained unmoved. "I'm going to kill every last one of you sons of bitches!" He had to get to Sloane. He couldn't fail him. Couldn't let them take him away.

"Sloane..."

The name was barely whispered, but Ash heard it clear as day. He stopped and turned to find Hobbs standing in his cage, his hands gripping the bars tight and his green eyes filled with terror as he watched them carrying Sloane to the chair. Ash turned his attention back to the men who'd finished strapping down Sloane's wrists and ankles. One guy was about to fasten a strap around Sloane's head when an alarm shrieked. Ash took a step back, preparing for a fight.

Shultzon smiled. "Looks like the boys have arrived with the package. Fuller, get your men into position. Retrieve the case. Keep Sparks and her agents busy until I administer the drug. I need to inject Sloane and Ash, get them ready for transport. They're our priority. Nothing else matters. You'll receive your payment once we're successful."

"Yeah, yeah. I heard you the first ten times. Maybe you should've been a little more careful," Fuller grumbled. "Then we wouldn't have a shitload of TIN operatives trying to castrate us."

Shultzon pushed his glasses up his nose. "I hardly expect you to understand. I suspected a traitor in the lab, and until I could discover who it was, I couldn't take any chances with the formula. I need to put in a call to the man upstairs and make sure the helicopter arrives on time."

Fuller headed for the door with Shultzon and the rest of

the men in tow. Shultzon paused and pointed a finger
at Ash.

"You behave yourself. Those steel bars are Therian
strength. So are the straps secured around Sloane. I'll be
back in a moment." He shook his head as he joined Fuller.
"We're going to have to sedate him. He's always been
temperamental."

The moment they left the room, Ash hurried to the door
of his cage. "Sloane," Ash hissed. He swiftly went about
removing his belt. "Sloane!"

Sloane groaned and moved his head, his eyes blinking
open. He looked confused and dazed. When he realized
something wasn't right, he tried to sit up but found himself
unable to.

"Sloane!"

"Ash?" Sloane pulled against the straps. "What the
fuck?" He gritted his teeth and jerked at his restraints. "Ash,
what's going on? Where are we?"

"We're in Shultzon's lab. Motherfucker was behind
this shit all along. We need to get the fuck out of here
before he comes back. I think the control drug is back in
the building. Shultzon's going to inject us with it for some
fucking program. I don't know. What I do know is
Shultzon was the one working on the drug, and that
asshole Fuller is here."

"Sloane?"

Sloane stilled. "Hobbs?" He cursed under his breath.
"It's okay, buddy. We're here with you. We'll find a way out
of this."

"Sloane, you have to shift," Ash said, taking apart his
belt buckle.

"I can't."

"You have to."

"I don't know if I'll be able to control him. What if I can't, and I end up hurting you or Hobbs?"

"Fuck that," Ash spat out. "You can control him. Look at me."

Sloane turned his head, his eyes filled with worry and fear. Ash understood. He was right there with his friend, but the alternative was worse. So much worse.

"Shultzon said the drug was here. Who do you think brought it? Who would be the first person to give everything in order to save you?"

Sloane's eyes widened.

"Your mate is out there. He needs you to get your shit together. Are you going to lie there and let those assholes get their hands on Dex? Do you know what Fuller will do to him for the sheer fuck of it? Dex helped put him in jail. Fuller will make him suffer. If you don't get your ass out of that chair right fucking now, the next screams you're going to hear will be coming from your boyfriend as Fuller tears him apart."

"No..." Sloane shook his head. He stared up at the ceiling, his teeth gritted. Sweat beaded Sloane's brow, and he flexed his fingers at his sides.

Ash hated what he was doing to his best friend, but it was the only way either of them had a chance of getting through this in time.

"Another Alpha is going to put his hands on your mate. Right now Fuller's probably already smelled you on Dex. We both know how ugly these things can get, and with no one there to stop him..."

Sloane pulled at the restraints, his canines elongating as he let out a feral roar. His back arched up off the chair as he bucked and convulsed, his claws piercing through his skin as he shifted. His black fur grew in as he screamed and roared, twisting his body in a frenzy to free himself. His mass shifted, and he was able to pull his paws free before rolling onto his stomach in his Therian form. Sloane hissed, massive fangs bare, before he let out a roar that echoed through the facility.

Ash turned to look at Hobbs. "You too."

Hobbs shook his head, his arms wrapping around himself as he backed into the farthest corner of the cage.

"Hobbs, look at me, pal. You need to shift and get the hell out of that cage. Your teammates—your *friends*—need you. You can do this. Fuck that asshole. He doesn't know shit about you. You're not broken. So you take meds. Who the fuck doesn't these days? Don't let that judgmental prick make you feel like shit for it. Does Calvin think you're broken?"

Hobbs shook his head.

"No, he doesn't. He thinks you're the coolest fucking guy to walk this earth. He's crazy about you, man."

Hobbs's head shot up to look at him, his eyes wide.

"Come on, bro. You can't hide that kind of shit. He's probably in a hospital somewhere terrified, wondering where the fuck his best friend is." Ash snapped the last piece of metal in his buckle, his fingers bleeding, but he didn't care. He had the pin. He wiped his hands on his pants, reached an arm through the bars, and stuck the pin in the lock to the sound of Hobbs screaming and shifting. Ash concentrated on trying to get the lock picked, his gaze landing on Sloane, who was pacing the floor in front of his cage. Ash had no idea if it was his friend pacing before him or the feral Therian inside Sloane, but right now he had to believe Sloane was stronger than that.

The lock on Ash's cage door clicked open, and he hurried out, coming to a halt when Sloane appeared in front of him. He sniffed the air and Ash before letting out a low mewl and sitting on his haunches. Relief washed through Ash, and he quickly went to work on the lock of Hobbs's cage. Hobbs hissed and paced back and forth.

"Yeah, hold your fucking horses," Ash grumbled. He went as fast as he could, satisfied when there was a click. He'd barely gotten the door open when Hobbs propelled himself against the door, knocking Ash onto his ass. Hobbs landed over him and licked his cheek.

"Fucking gross. Yeah, I'm happy too. Come on, get off." Ash stood and turned to his friends. "Ready?"

There was a collective round of hisses.

"Okay. Let's do this." He had no weapons, but that didn't mean he couldn't get his hands on some. He sidled up to the door and peeked out. The hall was wide, with several closed doors and too many corridors leading into other corridors. At the end there was another door, and on the other side of it an armed guard. It was now or never. He had to find Dex and whoever had come with him. As much as he wished Cael hadn't come, he knew Cael was somewhere in this building. Taking a deep breath, Ash broke into a run down the hallway, his feral teammates behind him. With a growl, Ash slammed into the door at the end, sending the guard on the other side tumbling down. One kick to the head, and the guy was out.

A guard came barreling through a glass door into the hall to his right, and Ash instinctively ducked for cover. An agent dressed in a black suit, tie, and shirt rolled out, got to his feet, and kept running, crossing the corridor and disappearing into another hall with two of Fuller's men on his tail. Who the fuck was that? All at once, everything went to hell, with Fuller's men and agents in black beating the tar out of each other.

Sloane sniffed the air and took off, with Hobbs darting after him. His best friend was trying to pick up Dex's scent. Wherever Dex was, Cael and Fuller would be there.

Ash ran as fast as he could after Sloane and Hobbs. His feral half wanted to break free, but he needed to be Human to confront Fuller.

Those who didn't want to die made a run for it. Feral Therian agents didn't handcuff their attackers. They put them out of commission.

Hobbs launched himself at an asshole with an MP5 machine gun. The guy hit the floor, the gun skidding away from him. Ash made a dive for the gun, snatching it up as he rolled and kept running. Behind him the sounds of men screaming and Felid roars echoed through the hall. Ash shot at anything that moved who wasn't his team or some dude dressed in a black suit. He had no idea who the hell they were, but if they were fighting Fuller's goons, then they were okay in Ash's book. For now. Ash managed to pick up some more ammo and a handheld tranq gun. He shot one large asshole in the leg before dragging him behind a wall. He jabbed the barrel of the MP5 against the guy's neck.

"You have five seconds to give me your vest. Five... Four..."

With a flurry of movement, the guy went to work removing his tac vest.

"Three... Two..."

"Here!" The vest was shoved at Ash, who snatched it up.

"Thanks." He slipped into it and fastened all the straps, finishing just as Hobbs and Sloane sped past him. Ash removed the tranq gun from his waistband and shot the guy in the neck. Hobbs roared, and Ash flinched. Fucking tiger Therians. He'd never get used to their roars. Lion Therians roared louder, but tiger Therians had the fucking scariest roars of all the Felids. There was something about the sound that turned your blood to ice.

Ash rushed out into the hall, not wasting more than one bullet per bastard. Then the piece of shit jammed on him. That was fine. He didn't need it. A small group of Humans approached, and Ash held back a smile. He tossed the gun before he held his hands up high in surrender. Five Humans against one Therian. Ash let out a snort.

"What's so fucking funny?" one growled, approaching him.

"I'm picturing what your face will look like after I've kicked your ass."

"Maybe you haven't noticed, but you're outnumbered. You're going down."

Ash grinned. Outnumbered but not outmatched. He puckered his lips and blew the guy a kiss. "I hope you plan on taking me out to dinner first. I may be fine, but I ain't easy."

The guy charged with a right hook. So fucking predictable. Clearly they'd been ordered to take him alive, or they'd have shot at him by now. Too bad for them. Ash grabbed his wrist with his left hand and thrust his right elbow in the guy's face, breaking his nose. He hung on to the guy and kicked back, catching a second goon in the chest and sending him hurtling to the floor. Spinning toward the guy in his grip, he thrust his elbow back again and caught a third gunman in the face while he front kicked a fourth in the chest. In between each gunman attempting to recover, Ash hit fast and hard. Punch in the kidneys to those stupid enough not to wear a vest, a kick to the knee, shattering it, the guy's howl echoing through the hall among his cohorts' screams. The fifth asshole wasn't as stupid. He came at Ash fast, trying to take out his knee since he couldn't get a hit in above the vest.

Ash put his fists up and shuffled back, parrying and dodging the large man's fists and kicks until the guy was out of breath. Ash grinned.

"My turn." No time to be fancy. Ash charged, threw his arms around his opponent's waist, and lifted him off his feet with a fierce cry. He slammed the guy into the wall with all his weight and swung his elbow against the side of the Human's head before kneeing him in the balls. The man crumpled to the floor as soon as Ash released him.

"Assholes." Ash turned and hurried down the hall, where Sloane had scratched the ever-living fuck out of a gunman who'd aimed his gun at Hobbs. Sloane scratched at the closed door leading to the stairs, and Ash opened the door. They all rushed through, and he followed Sloane as he leapt and ran down the stairs. Looked like they were heading down to the sublevel.

Hang on, sweetheart. I'm coming.

Ash had turned a corner where he ran into Sparks kicking a couple of Fuller's goons' asses. She swiped a leg out, knocking one off his feet and slamming him onto the floor before delivering a blow to the face that put the guy out. Casually, she stood and turned to him.

"Good. You're here."

Where the hell had Sparks learned to fight like that? And was that a bow attached to her thigh rig? He put all that aside. "Where's Cael?"

"Downstairs with Agent Daley."

Ash made to go around her when she stopped him.

"You can't go down there."

"What? Are you crazy? Fuller's down there."

Sloane hissed, and Sparks thrust her finger at him.

"Stand down, Agent Brodie. No one's going anywhere. Agent Maddock and Agent Daley are taking care of it. You will wait for my signal."

"We can't leave them down there alone to face Fuller," Ash growled. If he had to go through Sparks, then he would. He was about ready to when she put her hand on his shoulder.

"Do you have faith in him?"

Ash frowned. "Of course I do, but—"

"You either do or you don't, Keeler." She moved her hand away. "You need to let him fight his own battles."

Like hell he did. What Sparks was saying made sense, but that didn't mean he could stand here and let Cael face that bastard on his own. Cael had been doing great in their training, but they hadn't been at it very long. "I..." Fuck. What was he supposed to do?

"Trust him." Sparks insisted. "And in the meantime, you can help me keep those bastards from reaching your teammates." She nodded behind him to the hoard of goons coming their way. Ash looked down at Sloane.

"What do you say?"

Sloane looked past Sparks to the door that would lead into the subbasement, then behind him. He let out a roar and turned on his heels, charging toward the oncoming men. Ash gave Sparks one last glance.

"I hope you're right about this." With that, he followed Sloane and Hobbs.

CAEL HAD NEVER HATED ANYONE. He'd disliked some people, *really* disliked them, but never truly hated anyone. Until now. The thing Cael's nightmares were made of stood toward the end of the subbasement with a handful of goons. Around them, the place was filled with moldy brick pillars, pipes, crappy lighting, fuse boxes, and a couple of old turbines that looked like they came out of the industrial age.

"Nice to see you again, kitty cat. How's the lip?" Fuller asked with a laugh.

"Fuck you," Cael spat out, his grip tightening on the case in his hand.

"Ooh, isn't that precious. Now be a good boy and hand over the case." Fuller grinned widely as his men readied themselves.

Dex stepped in front of Cael. "If Shultzon wants it, he's going to have to come down here to get it himself."

"Yeah, that's not going to happen," Fuller drawled.

"If he wants this case, he needs to give us assurances that our teammates are safe. That's all we want. He can take whatever the fuck is in there and fuck off for all we care. We want our guys."

Fuller appeared to think about it. He turned and tapped his earpiece, speaking quietly. Cael waited with bated breath. *Please let this work.* With a deep frown, Fuller turned back to them.

"You're in luck," Fuller said gravely, heading for a pair of steel elevator doors to their right. "The doc is on his way."

They waited patiently for the elevator to arrive. When it pinged, the doors opened and Shultzon stepped out. The asshole had the audacity to smile at them.

"Cael, Dex. I would say it's lovely to see you, but I doubt the feeling is mutual. Now I'm in somewhat of a hurry, so if you don't mind." He motioned toward the case. "And please do spare me the speech regarding my betrayal. We'll simply have to agree to disagree on that matter."

Dex shook his head. "How do we know you'll release our teammates?"

Shultzon removed a small keypad from his pocket. "This here will open the cages, releasing your boyfriends. How about a trade? Their freedom for the case."

Cael gritted his teeth in order to keep his mouth shut. That bastard had locked them up in cages?

Dex nodded. "Okay." He turned to Cael. "You sure about this?"

Cael nodded. "Yeah." They didn't exactly have much of a choice. This was the only way to end this. He drew a deep breath and faced Shultzon.

"We meet in the middle. I give you the case, you give me the keypad."

"Deal. And please make it quick, my dear boy. My ride is waiting."

Cael took a deep breath. He thought about everything Fuller had done to him. For almost two years that asshole controlled every part of his life, from what he ate to who he talked to. He'd let Fuller in, let him hurt him, hurt his family, let him get in his head and make him feel worthless. Cael's anguish spread through him, and he used it to fuel his anger. He slowly walked toward Shultzon, who he trusted about as much as he did Fuller. Sparks was waiting on his word.

Cael was perfectly aware of Fuller discreetly shifting behind Shultzon, but Cael continued forward. He held his left hand out as Shultzon reached in his pocket and pulled out the keypad. He held it up for Cael to see. Cael held out the case. The rest went as expected.

Shultzon grabbed the case, and instead of releasing the keypad, he dropped it and snatched Cael's wrist, jerking him back and into Fuller's arms.

"Take care of it!" Shultzon shouted as he made a break for the elevator.

"Cael!" Dex broke into a run toward Cael, only to be waylaid by Fuller's men, who advanced on him. Fuller's arm wrapped around Cael's neck and lifted him off his feet. Cael's fingers dug into Fuller's arm as he coughed and sputtered, his legs kicking out. He stilled in Fuller's grip, ignoring his laughter as he took hold of Cael's head.

"I wish I could say I was sorry, but you and your brother put me in prison. I've been waiting a long time for this."

"Me too," Cael growled, snatching his tactical knife from his thigh rig and stabbing into Fuller's arm. With a howl, Fuller released him, and Cael landed on his feet. He dropped down and kicked back, catching Fuller on his knee and bringing him crashing to the floor. Cael sprang up, readying himself as Fuller pulled the knife from his arm.

"You stupid little shit!" Fuller threw the knife to one side. "I'm going to enjoy tearing you apart with my bare hands."

Cael could see Dex fighting from the corner of his eye. His brother was holding his own against the men. He'd already unarmed one and taken two down. With a grin, Cael motioned for Fuller to advance.

"Aren't we cocky?"

"I'm not afraid of you anymore, you prick."

"We'll see about that."

Fuller let out a fierce roar as he charged Cael, who spun to his side, missing Fuller, who ran past him. Fuller skidded to a halt and turned back, his frustration and growing ire clear on his face. He charged Cael again, and Cael remembered what Ash had told him about using his size to his advantage. He sped right for Fuller, dropping himself to the floor and sliding under Fuller, where he threw a fist, punching him in the balls. Fuller let out a strangled cry and grabbed his groin, his face contorted with pain and rage.

With Fuller doubled over, Cael snapped his fist forward, catching Fuller in the nose. Ash's words rang in his ears, and Cael delivered a fierce, unrelenting assault to Fuller's face and neck, and when Fuller pulled back, Cael jumped and brought down all his weight on Fuller's bent knee, shattering it.

Fuller hit the floor cursing and sputtering blood from his broken nose. He held on to his knee with one hand and reached for his gun with the other. Cael dove for the discarded knife, scooped it up, and hurled it at Fuller, catching him in the throat. A horrible gurgling sound met Cael's ears as Fuller stared wide-eyed at him, his hands grasping at his neck around the embedded knife.

The door ahead of them burst open, and Ash came running in with Sloane, Hobbs, and Sparks trailing behind. Sloane dispatched the last gunman trying to take Dex down. It was over.

Ash ran to Cael's side and threw his arms around him, holding him tight. "Oh thank God." He pulled back and looked him over. "Are you okay?"

Cael nodded, his gaze going to Fuller gurgling and sputtering his last breaths. Ash turned, his expression somber before he pulled Cael against him once more, kissing the top of his head. Dex and Sloane came to join them.

"You okay?" Cael asked his brother. Dex looked a little worse for wear, but other than that, he seemed fine.

Dex gave him a wink. "Never better." He threw his arm around Cael's neck and gave him a squeeze. "I'm real proud of you."

"Thanks, Dex."

Something seemed to dawn on Ash. "Fuck, Shultzon's getting away!"

"No, he's not," Sparks declared. She tapped her earpiece. "Is the package secure? Good." She turned to them with a smile. "Those were my operatives. They were waiting for Shultzon's transport to land on the roof. The moment they did, they subdued the pilot and took out the men on board. Then they took their place. Shultzon believes he's being transported to a secure location. He has no idea it's one of ours. Good work, gentlemen." She scratched the top of Hobbs's head, making him purr.

"So... you planned for him to get away with the case?" Ash asked.

"Yes. Shultzon knew you three had escaped, but he didn't know Cael and Dex were also aware. They acted as if they didn't know. We couldn't rouse Shultzon's suspicions. As far as he knew, Dex and Cael were desperate to get their lovers back alive. With the three of you free, his biggest concern was the drug. He could always get new candidates. He took the case and left Fuller to dispatch anyone left behind so he could get away. My operatives are sweeping the facility." With a scratch behind Sloane's ear, she headed for the doors they'd come in from.

"I want to see the five of you and Calvin in my office first thing in the morning."

"Calvin's in the hospital," Ash called out after her.

"No, he's at home. His injuries were minor and taken care of. Austen's looking after him, along with a private nurse. He'll be fine, and so will Seb. Someone will be along for Fuller. Go home and get some rest."

With that she disappeared, leaving them all stunned stupid.

Dex turned to them. "What do you think she wants to talk to us about?"

"I don't know, and I don't care." Ash put his arm around Cael. "Let's get the fuck out of here."

Cael paused. He went to Fuller and crouched down by his corpse. Ash joined him, speaking quietly.

"He left you no choice."

"He was going to kill me," Cael said. "I've never killed anyone before." The thought hadn't occurred to him until now. He'd fired his weapon plenty of times, tranqed perps, and shot in self-defense, but he'd never killed anyone.

"Whatever you need," Ash said, pulling Cael to his feet with him, "we're here for you, okay?"

Cael nodded, following Ash and the rest of his team out of the subbasement. Cael didn't know what to think about what had happened. He was still processing a good deal of it. But it also occurred to him that he'd stood up to Fuller. He'd stood up for himself and proved he was as fierce a Therian agent as any other Felid THIRDS agent. Cael felt a huge weight lift off his shoulders. He was capable, always had been. Smiling to himself, he put his arm around Ash's waist as they walked out of the facility.

He was going to be fine.

TWELVE

CAEL STOOD at attention inside Sparks's office with the rest of their team. They hadn't seen her since the facility. Last night after they'd showered and gotten into bed together, Cael and Ash had talked for some time, both wondering if they'd see Sparks again after that, considering who she really worked for. Yet here she was, carrying on with her lieutenant duties as if nothing had happened.

The office was in privacy mode, and Sparks sat calmly at her desk, stoic as usual in her signature white pantsuit.

"This team seems to have trouble obeying the rules. Why do you think that is, Agent Brodie?"

Dex held a hand up. "Lieutenant—"

"I believe I was addressing agent Brodie."

Dex quickly shut it.

"Could you be more specific?" Sloane asked, his expression giving nothing away.

Sparks cocked her head to one side before tapping her desk. The large screen on the wall above her head flickered to life. It split into numerous smaller screens showing different footage. To Cael's horror, he realized it was digital footage of their team, one of them time-stamped over a year ago of Dex and Sloane going at it in the parking garage. He did *not* need to see that.

Although the angle didn't catch them with their hands on each other—or rather in each other's pants—there was no question what was going on, especially with all the sucking face happening simultaneously. Another screen showed Calvin kissing Hobbs back when Hobbs was in the hospital, while a third screen showed Ash kissing Cael in his office, which had supposedly been on privacy mode. Jesus, when she said she knew everything, she hadn't been kidding.

"Did you honestly believe I wouldn't notice? Then there's this."

She tapped the screen, and Cael recognized the footage as "borrowed" camera feeds. Who the hell was behind all this? The screens changed, this time showing footage of them at various locations around the city as they went after Hogan. The ballroom, their surveillance van, the grain terminal.

"I believe Destructive Delta was put on leave."

Dex opened his mouth, and Sparks cut him off.

"I'm not going back on my word, Agent Daley. Seb will remain in his position. His work during this case, despite your interference, is still commendable, as is his solidarity. I've wanted to promote him for some time." She turned her attention back to Sloane. "Now, I ask again, Agent Brodie. This team seems to have trouble obeying the rules. Why do you think that is?"

Sloane seemed to think about it. "My team operates to the best of their ability within the limitations set by the laws they uphold, laws violated by the perpetrators we're tasked with detaining. There are times when in the pursuit of justice, the rules are bent, but only as a last recourse."

Sparks didn't look convinced.

Dex held a hand up, and Sparks let out a heavy sigh. "Yes, agent Daley?"

"The THIRDS is the only agency that allows family to work together. Why?"

"Research showed agents who belonged to a positive family dynamic had a higher rate of success in all areas of performance than the general employee population. Agents who had this type of positive support system at the workplace outside of their teams seemed to cope better with stress and produced higher results during psych evals. The THIRDS decided to allow it as long as agents were in different departments. It's been very effective."

"Right," Dex agreed. "My bond with my family keeps me sane. They share in my joy and pain. They understand what it's like to bleed for this job. They back me up and I back them up because of our bond. Because I will do whatever it takes not to let them down. Whatever we face, as long as there's breath in my body, I will fight for them."

"Admirable, agent Daley, but what are you getting at?"

"Destructive Delta is also my family. We might not be related by blood, but that doesn't make them any less family. Cael, Tony, and I aren't related by blood, but we're still family."

"That hardly sets my mind at ease, considering what I've seen."

"Okay, yes, somewhere along the line, things changed for some of us, but since that day, have Sloane or I done anything to impede our performance outside the normal levels of any partnership not involved in a romantic relationship? And let's face it, it's not like your agents aren't forming bonds or relationships. The rule was brought in because of what happened with Seb and Hudson. But that could have happened to anyone, whether they'd been in a relationship or not. We're all fallible."

"That's a very pretty speech, but I'm afraid you've left me no choice. Destructive Delta is unstable and insubordinate. Your unorthodox methods may bring results, but not without a great deal of chaos involved. You also seem incapable of working a case without blowing something up. I think it's time to consider disbanding the team."

The room was filled with gasps and curses.

"What?" Cael shook his head. She couldn't. After all these years? He couldn't be reassigned to another team. No one understood him like his team. His quirks, his weird inability to drink coffee, or his little spurts of hyperactivity. And Rosa? Sparks couldn't take Rosa away. She was his partner. They worked great together.

"Will that change be put forth by you or your replacement?" Sloane asked calmly.

Sparks narrowed her eyes at him. "Excuse me?"

"I assume now that your cover's been blown, TIN will pull you out of the THIRDS and move you elsewhere."

"My cover remains intact, Agent Brodie. The only ones who—" She closed her mouth, and her bright red lips spread into an approving smile. "I see. Do you honestly believe blackmail would make a difference to someone in my position?"

"No. And I have no intention of blackmailing you. You've worked damn hard to get where you are. So have we. Both our covers have been blown." Sloane shrugged. "Or maybe they haven't. Yes, our methods are unorthodox. Yes, we do seem to attract an unusual amount of crazy, but we're a damn good team, and we always come through for each other. We get the job done, we protect this city, and we bring down assholes like Isaac, Reyes, Collins, and Hogan. Maybe it's time the THIRDS removed, or at least amended, the no fraternizing rule. In all the years I've been team leader of Destructive Delta, we have *never* failed you. We may have disappointed you along the way. We might have stumbled. But we always get up. So please forgive me when I say it'll be a cold day in hell before I let you break up my team."

The room fell into silence, with all eyes moving from Sloane to Sparks, who was frowning deeply. She studied him closely before tapping away at her desk's interface. The screen behind her went black, one word appearing in the center of each screen.

Deleted.

With a sigh, she laced her fingers together on the desk's surface. She met Sloane's gaze. "I'll consider your request concerning the no fraternizing rule, agent Brodie. Perhaps in the meantime, you and your team can attempt to show a little discretion. Keep your personal activities out of the parking garage."

Sloane grinned broadly. "Yes, ma'am."

"Also, I think it's time Destructive Delta steps up its game. You've all been extremely lucky until now. Yes, a good deal of that has been skill, but you could do better. You're top agents on a top team. I don't want you to be the top. I want you to be the best. I expect you and Agent Keeler to get every member of your team up to your level."

Ash's jaw dropped. "But... We're talking over twenty years of field training and—"

Sparks arched an eyebrow at him. "I'm sorry, Agent Keeler. I believe the response you were looking for was 'yes, ma'am.'"

Ash swallowed hard, his voice gruff when he replied, "Yes, ma'am."

"You'll start receiving callouts on Monday. Enjoy your weekend. Dismissed."

Cael turned, waiting for the door to swish open before heading out with the rest of his team. He wondered if they were as confused as he was.

AUSTEN HEARD the door swish closed, and he stepped out from Sparks's personal bathroom. He sat down on the edge of her desk.

"You weren't really going to break them up, were you?"

Sparks waved a hand in dismissal. "Don't be ridiculous. Of course I wasn't. I needed to give them a little more motivation. There's a lot of potential there."

She got that familiar look in her eyes, and Austen groaned.

"Forget it. They'll never join TIN."

"I know that," she huffed, poking his leg with her pen. "Get your ass off my desk."

He hopped off and draped himself over one of the chairs across from her. "So, what then?"

"You don't have to be a TIN operative to work for TIN. You should know that better than anyone." She went to work tapping away at her desk and logging into the secure TIN communication system.

"You want them as freelancers?" Austen gaped at her.

"What? Don't look at me like that. With enough training, they could be exceptional. Look at Agent Maddock. He impressed me with the way he handled Fuller. And Keeler's barely scratched the surface with their training."

"Maybe."

"I think Sloane and Dex can do extraordinary things together." A slow smile crept onto her face. "They could be the first THIRDS power couple."

Austen gave a start. "You're really fucking scary when you're happy like that."

"Oh, shut up. You have no vision."

She brought up a THIRDS training schedule, and Austen thought about it. He knew Destructive Delta wouldn't join TIN. They had trouble with the whole means to an end thing. They weren't ruthless enough, couldn't shut off their emotions the way TIN operatives could. But as freelancers? Maybe. He couldn't help his smile

Looked like things just got a little bit more interesting.

CAEL WAS HEADED for the bullpen along with his team when Dex stopped in his tracks ahead of them and turned.

"What just happened?"

Sloane grabbed Dex's arm and continued walking. "I don't know but keep walking before she changes her mind."

Dex's mouth opened to reply, then closed. He turned and followed Sloane to their office, the rest of the team close on their heels. They had joined Sloane and Dex in their office when Ash's phone went off. He pulled out his smartphone and frowned at the screen.

"What is it?" Cael asked worriedly.

"Don't know. I don't recognize the number." Ash tapped the screen and put the phone to his ear. "Ash Keeler."

Cael watched Ash's eyes widen. He put a hand to his mouth, tears in his eyes. Cael was immediately at his side.

"Yes. Of course." A big smile spread across Ash's face, and he nodded, a tear rolling down his cheek. "That'd be great. I'll ask him. I look forward to it too." He ended the call and wiped his eyes and cheek.

"Everything okay?" Sloane asked.

Ash nodded, and Cael could tell he was trying hard to keep his emotions at bay. "Yeah, um. That was my mom. She's left my dad, and she wants to have brunch on Sunday."

"Oh, Ash! That's wonderful!"

Cael threw his arms around Ash and hugged him while the rest of the team patted him on the back and congratulated him. They all knew what this meant to him. Cael was so happy for him. After composing himself, Ash looked down at Cael.

"She wants you to come."

"Of course," Cael said. There was nothing he wouldn't do for Ash, and he was thrilled that his boyfriend wanted him there at his side when he saw his mother after so many years without her, thinking she hated him.

Sloane tapped his security code into his desk and brought up the team's training schedule on the large board across from them.

"Guess Monday's going to be a whole new world for all of us." He went to tap his desk when the board flickered and turned off. "What the hell?"

They all observed the darkened screen when it suddenly flickered to life. The whole schedule had been amended and filled in with a list of training requirements for each of them for next year, some of them with techniques Cael was quite sure weren't THIRDS requirements.

Dex stared at the screen. "Um... please tell me that was you."

Sloane shook his head. "Nope."

Cael frowned. "Wait, does that say mixed martial arts?"

"What's that?" Dex said, spotting a little icon on the bottom right of the schedule. He leaned in for a better look. "It looks like..." His frown deepened. "Ruby slippers?" He arched an eyebrow and tapped the screen. It went black, and Dex cringed. "Shit, I think I broke it."

Blue words started scrolling across the screen.

Welcome, Destructive Delta, to the TIN associate training program.

They all gaped at the screen, with Dex verbalizing their thoughts. "What the fuck?"

The door swished closed on its own, and the room went into privacy mode. Cael took a step closer to Ash. This whole thing was freaking him out. A small screen appeared in the corner of the board with Sparks waving at them.

"Destructive Delta, this is your new training schedule. Austen will be your contact from this point on."

Austen appeared behind Sparks and leaned over her shoulder to wave at them. "What's up, peeps?"

Sparks glared at him, and with a grin, he pulled away and out of sight.

"As I was saying. Austen will be your point of contact. Any time you see the symbol Agent Daley touched, it means you have a message from me not related to the THIRDS. The message will remain onscreen for a limited amount of time before it deletes itself permanently. All communication is untraceable. I have high hopes for Destructive Delta. I expect you won't disappoint me."

"What's going on?" Sloane asked. "What is all this?"

"You'll know more in due time. For now, continue with your duties and your training. Sparks out."

Before any of them could utter another word, the screen

returned to their training schedule. The icon that had been on the bottom right was no longer there. Dex dropped himself into his chair as the room came out of privacy mode and the door opened.

"So..." Dex said. "Who's up for a few drinks at Dekatria tonight?"

Everyone put their hands up.

"Good." Dex swiveled in his chair, a puzzled look on his face. "Good. Okay. Fuck, this place is weird."

Everyone promised to meet up tonight at Dekatria, and Cael headed for his office behind Rosa. He was actually looking forward to setting up some boring algorithms for a change. Ash caught up to him, leaning in to speak quietly.

"Pick you up at eight?"

Cael's pulse fluttered. "That sounds an awful lot like date talk, Agent Keeler." Ash wriggled his brows, and Cael laughed. "Eight it is."

With a wink, Ash was off, catching up to Letty and giving her a playful push. Cael could hardly wait. He knew Ash would still be reserved at the bar out in the open, but he was just glad to be spending time with him after everything that had happened. With a skip in his step, he followed Rosa into their office for a conversation on what he should wear tonight.

ASH TOOK a swig of his beer, his gaze on the dance floor, where Cael was dancing with their teammates. Everyone was out there, even Sloane and Dex, but Ash's eyes remained on Cael and the easy way his body moved to the rhythm of the music, as if he could feel it down to his soul. His smile showed how much he loved it. The beat picked up, and Cael bounced around with Rosa and her girlfriend, Milena, who finally managed to get some time away from her job as an antiques dealer. Ash had no idea there was even such a demand for antiques, but then what the hell did he know about it? Letty danced with Dimples the firefighter, and Calvin was off to one side dancing with Hobbs, who was back on his real medication. Lou was behind the bar with Bradley, while Seb chatted to Taylor at the bar.

Several guys had tried dancing with Cael, who'd politely declined. Ash wasn't overbearing. Cael could dance with whoever he liked, even if the thought of a guy getting close to Cael made Ash want to punch one of the asshats. They'd been having a great time. Dex did his stupid karaoke before everyone hit the dance floor except for Ash, who wasn't much into it. Not that he couldn't. He never really felt the urge to dance. Of course now...

Cael threw his head back and laughed at something his brother said to him. Ash took another swig of his beer and put it down. He worried his bottom lip.

"Fuck it." Ash got up and waded through the mass of bodies on the dance floor, pressed together as they moved to the sensual rhythm of the pop song. Cael was dressed in his gray Converse sneakers, charcoal jeans, and a black V-neck long-sleeved T-shirt that accentuated his sinewy frame. His jaw was covered in stubble, and his silvery eyes sparkled to rival diamonds, his lips wide in a gorgeous smile.

A Therian next to Cael with a wide grin was obviously flirting, his hand reaching out to take hold of Cael's waist. Ash clamped a hand down on his wrist and loomed over him with a sweet smile.

"Fuck off."

The guy swallowed hard and nodded fervently before taking off.

Turning to Cael, Ash gave him a sheepish grin. "Sorry. That was mean."

Cael laughed. "And that bothers you?"

"Nope," Ash said with a shrug. "I just don't want you to think I'm going to be some possessive Neanderthal."

Cael gave him a knowing look before asking, "So, what was that about?"

Ash slipped his hand over the exposed skin between the waistband of Cael's jeans and where his shirt had ridden up. "He was going to touch this. I didn't like it."

He stepped closer, his fingers brushing and caressing Cael's soft skin. Cael's pupils dilated, and he licked his bottom lip. He stood stock still, waiting for Ash to make a move. With a sinful grin, Ash put his hands on Cael's waist and pulled him up against him, his knee slipping between Cael's legs.

"Ash," Cael gasped, looking around them.

"What they think doesn't matter." Ash brushed his lips over Cael's. "You're what matters." He kissed Cael, ignoring the cheers and catcalls around them. A joy he'd never known swept through Ash as he squeezed Cael to him, kissing him passionately without a care for who the fuck was watching them. With a breathless laugh, he pulled back and met Cael's questioning gaze. "I love you, and I want everyone to know how damn lucky I am."

Cael threw his arms around Ash and kissed him. The world around them was reduced to nothing but music and the man in his arms. Ash knew he was an asshole. He was gruff and unapproachable. He did everything in his own belligerent way, but one thing he wasn't was a fool. Ash had been blessed with the love of the amazing man in his arms, and he had no intention of ever letting go.

What's next for Dex, Sloane, and the Destructive Delta crew? The adventure continues with Calvin and Ethan's story in *Catch a Tiger by the Tail*, the sixth book in the THIRDS series. Available on Amazon and KindleUnlimited.

A NOTE FROM THE AUTHOR

Thank you so much for reading *Against the Grain*, the fifth book in the THIRDS series. I hope you enjoyed Ash and Cael's story, and if you did, please consider leaving a review on Amazon. Reviews can have a significant impact on a book's visibility, so any support you show these fellas would be amazing. The adventure continues in *Catch a Tiger by the Tail*, book six in the series, available from Amazon and KindleUnlimited.

Want to stay up-to-date on my releases and receive exclusive content? Sign up for my newsletter.

Follow me on Amazon to be notified of a new releases, and connect with me on social media, including my fun Facebook group, Donuts, Dog Tags, and Day Dreams, where we chat books, post pictures, have giveaways, and more!

Looking for inspirational photos of my books? Visit my book boards on Pinterest.

Thank you again for joining the THIRDS crew on their adventures. We hope to see you soon!

CAST MEMBERS

You'll find these cast members throughout the whole THIRDS series. This list will continue to grow.

DESTRUCTIVE DELTA

Sloane Brodie—Defense agent. Team leader. Jaguar Therian.

Dexter J. Daley "Dex"—Defense agent. Former homicide detective for the Human Police Force. Older brother of Cael Maddock. Adopted by Anthony Maddock. Human.

Ash Keeler—Defense agent. Entry tactics and close-quarter combat expert. Lion Therian.

Julietta Guerrera "Letty"—Defense agent. Weapons expert. Human.

Calvin Summers—Defense agent. Sniper. Human.

Ethan Hobbs—Defense agent. Demolitions expert and public safety bomb technician. Has two older brothers: Rafe and Sebastian Hobbs. Tabby Tiger Therian.

Cael Maddock—Recon agent. Tech expert. Dex's

younger brother. Adopted by Anthony Maddock. Cheetah Therian.

Rosa Santiago—Recon agent. Crisis negotiator and medic. Human.

COMMANDING OFFICERS

Lieutenant Sonya Sparks—Lieutenant for Unit Alpha. Cougar Therian.

Sergeant Anthony Maddock "Tony"—Sergeant for Destructive Delta. Dex and Cael's adoptive father. Human.

MEDICAL EXAMINERS

Dr. Hudson Colbourn—Chief medical examiner for Destructive Delta. Wolf Therian.

Dr. Nina Bishop—Medical examiner for Destructive Delta. Human.

AGENTS FROM OTHER SQUADS

Ellis Taylor—Team leader for Beta Ambush. Leopard Therian.

Levi Stone—Team leader for Beta Pride. Arrested for being a mole inside the THIRDS and part of the Ikelos Coalition.

Rafe Hobbs—Team leader for Alpha Ambush. The oldest Hobbs brother. Tiger Therian.

Sebastian Hobbs "Seb"—Team leader for Theta Destructive. Was once on Destructive Delta but was transferred after his relationship to Hudson ended in a breach of protocol and civilian loss. Middle Hobbs brother. Tiger Therian.

Osmond Zachary "Zach"—Defense agent for

Alpha Sleuth in Unit Beta. Has six brothers working for the THIRDS. Brown bear Therian.

OTHER IMPORTANT CAST MEMBERS

Gabe Pearce—Sloane's ex-partner and ex-lover on Destructive Delta. Killed on duty. Human.

Isaac Pearce—Gabe's older brother. Was a detective for the Human Police Force who became leader of the Order of Adrasteia. Was killed by Destructive Delta during a hostage situation. Human.

Louis Huerta "Lou"—Dex's ex-boyfriend. Human.

Bradley Darcy—Bartender and owner of Bar Dekatria. Jaguar Therian.

Austen Payne—Squadron Specialist agent (SSA) for Destructive Delta. Cheetah Therian.

Dr. Abraham Shultzon—Head doctor during the First Gen Recruitment Program who was personally responsible for the wellbeing of the THIRDS First Gen Recruits. He was also responsible for the tests that were run on the Therian children.

Arlo Keeler—Ash's twin brother killed during the riots in the 1980s.

Felipe Bautista—Drew Collins's boyfriend.

EXTREMIST GROUPS AND GANGS

The Order of Adrasteia—Group of Humans against Therians. Leader was killed by Destructive Delta. THIRDS arrested its new leader along with remaining members.

The Ikelos Coalition—Vigilante group of Unregistered Therians fighting the Order. Leader was Beck Hogan. Beck's second-in-command Preston Merritt was killed by

Destructive Delta during a hostage negotiation. Most of the members of the group were arrested, leaving only Hogan, his new second-in-command Drew Collins, and a small group of Therians. Hogan and Collins were both killed during encounters with the THIRDS. The remaining group members were arrested.

Westward Creed—Gang of Human thugs who went around assaulting Therian citizens during the riots of 1985. Were arrested for causing the deaths of several Therians but released due to "missing" evidence. Eight members all together but only five became members of the Order: Angel Reyes, Alberto Cristo, Craig Martin, Toby Leith, Richard Esteban, Larry Berg, Ox Perry, Brick Jackson.

GLOSSARY

Melanoe Virus—A virus released during the Vietnam War through the use of chemical warfare infecting millions worldwide and killing hundreds of thousands.

Eppione.8—A vaccine created using strains from animals immune to the Melanoe virus. It awakened a dormant mutation within the virus, resulting in the alteration of human DNA and the birth of Therians.

Therians—Shifters brought about through the mutation of Human DNA as a result of the Eppione.8 vaccine.

Post-shift Trauma Care (PSTC)—The effects of Therian post-shift trauma are similar to the aftereffects of an epileptic seizure, only on a smaller scale, including muscle soreness, bruising, brief disorientation, and hunger. Eating after a shift is extremely important as not eating could lead to the Therian collapsing and a host of other health issues. PSTC is the care given to Therians after they shift back to Human form.

THIRDS (Therian-Human Intelligence Recon Defense Squadron)—An elite, military funded agency comprised of an equal number of Human and Therian agents and intended to uphold the law for all its citizens without prejudice.

Themis—A powerful, multimillion-dollar government interface used by the THIRDS. It's linked to numerous intelligence agencies across the globe and runs a series of highly advanced algorithms to scan surveillance submitted by agents.

First Gen—First Generation of purebred Therians born with a perfected version of the mutation. Any Therian born in 1976 is considered a First Generation Therian. Any Therian born after 1976 is simply considered Therian.

Pre-First Gen—Any Therian born before First Gen Therians. Known to have unstable versions of the mutation resulting in any number of health issues. Most possess the ability to shift, some don't. No medical research was available on Therians before 1976 as Humans were not classified as Therians until then.

BearCat—THIRDS tactical vehicle.

Human Police Force (HPF)—A branch of law enforcement consisting of Humans officials dealing only with crimes committed by Humans.

ALSO BY CHARLIE COCHET

FOUR KINGS SECURITY

Love in Spades

Be Still My Heart

Join the Club

Diamond in the Rough

FOUR KINGS SECURITY UNIVERSE

Beware of Geeks Bearing Gifts

THE KINGS: WILD CARDS

Stacking the Deck

LOCKE AND KEYES AGENCY

Kept in the Dark

PARANORMAL PRINCES

The Prince and His Bedeviled Bodyguard

The Prince and His Captivating Carpenter

The King and His Vigilant Valet

THIRDS

Hell & High Water

Blood & Thunder

Rack & Ruin

SOLDATI HEARTS

The Soldati Prince

The Foxling Soldati

STANDALONE

Forgive and Forget

Love in Retrograde

AUDIOBOOKS

Check out the audio versions on Audible.

ABOUT THE AUTHOR

Charlie Cochet is the international bestselling author of the THIRDS series. Born in Cuba and raised in the US, Charlie enjoys the best of both worlds, from her daily Cuban latte to her passion for classic rock.

Currently residing in Central Florida, Charlie is at the beck and call of a rascally Doxiepoo bent on world domination. When she isn't writing, she can usually be found devouring a book, releasing her creativity through art, or binge watching a new TV series. She runs on coffee, thrives on music, and loves to hear from readers.

www.charliecochet.com

Sign up for Charlie's newsletter:
https://newsletter.charliecochet.com

facebook.com/charliecochet

twitter.com/charliecochet

instagram.com/charliecochet

bookbub.com/authors/charliecochet

goodreads.com/CharlieCochet

pinterest.com/charliecochet

Made in the USA
Las Vegas, NV
08 March 2022

45246690R00173